NIGHTSHADOW

A Novel

M I A   R O G E R S

[[A Foggy Bay Book]]

Copyright © 2023 by Foggy Bay LLC

All rights reserved. No part of this publication may be reproduced, distributed, or transmitted in any form or by any means, including photocopying, recording, or other electronic or mechanical methods, without the prior written permission of the publisher, except as permitted by U.S. copyright law. For permission requests, contact Foggy Bay, LLC.

The story, all names, characters, and incidents portrayed in this production are fictitious. No identification with actual persons (living or deceased), places, buildings, and products is intended or should be inferred.

Book Design by Mia Rogers

Foggy Bay, LLC
foggybaypnw@gmail.com

For Mom, Dad, Ian, and Alyssa

PLACE OF TRUCE

FIRST FLOOR
EREBUS

SECOND FLOOR
Central Chamber
EREBUS

OUTSIDE VIEW
Central Chamber

SKY VIEW

CHAMBER
Diameter: 60ft
Radius: 3ft
Height: 50ft
Area: 2,827 sq ft

BUILDING
Diameter: 250ft
Radius: 125ft
Height: 50ft
Area: 43,338 sq ft

WALL

TABLE OF CONTENTS

ONE..1
TWO..24
THREE..48
FOUR...66
FIVE...80
SIX..103
SEVEN..128
EIGHT..134
NINE...148
TEN..166
ELEVEN...190
TWELVE...205
THIRTEEN.......................................224
FOURTEEN.......................................245
FIFTEEN..264
SIXTEEN..280
SEVENTEEN......................................293
REVIEWS..313
ACKNOWLEDGMENTS................................314
ABOUT THE AUTHOR...............................317

ONE

Boom. The room shakes. The ceiling tiles fall, shattering as they crash onto the hard floor. Screaming, crying and shouts for help. Yelling and chaos. She can't feel her hands, nor can she see them. It is like she's invisible, only able to sit and watch all the destruction and pain and agony. She tries to yell, but it comes out as a muffled grunt. Her ears are stinging from the loud echoes coming from the streets below, and the room smells of blood, dust, and as if something is burning. Smoke and ash cloud her senses, limiting her line of sight to only what is nearby.

She does not recognize the building, and its interior is destroyed, keeping her from telling what it once was. The concrete walls are painted black, and the windows are stained gray, the few remaining shattering at each new explosion inside the building.

A man crawls in front of her. He is bleeding and his leg twists in a way it shouldn't. His eyes are filled with pain and grief, his face marked with burns and soot, coated in a thin layer of dust from the falling rocks.

Another explosion goes off, rattling her ears when he speaks. "Help," he whispers, looking straight into her eyes. His voice is hoarse through the ash and smoke surrounding him. He lets out a pained cough, followed by a choked sob.

"I'm trying!" she wants to shout. "I can't!" she yells in her mind at him. She tries calling for help again, but no one is

there. There's no one else left alive in the building to help them.

Another explosion rocks the building, and the structure collapses, light blinding her vision. The man is crushed beneath layers of cement and wood and rock. Suddenly she's outside the building and can see the rest of the city. Buildings are crumbling down, killing all inside and around them. People are panicking, running and screaming, but no matter how much others might want to, they can't help. All they can do is try to stay alive themselves without success.

Fire engulfs her, and her vision turns dark.

I let out a gasp as I fully wake up. Dreams again. No, not dreams. *The* dream. The one that plays again and again in my head, each time from a different view of the same place. A dying city.

"Wake up. It's not real," I murmur to myself. But it felt real. It *feels* real, and it keeps happening. Maybe I'm going mad. I sigh and decide I can think about the dream later. It's not important at the moment, if it ever will be.

My bed is warm, and the scent of pine needles floats through the room. I stand up and walk to my window, seeing a very small city unlike the one in the dream in the distance. Looking beyond my neighborhood, light colored buildings stand tall in the near distance. I can see the roofs of shops along the main street of town. Each building features an abundance of windows, allowing as much sunlight in as possible. At the right angle, some windows reflect the forestlands that form a natural barrier behind my house. This is the only city I've ever seen, yet somehow deep down, I feel like I know the place in the dream. I wave away the thought and continue down the stairs to find the house is empty.

"Where is everyone?" Then it hits me. It's Friday. They're at Lily's doctor's appointment.

My brain immediately links that thought to a memory exactly six months ago, the last time I was in the hospital, and it still hurts. To think about it, to think about *him*. To hear all those things they said at his funeral... A tear rolls down my pale face. Maybe it's fine to cry for a moment. *No!* I can't cry. He'd want me to be strong.

"And that's what I'm trying to do, to move on like you said. But it's hard. I'll never forget you," I whisper to the empty house. Standing, I push my bright red hair out of my face and calm myself down. For a moment it feels like he is there, listening. But he's gone. Forever. Another tear escapes, and I wipe it away. I have to find something to do. To distract myself. Something to occupy my thoughts and my hands.

I make my way across the room to the front door. My mother, followed by my sister, father, and best friend, told me to skip today, anticipating a meltdown on a death anniversary, but I have to do *something*. Doing nothing is making it all worse. I make quick work of getting ready to go. Throwing on some clean clothes, I brush my teeth. My naturally pale skin still looks paler than normal. It makes my freckles stand out more than usual. My blue eyes look huge, ringed by dark circles, and deep sockets. I've lost weight over the last year, in stress, in grief, making me look almost gaunt. I quickly turn away from the mirror; the face looking back is no longer recognizable.

    My backpack is hanging on the coat rack where I left it yesterday. As I open the front door, a rush of cold March air hits me. I can drive, but it's a short distance. Not worth burning the gas. Making my way through the light layer of snow, I glance around the neighborhood. It's a quaint area, on the outskirts of the city, where all the houses are almost the same. Lined up in neat little rows, each one painted a warm, light color. Window boxes are empty this time of year, but in two months they'll hold cheerful flowers. The addition of snow makes the scene even more bright and immaculate. Only the gray-tinged snow lining the street mars the brilliance.

    I hear the speakers give out a speck of static before a voice booms across the plain and open street. "Fellow Aether, be sure to turn in your vote for our next representative. All votes must be submitted by noon. You may do so online or by visiting your local slip box, often found outside of libraries or major buildings in the community. And remember, if you ever see an Erebus, immediately run the opposite way and report them to the nearest law enforcement officer. May you find happiness if you deserve it, and if you don't, may you work to earn it. Thank you." The speakers release another burst of static as they shut off.

    That's right. It's voting day. Again.

    Every other year, each Aether fourteen and older must vote for a new representative, as our representatives are only allowed to serve one two-year term. The system works well if our representative is not fit for the spot, because he or she is not in power for too long. I haven't decided who to vote for yet. If it wasn't required, I wouldn't vote. I don't support any of the people who are running for representative this year, just like I didn't the last time we voted. They are all looking for money and power. The worst part is they already have more than most. But that isn't enough. They want *more* money and power, *more* control, which may only be gained by earning the title of representative.

I get tired of hearing the false propaganda and campaign promises. *"I will reinforce the wall, so that none shall ever pass it again."* Impossible. All Aether combined don't have a quarter of the money required to do that, nor the technology or time, for that matter. *"I have spies on the other side of the wall, living amongst the Erebus. They say the Erebus murder children ritualistically so they can bless themselves."* The spies wouldn't survive a day out there. I don't even have to mention the inability to get information back across the wall, because the spies would die before they could go ten feet. Anything and anyone who goes over, never comes back.

Our elected representative will meet a representative from the Erebus at the Place of Truce, a circular building built into the wall near Eos, one of our capital cities. We all call it the POT. It's the only place one may see a person from the other side without being killed, enslaved, or put in prison by whichever side owns the land that is trespassed on. The Erebus and Aether all know this law, and only representatives are allowed to enter the POT. This allows for the separation of the populations to continue, keeping outright worldwide war from erupting.

War makes me think of death, the very topic I'm trying to forget today. I sigh in relief when I reach my school and see my friend, Ivy, running towards me from the opposite side of the street.

"Maddie!" she yells. That's not actually my name, but she calls me that anyway.

Ivy's brown eyes are shining with happiness, and she's beaming with her smile stretching across her tan face, her dark hair flowing behind her. She's never this giddy, never bouncing up and down. Normally she's quiet except when alone with me or someone else she knows well. "Hey Ivy, you are positively vibrating excitement. What's going on?" I ask.

"You remember Will? That boy who lives down the street from me?"

Oh, great. It's about a boy. Shit. My face heats up, and I feel the tears waiting in my eyes as I remember when I was last excited over a boy. Why does everything remind me of him? Even a bagel reminds me of him. A *bagel*. How in the world would that remind you of another person?

"Well… oh." Ivy hesitates and flinches slightly as she takes in my face. "Sorry. I was worried about that. I'll tell you later."

"No, I want to hear." I'm lying. I really don't want to hear right now. Before I would have been begging her to tell me. But I don't want to think of…*him*. It hurts so much… She gives me a questioning look, so I continue.

"What happened with Will?" He's the guy she's had this massive crush on since the second grade.

"Well, he asked me out! He said he likes me and wished he'd had the courage to ask earlier. Can you believe it?

I thought he didn't even know I existed! I wonder why he asked now though, and what gave him the courage," Ivy quiets for a moment thinking.

I know why. Because when *he* died, everyone realized the one they love could suddenly go away forever without knowing their true feelings. Except *he* knew I loved him. He knew if he died, he would crush my soul. And he died anyway.

Ivy continues talking, and I'm hit with a wave of gratitude when she changes the subject. She knows when I can't handle hearing something and is always understanding about it. Some friends try to comfort you with hollow words and empty offers when you're in pieces. Best friends skip the quiet platitudes and soothing noises and start picking up the pieces you're too busy weeping over, slowly helping to put you back together before you even notice. They are the ones who help you rise when you've fallen and fix what has been broken. Ivy's that person, my piece picker-upper. I'm lucky to have her.

But she's also still the Ivy who's obsessed with boys and drama.

"Anyway, what are you writing your history essay on? I'm doing mine on that time when the Erebus…" She starts talking about our joint classes, and I force myself to answer her prompts in the conversation. By the time we reach our first classroom, our conversation is about the newest movie in theaters. She's great at distracting me, and I gladly take the distraction, moving my mind off *him*.

A first period test engages my mind for the next little while, and for a moment, I think maybe everything will be okay after all.

Forget what I said. Nothing will be okay. Everywhere I go people walk by me in couples. I feel the heartache return, the anger. Why do they get to keep their significant other while mine had to die? The stinging of a metal blade in my chest would be preferable to this pain.

I want to yell. I want to scream. Every square inch of this building brings back memories of him. The thought that he's gone buries me deep in a dark and cold pit with no escape. I reach my breaking point when I'm beginning my essay in history class and someone walks by me, talking about how he's going to ask the girl he likes to watch him play football at the field. The field. *The* field. *Our* field.

Ivy glances over at me, knowing that this is my trigger, watching me slowly fall apart. "Madrona," she starts with a worried look, but I'm already gone.

I explode out of my chair, throwing it back, grab my bag and run out the door. Tears swell in my eyes, and my chest feels tight as I hold on to them. My head throbs as I sprint down the halls, searching for a place where I can be left in peace, alone.

I notice Ivy doesn't follow me as I round the few corners needed to exit the building. *Good.* I escape out the front doors, breathing ragged and eyes slightly crazed. A group of juniors watch me leave and start whispering to themselves. I don't care if they're whispering about me. I'm all anyone talks about the last six months. The poor girl whose boyfriend died. The girl who can't get over it.

I run through the front lawn and around the school until I find the bleachers at the football field. The field, *our* field. *Our* place. I climb the creaky, loud steps until I find the fourth row, the place where I first sat with him. The place where we met, where he later asked me out, the place where we first kissed. This was our spot, our special place where we could talk when we worried our homes weren't safe from listening ears.

It's no longer snowing, and the morning accumulation has melted after three hours of sunlight. A small gust of wind blows my hair out of my face, and his scent fills my mind, the strong scent of pine trees. I always loved it; the calming scent of trees and earth always reminded me of life, of growth, of nature.

This is the place where I feel closest to him. It's open and empty, allowing sunlight to slowly heat the cold air. I let myself hurt. I let myself feel the pain of his loss in the warm sunlight as it heats the brittle, frost filled air. The seat is still wet from the earlier snow, but I don't care. It feels like he's sitting next to me, almost reading my thoughts as he had before.

I curl up into a ball, hugging my legs and try to hold myself together, my shoulders shaking under the weight as the cold kisses my cheeks. No one will bother me here. My teachers know what happened, everyone does. They know to leave me alone. That I'll be back when I'm ready. I'm not one to skip school often, since I enjoy most of my classes, but today is different. Today is the six-month anniversary of his death.

I finally let myself release the weight on my shoulders, in my heart. I let it all out, crying and letting it all out of the gash in my heart, releasing a small sliver of the pain that will never fully subside.

Suddenly, I hear footsteps behind me. I tense up, and suddenly I'm hit with a wave of anger. How dare they bother me here? Everyone knows this is our spot, this is my escape. The place I go when I want to be alone. Not comforted, but *alone*. I don't look up when I hear the footsteps climb the bleachers and approach me. Maybe if I pretend they aren't there, they'll go away and leave me in peace.

I feel an arm on my shoulder and another flare of anger erupts in me. My unwelcome guest is sitting in *his* seat, replacing *his* smell with an unfamiliar one. It's definitely not Ivy. The arm is too heavy, and a faint masculine scent reaches my nose. Plus, she would know better than to sit in *his* seat.

"I'm sorry. You don't deserve to go through this. You deserve to be happy, not ending each day in grief," says a male voice. I almost look up at him, but I just stay in my small, tiny ball, hoping he'll leave me be. I don't want to lash out and hurt him if he unknowingly says something wrong. "Sorry. I should just shut up. Words don't ever seem to be enough."

"I-I just need some time alone," I say through my sobs, trying to get him to leave.

"You don't have to be alone, Madrona," he answers. "Sometimes it's better not to."

I snap at him, head jerking out of my lap, grief turning into indignation. "What are you suggesting, then? I go find a new boyfriend who will only make it hurt more?" My tears are slowing as my anger builds.

A familiar face greets me in a dirty blonde-haired senior who has a look of empathy in his eyes. I think he goes to say something else, but clearly gets the message. Instead, he tries to give me a hug. *Wrong move.* I hurl my fist at his face. His eyes widen in surprise, but he doesn't move as it lands. A searing pain erupts from my fist, and I hear a small crack, followed by a muffled shout in pain. Great, I probably broke my wrist and his nose. There was more force in it than I thought.

Cradling my hand, I scream at him, "Please! Leave me alone!"

In the next instant, I go completely still when I realize what I've done. I broke one of the largest rules of the Aether. No violence. Only our law enforcement agents are permitted to carry weapons. Aethers are forbidden from any violent acts, punishable with death.

If it's possible to go beyond pale, I'm sure that's what I look like now. "I'm so sorry," I say, not intending for it to come out as a whisper, muted by my hoarse throat that still hurts from crying.

"It's fine," he winces, hands cradled around his nose. His eyes are full of hurt, and I hate myself for what I've done to him. Ivy's going to skin me alive.

"I have to go," I mumble and run, grabbing my bag as I rush home. I know who he is, and I know he didn't deserve to be punched in the face. He's a nice person, and I know Ivy is going to kill me for punching her brother, but I'll deal with that later.

When I reach my house, I quickly slam the door behind me. There's no one here, and I'm grateful. I head to my room and scream into my pillow, angry at myself. I shouldn't have punched him. I feel sick knowing I acted so rashly, so harshly. I don't know where that violent impulse came from, and it frightens me to think of the repercussions of my actions. Was it because this guy had the same hair as *he* did? The loosely cut waves curl down to his neck, shorter in the front. Was that the trigger? But should any Aether even have a violence trigger? No. It's simply unheard of. There's no excuse for punching him.

I move slightly, gripping my pillow tighter, which makes me realize my hand really hurts. I release a scream about that too, for being in pain and for being so stupid.

Suddenly I remember what *he* wanted. I have to be strong. I stop screaming and text Ivy to tell her brother I'm sorry. I can't tell her what for, as I don't want further proof of my mistake to be recorded. I'm sure it will be obvious as soon as she sees her brother. I hear constant buzzing for the next few minutes in response, as she blows up my phone, but I don't look at what she's saying.

I go to the bathroom sink and open the cupboard beneath it, finding tape for my wrist. My parents work at the hospital, and they have taught my sister and me how to identify and treat minor injuries, to check for broken bones, to manage a medical situation until help can arrive. Medical staff are spread thin in our city, and help isn't always quick to respond. I think it gives them peace of mind to know we can treat ourselves in case of an accident.

I slowly look over my wrist, testing its range of motion, and applying slight pressure in various spots. My verdict: I sprained it pretty badly. I also slightly dislocated a knuckle on my middle finger. I wrap the tape snuggly around my wrist and try to reset the knuckle through the pain.

Glancing at the clock, I know my family will be home in a few minutes. I don't want to talk to them or anyone yet, so I grab my hiking pack and leave the house. I loop around to the trail that leads into the forest behind our house and start walking. The movement helps me calm down. My shoes are quickly covered in mud, but I'll clean them later. I need to walk.

Soon the established trail ends, but I keep going. There are small deer trails if you know where to look. I know how to get back home. I know every inch of this forest. I go deeper into the woods, allowing the lush forest to envelop me until I reach the border wall that separates the two sides, the Erebus and Aether. It's a fifty-foot-tall barrier of smooth stone that runs for more than five thousand miles. We happen to live right next to it. I pull out a blanket from my pack, put my back against the wall, and sit down.

I refuse to cry, so I just listen. A few birds sing in the overhead branches as winter ends. There aren't many because of the cold, but there's one or two. I hear them chirp back and forth, and it makes me smile. The sun is gleaming through the branches, causing beautiful rays to shine through the leaves, illuminating portions of the forest floor. The forest is so quiet this time of year. Most of the small critters are still snuggled up in their dens, hiding from the winter. Hikers are few and far between, the wet and the cold keeping them home. A soft rustling slides past my ears as a breeze shifts leaves and branches.

The birds, the life, the trees and ferns and the light, all remind me of him, but not in a bad way. I take a deep breath, taking it all in. I look to my left and can almost see him sitting there, telling me what kind of bird is out this early in the year, how peaceful it is in this place, and how the wall interrupts the calmness of the forest. Then he goes quiet. *'When I go, I want you to be strong. I want you to move on, to be happy. But, don't... don't forget me. Just remember this moment. Be at peace. And remember I loved you,'* he said here, in this very spot, only seven months ago. I remember my response, but instead of thinking of it, I simply reply again, with a different answer.

"I'm trying, but it's so hard," I murmur. I can almost feel him hugging me, then replying, *'You are stronger than you think.'* Then, he disappears from my imagination.

"Aaron," I say quietly, almost hoping he's still there. But he's not, he's gone, never coming back except in my head.

I let go of one tear, then stand up. *It's time to head back, not to cry.* My phone is buzzing, my family probably wondering where I am. I take a few steps away from the wall, making my way through the bright and intense green forest, the tree trunks dark and wet making the green leaves and moss stand out even more. The air is damp, the sun reflecting off dew drops on the leaves of a nearby wild blackberry bush. I'm about to step over a fallen tree when I hear a thud behind me and feel a vibration in the ground.

"What the hell?" I say as I turn around. Back where there was only empty forest, now lies a large male body, on his side facing away from me. The person has long light brown hair and is wearing all black with a gun holster at his side. The unusual sight of a weapon sends fear spiking up my spine, and I nearly scream, but I don't want the person to know I'm here. That immediately strikes me as silly as I'm likely looking at a dead body. The only apparent injury is to his right leg, which is bent at an awkward angle. The impact from the ground must have killed him.

I'm about to slip away as quietly as I can, not sure how Law Enforcement would react to a strange girl standing next to a dead officer, when I hear a groan. *Wait. He's alive! How is he still alive? Did he fall from the top of the wall? Where else could he have come from? Is he okay?* I look again. He's not wearing an Aether uniform, and he's armed and wearing *black*. Black, the forbidden color. I feel my eyes go wide as it strikes me: Erebus!

What am I doing? Run! He's dangerous. Erebus are killers! Get out of here, my mind screams.

Another groan has me glancing back at his limp and broken body. *Even if he wanted to, could he hurt me?* I doubt it, with those injuries.

I feel something click, deep inside me. Almost like a switch connected to a very, very dim light that I thought died long ago. Even recognizing how stupid it is, I can't *not* pause. He's hurt. He needs help. Am I really going to just walk away? What if I'm wrong? What if he's really Aether? What if he's actually kind and gentle despite the gun strapped to his side? My mind may tell me to run, but my heart is fighting for him… why? I'm turning around to head back and check on him when I pause. *He has a gun! He might shoot you! He really does look Erebus!*

I look at his hand. It's still within reach of his gun holster, but he doesn't look like he's going to be moving anytime soon. Indecision nags at me as I watch him. If he dies, and I just stand here watching, it'll haunt me forever, knowing that I could have saved him, but I didn't.

Another groan escapes the injured man's mouth and I reach a decision.

"Screw it," I say and approach the figure. Up closer I can see blood on his shirt, barely discernible from the dark clothing. But before I get too distracted by his injuries, I grab the gun and throw it forty feet away. There. Safe from the gun. He appears too hurt to fight, but maybe it looks worse than it is. *What if he has a knife?* Damn, he probably does if he has a gun. Maybe this is a trick, and he's trying to get me close enough to stab me. I'm about to run back when he speaks.

"Wait…." murmurs a soft male voice.

"Who are you? What are you doing here? How did you get over the wall? You *did* fall from it, right? Are you here to kill me?" I ask, throwing questions at him.

"Please… help…. Don't tell... anyone I'm… here ...." his words quieting as he speaks, labored as his blood coats the green grass around him. "Not going… to… hurt you…." He struggles to roll onto his back. From what I can now see of his face, covered as it is in dirt and blood, he's younger than I expected.

I'm torn. Something deep inside me is shouting that this person has no intent of hurting me. But maybe that instinct, whatever it is, is wrong. *He's Erebus! He's probably a criminal, a killer! Only Erebus wear black, and he's definitely past the maximum male hair length for the Aether,* my head tells me. *But he's dying, bleeding out,* my heart counters. *Aether don't give second chances and Erebus get no chances,* my mind says again. *But he deserves one! What if he hasn't even done anything? He probably wouldn't jump fifty feet on purpose either, so what if he didn't want to come here?* My mind goes quiet at this. *Either way, he can't hurt you at the moment, and you can decide what to do with him later. But if he dies now and is innocent, you'll regret it.*

"Shit," I curse, and turn back to him. I kneel in the muck and ask, "Do you have a knife?"

"Yes," he replies, pulling it out of his side pocket with clear difficulty. I tense and go stiff at the sight of another weapon. He holds it out to me handle-side out.

"Any other weapons?" I ask, taking the first from him.

"One more," he says and hands me the second knife. I take a deep breath and toss the second one away with the gun. I feel marginally safer now that I'm the armed one.

"I need to check out your wounds," I tell him as I use the first knife to cut open his jacket since I'm clearly not getting it off him. His shirt is soaked in blood, and the scent makes me crinkle my nose. "Love the blood-soaked shirt, the dark red really emphasizes the black. What caused the wound?"

"Knife… Hence why I had a second one," he gasps out, as I check his pulse and forehead for a fever.

"Well, lucky for you, it's not a bullet I have to dig out. Though, it would be neater," I shake my head, then cut his shirt and slide it out from under him. He's fit and honestly his well-defined chest causes my breath to hitch just a bit. But that doesn't matter right now. He's bleeding out from the deep stab wound in his gut. It's an inch or two above the bottom of his ribcage. Two inches to his left and the knife would have missed him. I can't be fully sure without proper imaging, but the knife may have slightly punctured his spleen, having made it past his ribcage, but he's extremely lucky it didn't land anywhere else. You can live without a spleen if need be. If it had landed a little further south into his stomach or intestines, or north into his heart or lung, he'd be in big trouble. I took it as a good sign that he was still breathing and conscious.

I wad up his shirt and press it into the deep gash in his side, applying steady pressure, but I can't stop the bleeding. The shirt is turning bright red as it flows still. I look at my hiking pack.

"Dammit! How did I forget?!" With one hand, I reach into the large bag and, struggling slightly at the awkwardness, pull out my first-aid kit. Yes, I carry a first-aid kit, and not a small one. My parents' requirement for allowing me to hike alone. Makes my backpack fairly heavy, but it has come in handy more than once, so I keep it and deal with the size and weight. "I need to stop the bleeding. I have a stitches kit with me and know how to use it. But it's going to hurt because I don't have anything to numb the area."

He grunts, "I'm already hurting. Just do it," and struggles to lift the now-soaked shirt from his wound.

I quickly push gauze into the wound. It absorbs the blood for a moment as I grab the needle and prepare to stitch it up.

I feel a faint wave of nausea as blood runs over my hands while I sew together the wound, but I push it aside like everything else. When I am done, the wound is still seeping, but the stitches are holding and slowing the blood. I grab the bandage roll and wrap it around his chest after padding the area with fresh gauze, having a hell of a time getting it under him since all that muscle weighs like two hundred pounds.

The Erebus had done a remarkable job staying quiet and still while I stitched him back up. Too nervous to look in his face during the job, I take a peek now. Perspiration dots his upper lip, and his mouth forms a tight line as he bites down his pain. He sighs in relief as I repack my stitching kit. Utterly spent from his exertion and pain, he leans back and closes his eyes, falling asleep in seconds.

I try to wrap his destroyed jacket back around him since the temperature will drop soon. I grab the blanket from my pack and put it around him as well. He looks a little more comfortable, maybe slightly less pale, but it's hard to tell underneath all the dirt on his face. Unfortunately, he also looks too exposed. No one walking by would miss him. I grab mud and dump it on the blanket, breaking up the solid color and creating a make-shift camouflage, followed by a few branches to hide him until he wakes. He can be uncomfortable for now, as his contentment isn't my biggest worry.

His right leg is also broken, but I'll have to deal with that when I return. I don't have the proper gear to treat an injury that severe with me. Plus, my family is freaking out and the phone buzzing hasn't stopped. Hopefully, he'll sleep until I get back. Confident I've done all I can at the moment, I run back through the woods with my bag. When I walk through the door, my parents come at me.

"Where have you been?" Mom frets, brushing her long brown hair off her face.

"We were worried you ran into an… *Erebus*," Dad follows, whispering the last word. He's a blonde with broad shoulders, who gave my sister her own blonde locks. "You weren't answering your phone."

I freeze. *Do they know?* They better not know. They can't, can they?

"I'm fine. I was just taking a walk in the woods. I did what you said not to and went to school, and it was horrible. I couldn't stop thinking about him and…" I trailed off, letting the pain settle on my face.

"Oh, honey. I'm sorry. Ivy called asking if you were okay but didn't explain. What happened?" she asked.

"I… I punched Christopher. He showed up at a really bad time and tried to give me a hug and I just…snapped. I shouldn't have! I don't know what came over me. I already apologized to him and asked Ivy to tell him I'm sorry again."

"Madrona! You punched him? That qualifies as a violent act! One more birthday and you can spend the week in *jail* for punching someone!" Mom barks.

"You punched him?" Dad asked.

"Yeah," I reply, head down. "I think I broke his nose."

"Wow! That's a hard hit! Good job!"

"Michael! Encouraging this?" Mom snaps, turning to stare him down.

He ignores the strength of her glare and says, "What? Oh… no, I'm just amazed she had that much force in her. Is your hand okay?"

"Sprained my wrist and dislocated a knuckle, but I'll be fine. I got the joint reset."

"Let me see it," he orders, and I hold up my hand, glad I rinsed it off in a stream and replaced the blood-soaked tape on my way home. He slightly pushes on my taped-over wrist, and I wince at the pain. "Sorry," he replies, noticing my face.

"It looks like she took good care of it," Mom beams with pride.

"Yes, it does," Dad smiles.

"Alright. Well, next time let us know when you're leaving. Maybe leave a note or something?" she says, and I realize it isn't a question, but an order. "And answer your phone when we call."

"Okay, if everything is good here, I'm going back out to the woods to finish my walk then. It felt good to relax for a moment."

"Here," she comforts, giving me a hug. Dad follows. I let a few tears slide then notice Mom's eyes are wet too. "It's hard, I know. But we'll get through this."

I nod and break the hug. I don't want to cry anymore today.

"I just need to refresh my pack before I go," I tell them. "I used up my roll trying to tape my wrist correctly." I add a wince to show the false shame of an event that didn't happen.

Dad chuckles.

"You know where the extra supplies are in the bathroom cupboard," Mom offers with a sad smile.

"Thank you," I say. As they walk off towards the kitchen, I quickly grab additional bandage and tape rolls and a bottle of sedative my parents keep for emergencies. I'm out the door and back in the woods before they can question me further.

The temperature has already dropped a fair amount in the time I've been gone. I walk briskly as it's a fairly long walk back to the Erebus, so hopefully the blanket is working.

As I make my way back through the forest, I weigh my options for what to do about the Erebus. The punishment for helping him is death. I pause on that thought. If I die for helping him, I might see Aaron again, assuming there's some kind of afterlife. If I don't help him, he dies. No one will come for him here. Not his friends, not his family, and the guards will find him near the wall before too long.

I get a strange feeling. We aren't a secretive or dishonest family, sometimes even honest to a fault. I couldn't even keep my junior-high crush a secret from my parents! Luckily with Aaron, they weren't my secrets to tell, so it was easier to stay silent when he told me the things he did, rules he broke. But this time, it's me breaking the law. And not just a little. A regular violation would be not reporting the Erebus's presence to Law Enforcement. Tending his wounds is an even more grave offense. His life, and my own, are dependent on my ability to keep this a secret.

My heart rate picks up at the thought, but I force myself to calm down. "Why did I help him? I know why," I murmur the question and answer to myself. "Why did I walk here in the first place? I know that also. What's done is done." I continue down the trail, farther and deeper into the woods, to the place where I could die, if anything goes wrong.

TWO

By the time I get to the Erebus (an *Erebus*!), the sun has almost finished its journey across the sky. It takes me a moment to find the exact spot, but I spy a hint of the blanket peeking out beneath my pile of branches and know it has to be him. I remove the branches and mud-covered blanket to check his temperature and pulse. He opens his eyes and blinks at me as I'm checking him.

"I need to give you a sedative, so I can take care of your leg." He glances down and winces slightly at the sight of his limb. "Do I have your permission to stab you with a needle?" I try to make light of the moment.

He stares deep into my eyes, probably trying to figure out if it's a good idea to trust me, wondering if I'll just run and turn him in as soon as he's out. Either way, he doesn't have a choice, and clearly realizes this, as I hold the sedative above him. "Fine," he growls.

I inject the sedative and wait, but not for long, as he passes out in seconds. Most people who fall fifty feet wouldn't survive the journey, and this guy appears to have made it out with only a few bruised bones and a broken leg. That shouldn't be possible. Either it *is* impossible and I'm missing some critical injury, or he's really damn lucky. He definitely needs a CT scan to rule out internal bleeding.

"Okay. Let's see what I can do for you," I try to focus, putting my musings aside for later. First, I need to move the bone back into place. But if I do it wrong, it'll be worse. "No pressure or anything," I grunt in frustration. He'll also need a cast of sorts and eventually, a mobility aid. I look up at the sky that's steadily growing darker. I'll have to be quick.

As I reach for his leg, my breathing goes ragged as panic sets in. I have no experience setting bones. "I don't think I can do this," I gasp, stepping quickly away from his body at the hard, cold truth. "But I know, there's probably someone out there like me, who thinks she's lost this person, and I don't want her to go through what I am right now." I feel the breeze on my face, and the birds quiet for the night as the sky fills with color. If I stay perfectly still, I can almost feel Aaron's presence next to me offering comfort and support. I can just imagine him saying, *'You must save him. He's a person, just like you and me. You can help him get back home, and no one will know he was even here, but he'll be alive and back with those who love him.'*

A tear rolls down my face. "I miss you," I whisper to the empty air.

'I know. But I'm not gone. I'll be here as long as you need me,' his ghost assures, then disappears in the wind.

I take a breath. I can do this. I *will* do this.

Kneeling back down next to the Erebus's leg, I use the knife to cut the pant leg around his shin where the bone broke. A wave of nausea hits me as I see the swelling and bruising the break caused. His right leg is disfigured at the break point, bent in an awkward angle. Luckily, it didn't pierce through the skin of his lower leg. I study the break, carefully feeling the bone while I determine the best way to field dress it. It looks like a fairly clean break. He will need some kind of splint before I can even think about moving him.

Carefully, I place one hand on his ankle, below the break and the other just under his knee, above the break. I push down hard on the knee, bracing it in place while ever so slowly pull downward with the ankle to create separation at the break point. It's a bit tricky without help, and I end up sitting on his upper thigh, so I can use one hand to pull his lower leg while the other hand attempts to realign the bone. I take a deep breath and close my eyes briefly before forcing them open again. I feel for where the ends of the two pieces of the bone are and slowly shift the lower toward the upper. Even though he's sedated, I hear him grunt in pain. I can't imagine how much this would hurt if he was conscious. He'd probably pass out quickly, but before then…

The movement of the bone and muscle makes a horrifying sound as it shifts the small space of an inch back into place. I sigh in relief when I carefully check to make sure it's in the correct spot and feel everything line up.

"Holy shit! I just did that," I jump to my feet and take a few steps. I return to a crouch above the ground a few feet away as I try to release all the stress that has built up in my core. "Okay. Okay, okay, okay. Now for something to stop it from moving."

I don't have a splint, and obviously no material for a cast. I suddenly remember the extra bandages I grabbed when I was at home. I wrap an entire roll over his shin tightly, but not too tight. All the layers build up and create a hard cover, but I'm not completely satisfied. I grab the piece of his pant leg I cut off and wrap it around tightly, then duct tape another layer over that. This builds a protective layer around the area, so the bones hopefully won't shift. I grab four flat sticks and line them up with his shin, then tape them to my mess of a cast. I nod with pride at my work. He should be alright. His leg might not heal perfectly, and he'll probably be in a world of pain when he wakes, but he'll live, and he *will* walk again.

Now I have to hide him again because he can't lie out in the open overnight. I place the reflective blanket and mud back on him, trying to keep him as warm as possible during the cold night. I grab branches and tie them together with string. Propping up my tied together sticks against a tree on the other side of him, it forms a small area of cover. I cover the sticks in fallen leaves and cover the open sides with tall grasses I dug up.

It doesn't look quite right, but you'd only realize this after inspecting it carefully. At a glance, it appears like another thick, overgrown bush, not a makeshift cover for an injured Erebus. The darkness should further help disguise its true purpose. It's a few feet from the wall, but should be enough since the guards get lazy, and they won't see it due to the tree cover anyway, but I'm not taking any chances. The night guards are ordered to kill Erebus on sight, while during the day, they take them to court to determine their fate. Most end up being sentenced to death there as well, but the ones that are considered fit for work might be enslaved or thrown in prison.

"Okay. I have to go. My parents will freak out if I'm gone any longer," I state to the unconscious body that's hidden from sight. He'll be awake by morning but should have enough sense to stay put. Not like he's going anywhere without help anytime soon. I grab my bag and start making my way back on the trail. I'll return tomorrow with more supplies.

The half hour of walking passes fast as I try to think of a reason to be out in the woods again tomorrow, but I can't think of anything. All the excuses I come up with aren't realistic or don't make sense. Eventually I decide that I shouldn't need an excuse, and that I can just blame it on my grief that I need the space and quiet of the woods.

I walk in the door and sit down with my family for dinner. My parents, little sister, and I all eat in silence. If I'm going to cover this up, I'll have to do nothing out of the ordinary. I'll pretend to hide in a world of mourning and grief, but I already am, so I guess it's not really pretending. I'll have to do what Aaron had to do, lie to family, for their sake and mine.

It's not going to be easy. Not that life has been a walk in the park recently. Is it worth the risk? The danger? All this lying and deception to save an Erebus who might kill me afterwards. Is it the right thing? Aaron would have done it. He would have done whatever it took. He would be proud of me for trying to save another's life, but he wouldn't want me to risk my own. And because of that, he would tell me not to do any of this. But I'm not listening to that side of him.

I'm not afraid of death. Aaron wasn't either. I wish he had been. Maybe he would have tried harder to live. Maybe he would have fought harder rather than give up. For that, I hate him... No, I don't. I could never hate him, no matter how hard I tried. Everything is so confusing right now. It's like someone tied my string of thoughts in knots, disrupting it, making it short and unusable.

I sigh to myself and realize Mom's trying to start a conversation. I stick with my plan and pretend to enter my world of grief and suffering. After a few moments, I'm not pretending anymore. The feeling of loss comes back and punches me in the heart. Again and again. Suddenly everything loses meaning. Why keep the secret? If I'm sentenced to death, I have a chance of seeing Aaron again in the next life, if there is one. *Stop*. If I don't stay silent, I won't be the only one to die. The guy in the woods has no worth to the Aether. He's unable to work, and they rarely put Erebus in prison. Even if they did, he'd likely die there anyway.

I walk to my room and lay down on the soft and cozy bed. I let my grief overtake my thoughts, and I cry myself to sleep through exhaustion and stress from the strange day.

When I wake up the following morning, my pillow is still wet. Apparently, my tears continued while I slept, my dreams containing a litany of memories. I stuff down my emotions and stand up. Walking down the stairs, I find my little sister awake.

"Hi Madrona," she yawns.

"Hey Lily," I say, almost whispering. My early morning vision is covered in a layer of fog, blurring her face. I blink a few times, and it slowly starts to go away.

Lily may be four years younger than me, but she still takes care of me. "I heard you moving around, so I threw a bagel in the toaster for you," she announces, nodding her head towards the toaster at the far end of the room. "Figured you'd be down soon."

"Thanks." She smiles and quietly climbs the stairs to hide in her room. For a moment I wonder why she isn't getting ready for school, then realize it's the weekend. My sense of time is destroyed. I used to keep the family's schedule, always keeping everyone on track and organized. Now, I'm a mess. Can't even remember what day it is. Thankfully, Lily stepped up and is now taking care of everyone.

The bagel pops up, and I cover it in butter. Then it hits me: the Erebus! He's awake and stranded in the woods. *Hurry the hell up!* I shove the bagel into my mouth then grab my coat. I hesitate before exiting the door, remembering they'll question my absence. I scribble a note out, telling them I'm back walking in the woods again before heading out the door.

Wait! I stop again. Making a one-eighty turn, I grab three plastic water bottles and throw together two sandwiches, along with some pain meds since he's probably hurting. I stop to consider for a moment before grabbing an ice pack. He was pretty beat up when I saw him yesterday.

All but running out the door, I start my trek through the forest. He can't stay in his current hiding place forever. I'll have to figure out what to do with him.

It's a misty, chilly Saturday morning, but the sun is just breaking on the horizon, and its warmth should heat the ground soon enough. More birds are out this morning, chirping away at the start of spring, after the last small snowfall yesterday. A deer leaps over a fallen tree and undergrowth, quickly followed by another. An owl cries somewhere above, probably giving out warnings to those below.

Ferns and small trees cover the ground, followed by various wildflowers adding a few colors to the green and brown backdrop. They add brightness to the already lively forest, giving it a sense of depth, as they glow in the sunlight and dew drips from their petals. The smell of wet wood floats through the air, the trees soaked with melted snow, as the sun extends hands of soft light towards me. Its rays comfort me as I creep closer and closer to what may very well be my end, and I smile at the forest's beauty despite the danger.

I continue down the path and see a light brownish-orange, almost copper-colored tree with bright green leaves. I smile at the wondrous growth, its careful branches reaching out in every direction. This is my tree, this tree is me, the tree I was named after. *Arbutus menziesii*, the Madrona tree. The tree whose bark can be used as paper, the tree that grows through the year, through the cold and is beautiful no matter the season.

Continuing down the path, I only know one thing. I am not afraid.

Eventually, I reach my makeshift hideout, my footsteps barely audible on the leaves and twigs lying on the ground. I stop a good fifteen feet away, giving him space. He *is* likely a killer, after all, and while it may seem like it, I don't actually have a death wish.

"Hello?" I whisper.

"Who's there?" The voice is deep, but still young. Stronger, tougher, more armored, and less labored than it was yesterday. He's gotten much better overnight.

"It's me," I reply, then remember that he doesn't know who I am and nearly slap myself in the face.

"Are you the girl?"

"Yes," I sigh, approaching and lifting my tied-together sticks to reveal the guy from yesterday. He supports his body with his elbow, his legs sprawling across the ground in the same place they were before. His light brown bangs almost cover his deep blue eyes. Definitely not an Aether hairstyle. His skin isn't quite white but has a slight tan coloring.

"You sound better," I remark, untying the branches. Don't want to litter, right? Besides the movement, the fact that I'm doing *something* calms me down.

"Well, I'm not dying at the moment," he replies with a smile. I turn away as I start to see his mouth change shape. He's an Erebus. He's not supposed to smile. I halt my untying and throw him a bottle and sandwich. He catches them eagerly and drinks the full bottle, devouring the sandwich afterwards.

"Thanks. Haven't eaten in a day or two."

What? Why? "You can have mine, too then," I state carefully and toss him the second sandwich, and he inhales it just as quickly as the first.

"Thank you," he repeats. He's polite. Well, he's already *not* half of what Law Enforcement told us the Erebus were: ruthless, murderous, uncivilized, destructive, horrible, and cruel. He's definitely not uncivilized or horrible, and I'm guessing he could have killed me by now if he wanted me dead. But hey, I could be judging too early.

He struggles to shift his position without moving his leg, trying to use the tree next to him as a backrest. He groans when he moves his leg slightly, dragging my makeshift cast across the forest ground.

"Does it hurt?" I inquire, suddenly glad I brought the pain meds.

"No more than anything else," he explains. I grab my bag and kneel by his side, handing him the meds and ice pack.

He hesitates before swallowing them but eagerly grabs the ice pack, throwing off his jacket and placing it on his bare left shoulder blade.

I have a fairly hard time looking away, since the one moment I allow myself a glance, he's covered in large muscles that cover his back and chest. He is utterly and absolutely *beautiful*. This is a guy most girls only *dream* about.

I quickly shake the thought from my mind. "What happened to you? And how did you survive the fall? It should have killed you," I interrogate, breaking the moment of silence.

"I was attacked and went over during the fight. As for the fall, guess I was just lucky," he answers.

He's hiding something. I consider asking further about who attacked him and how he was 'just lucky', since even luck's odds probably couldn't save him from that fall but decide I can ply him with questions later.

"That reminds me," he ponders. "Why did you help me? You are obviously Aether."

I stop and think about how to answer. "Have you ever lost someone you loved?" I finally ask, deciding to tell him the easiest explanation, rather than the one I'm still unsure about.

Giving a confused face, he replies, "Yes."

"My boyfriend died six months ago. I'm still not even close to getting over it. I couldn't imagine someone grieving for you. Too much death. Too much loss. I just couldn't walk away and not try. By helping you, I'm giving your loved ones a chance to see you again. Besides, if I get caught, they'll kill me too, and then I'll be with him again, right?" I reply.

His eyebrows knit themselves together, forming a look of pain as he stares deep into my eyes, and I try to stare back into his. For a second, I wonder if he's reading my mind.

He turns away quickly, breaking the lock. "I'm sorry for your loss," he murmurs, a blank expression coming onto his face. A mask. I can't see past it, frustratingly. "As an Aether, you have a name, correct?"

"Yes. I'm Madrona. And you are?"

"L26."

"Nice to meet you, L26," I answer, the letter and two digits sounding strange in my mouth. We sit in an awkward silence for a moment, and I vaguely remember from class that Erebus don't have names, only an assigned letter followed by two to seven digits, supposedly depending on where the person is from. Occasionally they will repeat codes, but it doesn't happen very often.

"Well, thank you, Madrona. For not letting me bleed to death and repairing my broken leg."

I nod in acknowledgement. He turns to look at his shoulder, revealing a large purple and blue bruise twice the size of my hand. I gasp, having never seen a bruise so large.

"Holy shit! What happened?"

"As I said, I was attacked. Specifically, I was stabbed, kicked, and then beaten repeatedly until I fell off the wall, and *then* I nearly died from the impact. Yeah, I had a rough day."

I smile, letting out a quiet chuckle, and he smiles back in response. Oh god, that smile. *And I thought he was beautiful before.* Realizing the thought that just entered my head, I scowl at myself for thinking such a thing, instantly averting my eyes, and not meeting his gaze.

"That bruise doesn't look good. Let me see it," I command, avoiding his gaze. He grimaces, turning to reveal more bruises and cuts, though the bruise on his shoulder blade is by far the biggest.

I grab band-aids and gauze from my bag, along with another water bottle and some antibacterial ointment. Pouring a bit of water on his skin, I very carefully clean his cuts before throwing a band-aid with the ointment on the larger cuts. He hands me the icepack, and I hold it to each of his larger bruises that he can't reach for a few minutes.

I notice another bruise slightly hidden beneath his light brown hair on his lower neck. When I lift it out of the way, I notice a crescent moon tattoo on the back of his neck. I place the icepack on the bruise next to it, and his hair falls back into place.

Noticing my hesitation and guessing the cause of it, L26 says, "My brother… My brother and I got identical tattoos when I turned sixteen. He had just turned eighteen, as he is two years older than me. Told me that whenever I'm lost, whenever I'm alone, there will always be a mark to help me remember, to help me continue on. To help me come home." His voice cracks at the last sentence, and I gulp down the pain I feel for him.

"He sounds like an awesome brother," I smile.

"He-" L26 goes quiet for a moment. I'm about to ask if he's alright when he speaks again. "He is," he replies, his voice hardly audible. I decide it's not the time to ask and hand him the icepack when I finish after the next few minutes are spent in silence. He places it back on the large bruise on his shoulder.

"How did you know what to do about my leg and all? Are you a healer or something?"

"No. My parents taught my sister and me basic medical skills. They're both docs," I admit, noting his use of the word 'healer.' "Which brings me to your current problem. You can't stay here in the woods forever. Are you planning to go back over the wall? And if so, how?"

"I want to go back, yes, but I don't think it's safe. Our representative is the one who sent my attackers. I would like to stay here until I find out why," L26 responds. Having picked up a plastic bottle, I nearly choke on the water.

"What?" The main job of a representative is to *help* and *protect* the people. Not throw them over a fifty-foot wall. *Maybe it's an Erebus thing?* I shake my head. *Not important right now,* I conclude.

"And how long would that take?"

"I... don't know. Maybe two days, maybe two months. I'll definitely go back when we re-elect in eighteen months, and he loses power." *They had their election six months ago, while we are doing so now... So, we* aren't *on the same schedule.* Well, such should be expected.

"Well, I'm guessing it's going to take more than two days, and tomorrow the Aether guards are going to do their routine sweep of the area, so we need to get you out of here," I mention. My uncle was a guard; he used to patrol the wall until he was upgraded to guarding the POT, the Place of Truce. I pace in consideration. I'll have to move L26 somewhere else. But where? Then he interrupts my thinking.

"What if I dressed up as one of you?"

I stop in my tracks and glance at him, considering his proposal. After a moment of silence and going through all possible outcomes, I come to a conclusion. "That might just work. You'd need a name, and we'd have to make a cover story for... this," I state, motioning at his injuries. "And you'd need a haircut, the correct clothes, a way to hide your tattoo... I'll have to instruct you on how to act like us, but it might work. It might just work," I muse. "Where would you stay though?"

"Maybe I could stay with you... But only if you're fine with that, of course," he proposes.

Stunned by the idea, I hesitate before considering it. *You still don't know if you can trust him,* a small part of me says. "I... I don't know."

"You think I'd kill or harm you and your family?" he asks, giving me a '*seriously*' look.

"I don't know," I reply. "I know absolutely nothing about you." He just stares at me. "I can't trust you, and you're asking me to place my family at risk."

"True," he concedes. "Alright.... Hmm... I love to cook."

"What?" I startle, both from the rapid subject change and because he doesn't strike me as a guy who'd spend time in a kitchen.

"Yep, I love to cook," he admits. "What, your Erebus stereotypes not lining up?"

"Nope, but... still."

"Okay... uh... let me think," he states. After a moment he finally speaks again. "Okay. I love music, art, all of it. Some nights I'd play guitar for my family underneath the stars, and afterwards my parents would tell ancient stories of the night sky. My sister would beg me to braid her hair while we listened, ashes from the fire dancing in the air before sprinkling the ground." He smiles at the memory, then it quickly fades, and he closes his eyes in sorrow.

"We'll get you back to them," I comfort. He answers with a sad smile. He's lost and alone. His eyes and body language say it is the truth, and he's young, maybe a year older than me. The way he speaks of his family tells me that I can trust him with mine.

"Thank you," he replies. "For taking care of me, for not turning me in."

"I couldn't have... I have trouble not helping someone in need," I say truthfully. "But more than that, there's something about you that I can't put my finger on, something different. Something that drew me back when I was going to walk away..." I trail off, slightly embarrassed to say so much and partially because I haven't quite yet figured it out myself.

"Whatever the reason, I am grateful."

His face is closed off where moments ago it was open and friendly. I try to recall the moment it changed during my stumbling confession, but after a moment of staring deep into his eyes, trying to read him, I finally give up. "Alright, alright. I'll let you stay with us, but it's not really my decision. You'll have to convince my parents..." I trail off.

"I can be pretty convincing," he assures, flashing me a perfect smile.

Oh, man! I feel heat rush into my face as I turn around and try to hide my reaction. Damn! He was handsome before, but add in that smile... Heck, with just that smile he could probably convince anyone to do anything. My mother will probably sway towards helping him after seeing that smile. Dad will be the harder one to win over. He'll want to help, but he will be confused about why we're letting a complete stranger his daughter found on the 'street' stay in our house.

"Either way, you'll need a story. Something to cover up why no one knows you, why you're so beat up, and this will all have to include a reason to let you stay with us. It'll have to be something good."

"What if I'm a guy who just moved here and that's why I'm not in the city records yet? What if I'm alone because my parents died in a car crash on the way here, and I was in too much grief to go to a hospital? Then, you found me on the street hobbling through the neighborhood using a branch as a walking stick," he puts forth.

"They'll take you to the hospital the second they see you. I guess you could guilt trip them afterwards."

"Great! Story, done. Name, uhh… What's a good male Aether name?"

I snap my attention back when I notice he's talking to me again. It hurts, plotting against my family, using them like this… I throw it deep down in my mind for later, as now isn't the time. "Will, Thomas, Jacob, Sam, Anthony…" I start listing off names when he stops me.

"Wait, what was that one, the one with the 'J' sound?"

"Jacob?" I repeat.

"Jacob. I'm kind of liking that."

I don't know what it is, but something about this moment makes me smile. "And for your last name?" I chuckle quietly.

"Last name? You have multiple?" L26, now Jacob, wears a horrified expression.

"Most have three," I explain, keeping the fact that others have four to myself.

"What? Why so many?"

"I don't know, honestly."

"Okay. How about Jacob Anthony Thomas?"

I stop for a second. It isn't bad. He looks like a Jacob and seems like a Thomas. Not sure about Anthony, but most middle names don't make sense, so it'll be fine. "Sure. Now every time someone calls 'Jacob,' you'll have to react as if they said L26."

"I can do that," he promises.

"I'll go grab some clothes and scissors and see what I get my hands on to cover that tattoo. Stay here, and I should be back in an hour."

"Okay," L26, or Jacob - guess I should start calling him that too - answers. I grab my bag and start heading back through the lush, green forest, the comforting and familiar smell of wet and rotting wood following me home.

· 〜 ∘ ✦ ☾ · ☼ · ☽ ✦ ∘ 〜 ·

It takes me a bit to find men's clothes that will fit him, but eventually I find a shirt and pair of pants in a dumpster around the block. They might be a bit small, but they'll work. We'll have to tear them a bit anyway, so hopefully that'll make them fit better. They don't smell great, but if the story's going to fit, they can't anyway. I grab scissors and dig through my extremely cheap make-up set that contains four different skin shades. I dislike using it and haven't in a long time since Aaron convinced me I didn't need it. He believed it made me look like a Barbie doll. He wasn't wrong. I grab something that looks close to Jacob's skin tone and run out the door.

My parents are at work, and there's a note on the door I must have missed when I first came in. *'Have a good day. Remember to let us know if you need anything. Love you, Mom and Dad,'* it reads. I smile. They used to leave notes for us every morning before work. They stopped doing it as we got older.

I run out the door and back into the forest, following the path and then jumping over ferns, bushes, and fallen trees when I reach the end.

Jacob is right where I left him, leaning against the tree. He must have gotten cold because he's wearing his jacket again.

"Hi," he says.

"Hi. I brought you some clothes. I think you need the haircut first though. Ready?" I ask, pulling out my scissors.

"I don't know. Just make sure I don't look too bad," he pleads, warily eyeing the connected twin blades in my hand.

I smile before answering. "Hey, I know what I'm doing. I've done this a total of zero times."

"I'm not going to lie and tell you I'm feeling good about this," he chuckles.

"I'll do my best," I smile, kneel next to him, and set to work cutting his long light brown hair.

It's hard to do, watching the beautiful locks fall to the ground. He looked pretty good with long hair, but it just screams 'Erebus', so it has to go. I trim the sides of his head to be short, cutting off years of growth. I trim his bangs and they start to naturally rise, standing up on his head at the loss of weight. The back of his head is hard, since I don't know this style too well, so I try doing the same thing I did for the sides of his head, and it seems to work. Locks of his long hair fall to the ground.

When I'm done, I drop the scissors and try to style his hair, running my fingers through it so it fits the cut. His smooth and soft light brown hair naturally builds, so it's not hard to fix.

I step back and admire my work. Now his hair screams 'Aether.' I've given him a tapered undercut to go with his very light and thin beard. His slightly shorter bangs in the front stand up slightly, smoothly flowing off to the side in the direction I combed it, making the look fit him even better. I smile. He still looks good, so I can't have done too badly.

"So... how do I look?" he asks.

"Good. Different, which was the goal, but still good. You look Aether. Well, except for the gun holster, torn black jacket and pants that are covered in blood, and the tattoo," I list. Then it strikes me. Is he going to be able to change his clothes on his own? I hope so because I am not helping him, that's for sure.

"Alright. Tattoo next?" he asks. It's probably better to do the tattoo last, so it's not smeared, but I can see he's delaying the changing bit. The make-up should dry quickly, so it might not even be a problem.

"Yeah," I agree, pulling out my bottle of BarbieMaker2000. He turns his back to me, so I can work easier. The tattoo is much more obvious without his long hair. I open the bottle and start rubbing the makeup onto his neck. I force away thoughts of how smooth his skin is, and the black tattoo slowly disappears beneath the layers of makeup. I didn't get the perfect shade, but it's so close you wouldn't notice unless you were looking for it and maybe not even then.

"Okay, done. Here's the clothes. Good luck getting them on," I comment. "Yell for me when you're done." I start walking back down the path after handing him the white shirt and jeans. Once I'm out of view, I sit on a log and wait, watching the sun disappear behind a cloud, listening to the birds.

A few minutes later, he calls out and I make my way back. Unlike the jacket, the shirt shows how fit he is. The blue jeans complement the white shirt, and a wave of recognition hits me. He almost looks like Aaron at that moment in his expression and with eyes so similar... A tear starts down my face, but I turn my back to him and wipe it away before it can go anywhere. Okay. Back to the moment.

I grab the scissors and tear holes in the shirt where he was stabbed and cut, adding a few extra tears for good measure. I lift my gaze up to Jacob's and see he's smiling. Smiling that killer smile.

"What?" I demand, noticing his attention to me, butterflies sprouting in my stomach.

He shakes his head, chuckling. "Nothing."

I smile back at him and choose to move on. "You look… Aether. Now, ready to meet my family?"

"I don't know," he pales. "Am I?"

"I honestly don't know either. Just remember the story and flash that smile when appropriate," I tell him, then kneel next to him on his right side. "Arm around my shoulder, and I'll carry half your weight." He obeys and puts his arm around my shoulder, and we attempt to rise together. I consider those words, 'rise together,' and what they mean. Literally and metaphorically. Once my family gets involved, there's no turning back. We're in this, whatever 'this' is, together.

Jacob's wincing the whole time it takes to stand, but eventually we're up and moving. He's heavy, relying on me to help support him, as he can't put any weight on his broken leg. I may be five-five and considerably shorter, but I'm stronger than I look. His arm is around my waist, my bright red hair flowing in the wind, as we slowly work our way through the forest, stumbling on occasion on undergrowth or a hidden tree root. Several times he almost falls over, but each time I manage to catch him until he regains his balance.

The journey is long and tiring for both of us, but we make it to my house. We approach the doorstep and I notice what time it is. The sun is past its halfway point in the sky so we must have taken two hours to get through the forest. My parents took the shorter morning shift today, so they should be home by now.

Just as we're climbing the steps to my house, Lily runs by the door and opens it for us with a worried look on her face, eyes going wide at the sight of Jacob.

"Madrona? What's going on?" she questions loudly.

Jacob glances down at me as if to say, *I didn't know you had a sister*. I just smile back with a slight shrug. Mom and Dad, who must have been in the kitchen to the left of the door, run over after hearing Lily, and gasp when they see Jacob.

"Broken leg and puncture wound to the torso, multiple contusions," I quickly launch into a litany of Jacob's injuries. "Car crash survivor. I found him on the street as I was walking home."

"Let's get him to the hospital," Mom insists. "A car crash could mean internal injuries too."

"How long since the crash?" Dad questions, as we change direction heading towards my parents' car instead of inside the house.

"Eight hours," Jacob replies, wincing at the movement when he tries to bend at the waist to get inside the car.

"Why didn't you go straight to a hospital? Wait for an ambulance?" Mom lectures as we help him into the back seat.

"My parents… didn't survive. And I-I just… I wasn't thinking. I bandaged what I could and then got away from there as fast as I could. I just… I just couldn't sit there with their bodies and wait for someone to come along. I guess I wanted to pretend they were still alive, and I was just walking home…" he lets a few tears slip, selling the story completely.

"Oh, sweetie, I'm so sorry. We'll get you fixed up. If you need to talk about it feel free, and if you don't want to, you don't have to," Mom replies. Jacob nods and lets out a quiet cry as they shift his leg into the car. I run to the other side and sit in the seat beside him, keeping him upright, while Mom and Dad take the front seats.

When we reach the hospital, Dad almost sprints in and comes back with four workers wheeling a stretcher. They get Jacob onto the stretcher and take him inside, Mom and I following.

"What happened?" a nurse interrogates Mom, as she attempts to cut off Jacob's shirt with scissors to reveal my messy bandaging.

"Car crash," she replies. They both gasp when they see the bloody bandage that was hidden underneath his shirt. "Head straight to imaging. We need to check for internal bleeding and the positioning of his broken leg, then possibly surgery afterwards if that abdominal wound looks concerning. Or if we need to reset his leg. Reserve us an operating suite as soon as there's availability. And call Dr. Davies. I believe he's the general surgeon on duty today. Tell him we might have a case for him."

One of the workers looks at me. "Miss, I'll have to ask you to wait here. We'll take it from here, and let you know how he's doing," he says.

"Please let me come along," I beg.

"I'm sorry, but I didn't make the rules. Staff only," the worker claims.

Mom and Dad glance back at me but are already in full doctor mode. "We'll get him situated and in good hands. Then we'll come back to take you home."

I slow my walk and let them wheel Jacob down the hall. He glances back at me as I stand there, a look of worry on his face as he's moved around the corner and out of my view. What if the makeup rubs off and they find the tattoo? It won't. That's heavy-duty makeup; it takes hours of hot water to come off. It could last a week if handled correctly. What if they find out another way? They'll report him, and he'll die!

I search my mind for ways they could find out he's Erebus and can't come up with anything. He'll be fine, I tell myself, and sit down in the waiting room, preparing for a long wait. Mom, Dad, and I will head home in a couple of hours, then come back in the morning. This has happened before, although that time, it was obviously with another Aether.

I stop for a moment, realizing something. Less than a tenth of one percent of Aethers ever see someone from the other side even once in their lives. The chance of someone finding Jacob who wouldn't report him on sight, the chance of him being found before he bled out, the chance of being found by a person trained in basic medical care, the chance of *me* being the one to find him, are all impossibly low. Jacob might be the luckiest person to walk the earth.

I attempt to get comfy in my chair and begin to wait.

THREE

I wake up at five o'clock in the evening, still in the waiting room, when my parents come down the hall saying it's time to go home. I hadn't planned to sleep, but it is a faster way to pass the time than staring at a wall.

A wave of worry hits me. Will he be okay? What if they figure it out? I finally decide there's nothing I can do about it at the moment, and therefore shouldn't think about it, because it'll just cause unneeded stress.

We jump in the car and head home, the ride quiet as we are all drained from the day's events. When we return, Lily is on the couch playing video games with a bowl of popcorn.

"Is he going to be okay?" I finally ask, breaking the silence as we walk inside. I try to hide the hint of worry in my voice but end up failing.

"He'll be fine. He was stabbed with shattered glass from the car windows, but he'll live. Lucky guy, he is. The shard didn't hurt anything important, and it sounds like he yanked it out so he could bandage it," Mom assures me. "He did a good job taking care of his injuries."

"As for his leg, it looks like he somehow got it lined up again. I can't imagine how painful that must have been," Dad shutters slightly. "His messy support kept it from moving out of place, but the movement put pressure on it and bumped it over slightly, so we corrected it. He just needs time to heal, for the moment."

"Good." I don't know what else to say.

"The boy didn't know where the crash was. Makes sense since he's new to the area. Said he just started walking after dragging himself out of the car. He thinks he remembers the car swerving, trying not to hit something, before the crash. The hospital hasn't received any reports of car wrecks today, so they must have been out in the middle of nowhere. Law Enforcement will probably find it at some point, but if it was closer to another town, we won't get the report. Then again, that's a long way to walk, especially with a broken leg," Mom ponders aloud. Hearing her logic through the details worries me. She might very well find out the inconsistencies of Jacob's story on her own, just by thinking it over.

Dad sighs. "The poor kid. Doesn't have any other family to go to. No aunts or uncles, and his grandparents are likely dead. Where's he going to live? He was just moving here, so he doesn't know anyone, either."

There's a moment of silence, and I know what my parents are thinking. Exactly what Jacob and I were hoping they would. When they remain silent, I decide it has to be said, because if it isn't spoken aloud, it won't happen. "What if he stayed with us? I mean, until he's an adult. Isn't he almost eighteen?"

"He said he turned seventeen a month ago. That's almost a full year," Mom exclaims. I make a mental note-to-self that he's only a year older than me. "We don't want to do that to you girls. We know it'd be a hard change to adapt to, and we don't know anything about him anyway. He's a random boy."

"He lost his family and doesn't know anyone here. As for the safety concern, would a boy my age do anything against the law that could risk death?" I ask. "He's just looking for help. At least talk to him first."

Mom sighs, and finally gives in to the urge to help. "Okay, I'll talk to him, and yes, you're right. He's probably not a concern, but as your mother, it's my job to worry."

I give her a large hug. "I know."

"Lily, what do you think about this?"

Lily puts down her game and says, "Cute guy living with us? I'm up for it!" This makes all of us smile. I release a small chuckle because Jacob is *far* past 'cute.'

"Maybe it'll be for the better, provide a nice distraction from other things…" I insist. Mom and Dad look at each other. I know what they're thinking. Maybe Jacob and I can grieve together, or the distraction will keep me grounded or maybe even turn me back into my previous self. I know I'll never be the same though. They're wondering if he'll pull me out of my world of depression, this deep, dark pit inside me where my heart used to be. And honestly, I am too. I remember the moment in the forest as we tried to stand together. To rise, together. To overcome the weight holding us down, as one.

I know I want to be single for the rest of my life because the pain of Aaron's death was too much. But maybe Jacob can help me recover, while he tries to figure out what's going on.

"Where would he stay though?" Mom whispers to Dad.

"He could take one of the girls' rooms or the couch. Wait, don't we still have that old mattress? He could take the attic. Someone would have to clean it out first, but it could work," he answers, glancing upstairs at the attic door that's hidden from view.

"Do we have enough food to support a teenage boy? Don't they eat like pigs?" Mom asks quietly. I laugh, and she looks over, realizing we can hear them just fine.

"Yes, they do. But I'm sure we have enough food. We've done this before, so I'm not really worried about it."

"But last time it was for two weeks! Not several months!"

"We'll make it work. Besides, he could help... *someone-*," he motions with his head in my direction, "recover."

"True. I don't know though. It's still a long time."

"He just needs some help right now. Once he recovers, if things aren't working, we can always kick him out once he gets a job."

"Alright," Mom gives in. Honestly, I thought it'd be Dad who didn't approve. Mom disapproving is a first.

Dad turns to us. "We'll talk to him, and if we approve, we'll invite him, but he probably won't accept. I know I wouldn't if I were in his place," Dad admits.

"Yay," Lily cheers.

I can't tell if she's being sarcastic or not. I throw together a sandwich and climb the stairs to hide in my room. Lying to my family is wearing me down. It's stressful, and I can't imagine what they would say if they found out.

I sit in a corner of my small closet, curling myself into a ball after eating my plain sandwich. I like this spot, it's cozy and comforting. It makes me feel small and insignificant, like every time I screw up, it won't have too big of a consequence. Aaron hits me like a bowling ball going a hundred miles an hour, and the weight of memories is too much to bear. The moment I first saw him, the moment he asked me out, the moment he first vented to me about all his hardships, the moment I first confided in him. The time in the meadow when I first told him about my self-doubt, and he hugged me telling me I'm perfect in every way. *'Except the fact that you hate peaches.'* I remember laughing after that comment. *'Who likes peaches?'* I asked him. *'Everyone!'* he answered. *'Everyone likes peaches!' 'That can't be right,'* I'd said. I smile at the memory, though my tears begin to flow faster.

Somehow, I see Aaron sitting next to me, squished between me and the wall. *'A little space here?'* he requests. I smile and move over. He's still shoulder to shoulder with me, but there just isn't any more room. I know I'm likely going crazy, but if it's the only way to see him, I'm fine with it.

"Why did you have to die? Why did you just give up?"

'You think I gave up?'

"Yes," I say, though I know it's not true the moment it leaves my mouth. But still, I need to know I'm right.

'I fought 'till the end. It might not have looked like that, but I knew what I'd put you through if I died, so I did my best to avoid it.'

"Wish there was something I could have done," I murmur, hardly a whisper.

'You did do something. You were with me until the end, which was more than I could have ever hoped for. You helped me fight; you helped me fight my hardest, harder than ever before. It was just a battle that couldn't be won.' In my mind I see him put his arm around me, but I can't feel it, no matter how much I want to, how much I need to. *'We can't undo the*

past, so we must make do with a better future.' He fades away, dispersing into nothing.

I smile at the thought. It's such an Aaron thing to say. I let it rest in my mind, as I consider the meaning. Then I feel silly, as I know he isn't real, but I want him to come back anyway. Tears are still rolling down my cheeks. Why? Why did he have to die? I have to stop crying. I wipe my tears away with my sleeve and decide to go to bed early. My eyes close and sleep carries me away into a dreamless, peaceful, and quiet sleep.

The next morning, I climb down the stairs to find Mom, Dad, and Lily talking in the kitchen. Something about school and her homework.

"Morning," I say.

"Good morning, Madrona," Dad replies.

"Do you have the morning shift?" I inquire, noticing their hospital scrubs.

"We're going back to the hospital to put a cast on Jacob's leg," Mom informs us. My parents are orthopedists and were chosen to work on Jacob's leg. "We had to wait for the swelling to go down before we could properly treat it."

"Did you turn in your vote for representative?" Dad inquires.

"No," I answer, surprised at the change of subject. Shit, I forgot! If I don't turn it in soon, Law Enforcement will come banging on our door asking for it. It's Sunday, so I'm already over a day late. "I'll do it today."

I move the subject back. "Is Jacob allowed visitors?"

"Not yet. Once we get him a cast, he should be."

"How long will he have to be in the hospital?"

"He'll need a few days to recover his strength from the blood loss. Once he's moving in the right direction, they'll allow him to leave," Dad explains.

"Okay." I need to introduce him to our customs soon before he screws up without knowing it.

"We need to get going," Mom points out. "Have fun today; love you both." They head out the door, closing it behind them.

I turn to Lily. "So… What do you want to do today?"

"I don't know."

"Well, let me know when you think of something," I tell her and go back upstairs. I have homework: Calculus, History, Spanish, English… I sigh. I might be fast when it comes to getting work done, but this could still take a while. I dig through my backpack and pull out my computer. I put in my earbuds and set to work on writing about the last war between the Erebus and Aether over a hundred years ago.

The Aether and Erebus are pure opposites. Day and night. Happiness and suffering. Even our namesakes are opposites: Greek gods of light and dark. Good and evil. Erebus carry weapons everywhere they go, while violence is strictly forbidden for Aethers. Rumors abound since very few citizens ever get to talk or even see someone from the other side. Some say the Erebus live underground. Others believe they live in skyscrapers, built on the highest mountain peaks, so they can be closest to the moon and stars. Most agree that they are just like us but live in anarchy rather than order and law.

It was this last war that built the wall. The war that made it illegal to even *look* at someone from the other side unless you turn them in within minutes of seeing them. The war that *no one* won. The war that launched the nuclear bombs which killed off almost ninety-nine percent of the world population, leaving only eighty-two million alive. The war that forced the survivors to come together to the only part of the planet that remained free of radiation.

By the time I finish my essay, it's noon, and I have to make Lily lunch. I throw some vegetables and lettuce together to make salads. She doesn't like the everyday plain sandwich I normally have, so I try to make her something different each day.

Once we're done eating, I finally speak. "I'm going to head to the hospital to check on Mom and Dad, okay? Can you hold up the fort?"

"Haven't burned it down yet," she chuckles.

I smile and grab my bag, then head out the door, making sure to grab the important sheet Mom tapped to the door.

My vote slip is shoved in my bag, followed by my car keys. I haven't driven in a while, having not gone anywhere except for walking to school. I sigh as I jump into my old Volkswagen and start up the engine. I've always loved this car.

My sweet, old beat-up Volkswagen. When everything was different and horrible, my good old light blue car was always there. I place my hands on the wheel and take a breath, then drag my old-fashioned stick shift into reverse and back out of the driveway.

Shifting the gears and putting my feet on the pedals calms me. I may not know much about cars, but it's one of those subjects I've always wanted to learn more about. Watching for stop signs and speed limits isn't needed. I've lived here my whole life, so everything is laid out in my head, memorized. I could walk to the library two miles away with my eyes closed. Driving I'd probably crash, since I don't have as much practice. The constant scanning and awareness of my surroundings keep my mind occupied, and the comfort of the wheel in my hands keeps me steady. Grief can't reach me here. And it's mobile.

I take a right turn followed by a left, and I'm on the street that runs through downtown. I drive by the vote box and reach through the window to drop my ballot into the slot, then continue on, passing all the small shops and businesses, along with the larger ones. The purple donut shop where we go every year for birthday donuts, the library where I spend my summer days, the sushi restaurant that makes the worst sushi and the best pasta, the park where Ivy and I would spend our middle school weekends… This is my hometown. And I love it.

Eventually I reach the local hospital. One of the larger buildings in town, the white walls have accents of yellow and blue in addition to the big red cross painted on the front. I park in the back of the employee parking lot because I don't want door dings from the crowded visitor lot. The longer walk inside is worth it to keep my baby looking good.

Jacob should have a cast on by now, meaning I should be able to see him. I have to start coaching him on how to act Aether. Hopefully there won't be any nurses or anyone else in the room, so I can start today.

Having been here many times to see my parents, lots of the doctors and nurses know me. I pass several in the hallway, and we exchange greetings, then I continue down the maze inside the hospital. New hires will often get lost in these hallways, but I never have.

The front desk tells me Jacob is in room three sixty-five. Odd numbers mean the left side of the hall when you're heading away from the desk. Three sixty-one, three sixty-three, three sixty-five. The door is open, and I see my mom in the room talking with Jacob, who's lying in the hospital bed with his leg held up in a cast, propped up on a pillow. The room is covered in ugly yellow wallpaper covered in darker yellow outlined roses. The hospital bed lies next to the window, allowing Jacob to have a nice view of the town and a forest of evergreen trees extending as far as the eye can see. Near his bed sits a small side table with a stack of books, water cup, and television remote. The air is thick with the scent of cedar trees, and a small fan in the corner gives a quiet breeze.

"Hello," Mom greets me, noticing me in the doorway.

"Hi, Mom."

"Jacob and I were just talking about what he's going to do when he gets out of here. He doesn't know where he's going to stay. His parents hadn't bought a place here yet. Would you like to offer what we discussed earlier?"

"She's trying to say you're welcome to stay with us, if need be," I explain. Everything according to our plan. "Until you either turn eighteen or want to take off on your own, you can stay with us."

Jacob looks at me then my mom, giving us a small but hesitant smile. "Thank you for the invitation. It is a very kind offer, but I don't want to intrude in your lives. You've already done so much for me."

"You won't be intruding," I assure him.

"Yes," Mom follows. "We have space for another person, and besides, maybe it'd be a change for the better."

Jacob glances at me. He knows how I convinced them. I quickly move my gaze away, avoiding eye contact, and he does the same, turning to my mother. "Thank you, Doctor Ann. I'm grateful people in this town are so willing to help me. I accept your invitation," he smiles. "Sorry, but I don't believe I know your name."

"Madrona Carter," I tell him, for the second time. We must act it out again. This has to be convincing.

"Jacob," he smiles. "Jacob Thomas." I can tell we're both thinking the same thing. He is no longer L26, no longer an Erebus. He must become an Aether. His life depends on it. And so does mine.

"Well, why don't you two get to know each other better. I'll be in the room next door if you need me," Mom declares, walking out of the room. I wait until the door closes behind her.

I sigh in relief, letting out the breath I'd been holding in. "Damn, this is hard," I blurt out.

"Well, how Aether did I sound?"

"Far too formal. You'll need to tone it down. Otherwise, the whole not-wanting-to-intrude part was pretty convincing, and the smile was the cherry on top," I claim.

"Well, if you could coach me on the whole Aether thing, beliefs, sayings, stuff like that, it would probably be a good idea."

"Exactly why I'm here. First, the most important thing is that we believe happiness should be earned. If someone says to you, 'May you find happiness if you deserve it,' then you should reply with, 'and if you don't, may you work to earn it.' It's the main belief of the Aether. Almost like karma, essentially. When you must be formal, you should always end with this."

"Alright. I think I can do that."

"Also, if you have a weapon of any sort on you, they'll assume you're Erebus unless you're part of Law Enforcement. You definitely aren't military here, so no weapons, okay?" I spend the next fifteen or twenty minutes explaining basic things the Aether do and don't do, things that are different from what I know of the Erebus. Finally, I reach the end of my lecture. "I think that's all that matters for the moment."

"Doesn't sound too hard," he admits. "Honestly, I was expecting to have to learn a whole religion or something."

"No, we don't have a state religion. I mean, if your family does have a religion, you are allowed to practice it, but most Aethers are agnostic or atheist."

"How long do you think I'm going to be here, in the hospital?"

"My parents believe you'll need a few days to get set on the correct healing path for your wound. Apparently, it punctured your spleen, and they had to patch it up or remove it or something, probably remove it. They are much more worried about the wound and possible infection than your broken leg, especially now that it's in a cast," I explain. "Should be less than a week. Our doctors are really good at what they do."

"Good, because I think staring at the ceiling will get old pretty fast."

I smile. "Been there, done that." We sit in silence for a moment. He looks much better than he did when he was in the forest. He was pale before, due to loss of blood, and now the color has returned to his face. If he didn't look good before, which he did, then he definitely does now. His new haircut fits him, the short beard he's growing adding to the whole Aether look.

"Can I ask you something?"

Our eyes meet, and I hesitate for a moment before responding, "Sure."

"How did he die, your boyfriend? You don't have to answer if you don't want to…" he trails off, slowly, carefully.

"Cancer," I reply, all the painful memories returning. "Leukemia. Acute Lymphocytic Leukemia or ALL, specifically. He had almost a seventy percent chance of survival," I whisper, my voice cracking more than once, and I let one tear run, then erase the others from existence. "I guess the odds were holding something against him."

Rather than saying, 'I'm sorry' or 'That's horrible,' he instead answers with a moment of silence, afterwards saying something I wasn't expecting. "My mother, she had cancer. She had a ninety-six percent chance of surviving. And… well, she didn't. She was there one day, recovering smoothly. They were going to send her home within the week, and the next day she was… gone. She passed away when I was twelve, five years ago."

Everyone else had said, 'I understand,' but they didn't truly understand. Jacob does, though. He does understand that feeling of loss, of insignificance, of helplessness. That someone you loved was reduced to statistical odds and buried under hours of cancer treatment that did nothing to help. The overwhelming knowledge that someone you loved is gone forever.

I nod. I know better than to say, 'I'm sorry,' the words I hate more than any others. I know they don't need to be said; the message is obvious already.

We are sitting in silence again when my mother comes back through the door.

"Jacob, I've got you an official update. You can get out of here in four or five days. Based on your current healing rate, which will probably change but is currently incredible, you'll be fine to go in three, but general surgery just wants to be sure. Madrona, why don't we let him rest? You can go tell your sister we'll be having company, and if you'd like, you can start preparing his room."

I nod and make my way through the door when Jacob speaks, "Thank you for visiting me. It's nice to have someone to talk to." I know he means it's nice to know someone else understands.

I turn, smiling and answer with, "Of course. The feeling is mutual." To give him some practice, I decide to throw in some formality. "May you find happiness if you deserve it."

"And if you don't, may you work to earn it."

Perfect. There is no doubt he's Aether now. I continue out the door, out of the hospital, and to my car. As I climb in and start the motor, Aaron's voice comes into my head, though I can't see him.

'I'm glad you found someone who understands,' he says, interrupting my flow of thought.

"I wouldn't have, without you," I murmur.

'Just know there are people other than me. There are other guys out there.'

No. Absolutely not. "I don't like him. Not in that way. He's strictly a friend, if even that," I fume. "I'm not dating anyone. I don't want to lose what I have left of you. And it's still way too early. I'm not ready… I don't think I'll ever be ready."

I hear him sigh. *'I'm only here as long as you need me. You need to move on. You can't let my death hold you back.'*

"Either way, it's *illegal* for me to like him. It's illegal for me to even talk to him, to *not* run from him," I play my trump card.

'Still,' he repeats, his words echoing as his voice fades from my mind.

I drive home and tell Lily we are expecting a new housemate, and she smiles. "Want to help me prepare the attic?"

"Sure."

We climb the stairs, reaching the end of the hallway and entering the door to the left. Dust floats through the air of the dark room.

"I thought I didn't believe in monsters hiding in dark places anymore," Lily shudders.

I smile and grab a flashlight. It illuminates the dark room filled with boxes and bins, all covered in a thin layer of dust. There's a window at the far end of the room, but the light doesn't reach past a frame leaning in front of it, and we can't reach it for the moment.

"Okay, let's start by making some space. We can clean after that, then make it more... *homey*." Lily nods and follows me, grabbing bins of stuff and carrying them down the stairs to the front door. From there she takes the boxes and moves them to the garage, while I repeat my cycle of picking up boxes in the attic and moving them to the front door. This method allows us to move faster, as we don't have to pass each other on the stairs.

We spend twenty minutes just clearing out boxes in the attic. I find the mattress Dad was talking about beneath a few crates of old family photos. I also unbury a desk, which I figure can stay too. After all the boxes are out, there is a lot of space despite a few random items lying all over the floor, including a rolled-up rug I stash in a corner.

Lily and I struggle to get frames, surfboards, medical equipment, and other large items out the door and down the stairs. After we move the last large picture frame, she grabs a vacuum while I pick up a towel and cleaning spray. Lily vacuums the wood floors while I wipe up all the dust. I move towards the window, light spilling into the room now that the stuff has all been removed. I spray and wipe the glass, removing years of grime, opening it afterwards and taking a deep breath of fresh air. My sister puts down the vacuum and comes over to join me.

"Dang, it's stuffy in here," I pant, the warm, sweat-filled air leaving my lungs, allowing for fresh air to move in.

"We should have opened the window first!" she laughs.

"Probably," I agree. "Okay. Let's move the vacuum, then lay down this rug." She moves the vacuum off to the side while I get the plastic cover off the roll of fabric. We lie it down at the far side of the room, then roll it out to reveal a soft light blue color. The rug covers nearly the whole floor. Considering how small it looked rolled up, I'm surprised it's so big.

Lily goes back to vacuuming, this time working on the rug, and I work on clearing all the spiderwebs. We never find a bed frame, so we just set the mattress directly onto the freshly vacuumed rug. The mattress is dusty too, so I have her run the hand vacuum over it while I go searching for sheets and a pillow.

Lily helps me make the bed, then we take a step back. The only light is coming from the window, but it's just enough. The room doesn't look like an attic anymore. With the desk in the corner next to the window, the bed next to it, and the rug giving the room some color, it looks like a proper bedroom. Still pretty empty though. And dark.

Lily and I search through our rooms for light sources. I find some decorative lights, and she finds an old lamp from the back of her closet. Luckily there's an outlet next to the desk, so she places the lamp on the clean surface and plugs it in. We string up the decorative lights along the ceiling, then step back again. Colorful light fills the attic, now warm and bright, the room almost seems to be smiling at us. With all the additional lights, we can truly see our work. The open window and sunlight, the lamp and twinkle lights, the light-colored rug, the whole setup represents daylight. Aether. He'll probably hate the bright feeling at first, but hopefully he will learn to like it, assuming he's here for a while.

I turn to Lily and hold up my hand. She smacks it and a sharp pain flows up my arm. She cradles her hand too, and we start laughing.

"Damn, you hit hard!" I chuckle. We head down the stairs, proud of our work, and sit on the couch, exhausted from moving all the boxes.

FOUR

The next morning Ivy knocks on my door at seven thirty, half an hour before school starts.

"You coming?"

I was going to skip school to visit Jacob again, but I guess I probably need to show up after what happened on Friday. "Let me grab my stuff." I throw on a pair of shoes and grab my bag and coat, then follow her out the door. We walk in silence for a moment, then of course she has to start with the obvious conversation.

"So… you punched Chris," she states.

"Ugh," I grumble. "Did you tell him I'm sorry?"

"Yes, I did. He said he was pretty sure you weren't though," she smirks as we turn a corner.

I sigh in regret. "I'm pretty sure I am."

"Well, he also said he deserved it and wanted to know if your hand was okay," she glances at my taped wrist. "And, being his younger sibling, whether he deserved it or not, I still have to congratulate you. I got to pick on him all weekend for the green and purple bruise on his pretty face," she grins with a smug expression. "It was the perfect payback for him picking on me and Will." We both laugh for a moment. "What did he do anyway?" she asked.

"I went out to the field, and he followed. He tried to comfort me the way Aaron did, said the wrong words, and did the wrong things at the wrong time. He knew what was coming."

"He followed you to comfort you," Ivy repeats, then bursts into laughter. "Damn, he's stupid. Wrong time to make it obvious." Her laughter continues.

"What?" I ask, confused.

"Can you not see it? He *likes* you!" she exclaims.

I almost miss a step before I come to a sudden stop. *How am I so blind?* He came to sit with me, to comfort me. This is the same guy who always compliments me at school or at Ivy's house. And now he's more worried about my *hand* than his *face*.

My hand flies to my forehead and Ivy smirks. "How did I not see it?"

"Well, you had more pressing things on your mind. I'm sure you weren't really paying attention or caring at the time anyway," she muses. "And guess what! You can tell him you're sorry in person, and that your wrist is fine, and maybe he'll ask you out now that he's made it obvious he likes you!"

"Uhh, Ivy, I don't want to go out with him. It's just too soon. I don't know if I want to go out with *anyone* anymore," I admit, finally telling her what's been weighing on my mind.

"Well, maybe it is too soon, and he should give you a bit more time, but you should *try* to move on. Go out with someone at *some* point."

No, I'm never going to date anyone else. I will not go through that pain again, I won't risk it.

"Maybe," I lie, knowing she won't allow any other answer. "But not now, not for a while. And I really don't want to talk to Chris anyway."

I should have stayed home.

"Alright, but I'm sure he's going to want to talk to you," she giggles as we walk up to the front of the school. We start heading toward the doors when I notice Chris talking with his group of friends thirty feet away. Shit. I put my head down and pull up my hood, trying to hide from him. I begin to speed up my pace. I almost make it to the door.

"Hey, Madrona!" he yells in his happy, rich voice.

Dammit. There goes that. I pull my hood back down and turn to face him. Ivy is right about the large bruise being green and purple. I must have hit him harder than I thought. "Hey, Chris," I mumble unenthusiastically. "Look, I'm sorry about your face. You didn't deserve it, and I overacted. I wasn't thinking--"

"It's fine," he interrupts. "I did deserve it. You were in pain, and I walked up and intruded. You wanted to be alone, and I screwed up. How's your hand, by the way?"

I hold up my taped wrist. "I slightly sprained it, but that's not important. Look at your face! That's a massive bruise." He puts his hands around my wrist, and I fight the oncoming wince of slight pain.

"I'm fine. I'm still more worried about you than me." His hands are warm around mine, but his use of the word 'still' sends a shiver up my arm. *Still? What's that supposed to mean?* I try to pull my hand free, but he holds it tight, staring deep into my eyes. It's like he's seeing through me. He frowns, a sad thing on that handsome face. "Are you sure you're alright? You look tired and stressed."

I tear my hand away and lower my eyes, hating that he can read me like that. "I'm fine," I lie. I walk straight into the building with Ivy following, without looking over my shoulder to see if he's trailing me also. I'm not worried about him following me. What I'm worried about is that he knows I'm lying; I just don't know how much else he knows.

"What was that?" Ivy asks when she catches up to me. "I mean, what was he implying when he said you looked stressed?"

"I... I don't know," I lie again.

"You're lying. Don't lie to me," she commands, standing in front of me. "My brother can see through anyone, and he's almost never wrong."

"You're right. I'm lying, and I shouldn't lie to you. I'm torn. I know I should move on, but I don't want to. Everything reminds me of Aaron, so the pain of his loss gets revisited over and over again. I don't want to go through that again. I *can't* go through it again. Sometimes, I can almost hear him talking to me, helping me through. Maybe I'm losing my mind," I whisper with a small grimace. "I haven't been getting enough sleep, and I'm stressed and... a guy's moving in with us," I burst out, telling her everything. Plus, she'll find out about Jacob eventually. Better to tell her now.

"Wait. What?" She squeals, her eyes going wide. Once you mention the word 'guy,' she goes ballistic. "Who? Why? When? How?" she interrogates, her hands on my shoulders, trying to shake the answers from me.

"I found him on the street, literally lying in the street. He and his family were moving here when they were in a car accident. His parents died, and he's in the hospital. We offered to let him stay with us until he's eighteen or wants to leave," I wince, painfully repeating the lie. She won't question the truth of it. It's too good, woven into perfection by Jacob himself.

"How old is he?" she screams at me.

"Seventeen, I think."

Ivy's giddy with excitement. Suddenly she halts and gasps, "You're going to have a love triangle!"

"No! Hell, no! I don't like either of them!" I am adamant. Oops. Too fast of a reaction.

"Whoop! Yes, you do! Ooh, which one? Or is it both?" she croons. "Tell me!"

"Woah, slow down. I don't like either," I repeat.

"What does he look like? What's his name?"

"Light, short brown hair with a thin beard. He's pretty fit and maybe six-three or four," I tell her. "His name is Jacob Thomas."

"He sounds handsome. Is he?" She stares me down, trying to force the words from me.

"He doesn't look too bad--" she squeals in excitement before I can continue, "But I still don't like him, not like that!"

"I bet five dollars that four months from now you're dating either him or my brother," she grins uncontrollably. I consider trying to convince her that's not going to happen, but there's no point. She won't believe it.

"Enough about me. How are you and Will? How was your date this weekend?" I ask, quickly changing the subject. I know I've hit the right mark when she launches into telling me about how amazing it was and how good of a time she had, even though the car tire popped, and they had to wait by the road for an hour.

"Anyway, we're planning a second date, this time to the movies!" She exclaims as we approach our Spanish class.

I smile, "That's exciting! You two are the perfect couple," which is exactly what she wants to hear. She beams as we enter the class, and I sit at my desk in the very back of the room, preparing for a class lecture. The whole time I'm only half listening to what my teacher is explaining, thinking more of Chris and Jacob, Ivy's words, the fact that an Erebus, *an Erebus*, is coming to live with us. Everything I can't tell; everyone I'm lying to.

It's weighing me down, the stress and the struggle. I'm not sure if I regret the decision to help Jacob or not. One moment I do, and the next I don't. I feel this strange connection to him when we're together, and I know it must have been the right decision because if I didn't choose to help him, he would be dead.

I know I need to talk to someone about everything that's happening, having an Erebus in my house, representatives attacking their own people, dealing with Chris and recovering from Aaron, otherwise I'll go crazy. And I know the only person I can talk to is one of the two people Ivy thinks I'm going to be dating in four months. I sigh and begin taking notes on the lecture, pushing the thoughts away.

·〜 ∘ ✦ ☾ ∘ ☼ ∘ ☽ ✦ ∘ 〜·

The next two days are almost identical. Ivy walks with me to school in the morning, and we talk about what's happening between her and Will. Chris is giving me a break, keeping his distance, though he's never too far away. After school I visit Jacob in the hospital. I teach him something else about the Aether he needs to know, and afterwards, we just talk. Sometimes I tell him about my family, so he'll know how to act and how not to act while he's with us. Sometimes he tells me something about the Erebus. Then I'll head home and do homework, sometimes helping Lily with hers.

When Thursday finally comes, it's Jacob's release day. Ivy knocks on my door and blurts, "His first day with you guys!"

"Yep." Honestly, I'm a little excited too. It'll be different. Whether it's *good* different or *bad* different, I'm not sure yet. Plus, I'm wondering if he'll like what we did with the attic. He'll probably be surprised to get his own room rather than the couch or a closet. More importantly, we'll be able to start trying to figure out what the hell is going on in Erebus territory, so we can get him home. My heart quietly sinks a bit, and I don't let myself consider why.

I walk with Ivy out to the sidewalk, and nearly turn around to run back inside. Chris is waiting next to our mailbox, the bruise almost entirely gone from his face. Only a slight yellow mark remains. He smiles, and I interpret it as if he's saying, "Don't worry about a thing." Like I could do that.

Ivy saves me the question by answering it, "He asked to walk with us today."

"Okay," I reply. Because there isn't anything else to be said. I try to walk next to Ivy, but being the annoying friend she is, she keeps changing her pace, trying to get me to walk next to Chris on the sidewalk that can only fit two people side to side. The battle is constant and obvious, so when Ivy finally achieves her goal, Chris grabs his chance.

"Hey," he starts. And... I'm stuck. Ivy is behind me and won't let me slow down, forcing me to walk next to him. I try speeding up, but he matches my pace.

"Hi," I finally answer.

"How's your wrist?" I glance down at my wrist. I removed the tape just minutes ago before walking out the door, so the marks from it are still there.

"Fine. How's your face?" I wince at the tone coming from my mouth.

"Fine, but holy hell, you have a strong arm," he chuckles.

I feel more regret explode in my chest. I still feel horrible about punching him, as I should. "I'm so sorry."

"Stop apologizing," he counters. "It was my fault. I should have left you alone."

"No, it was mine. You were trying to help, and I blew a fuse at the wrong time."

"Okay," he gives in. *Wait, what?* I can feel Ivy's look of astonishment behind me. He just gave in. Well, I'm glad he did, but I wasn't expecting it.

I don't have time to overthink his lack of a response because we're already arriving at school. Chris breaks off before I can think of something else to say and joins his group of waiting friends. He smiles in greeting, and they slap his back in welcome.

Ivy finally comes up even to me, muttering about idiot brothers and blown chances.

After school I walk home to get my car. I'm supposed to pick up Jacob from the hospital. The feel of the wheel in my hands is calming, as it always has been. "You still there?" I ask the empty air, double checking.

'Always.'

I smile. I will be strong. I will keep Jacob's secret. Aaron will help me stay together. "Okay, time to go." I pull out of the driveway.

When I get to the hospital, Jacob is already sitting on a bench in front of the building, two crutches lying next to him, his leg in a thick cast.

"Hey," I smile.

"Hey."

"You ready?"

"I don't know."

I walk over to help him into the car. He gets his crutches under his arms, and I help him onto his feet, opening the door for him. He winces when using his core muscles, as he's still healing from the "glass" wound.

Once we're in the car, I turn us around, and we start the trip home. He's sitting next to me in the passenger seat, the cast taking so much space we had to move the seat as far back as possible. When I glance at him, I see the nurses did a great job of cleaning him up. His short hair is perked up naturally, flowing to the side smoother than it had been before, and his face is calm with his eyes on the horizon. The thin long-sleeve shirt shows how fit he is, how strong he is. I smile and turn my eyes back to the road. His hand goes to the radio and turns up the music. The station features a solo guitarist singing about the wonders of life.

"You play?" I ask him. He looks up and our eyes meet.

"Guitar? I used to. Not so much anymore," he admits, frowning. "You?"

"Nah, I've always wanted to learn though. My dad plays every once in a while. During the summer he'll go out on the front porch and play for the neighbors."

He smiles. "My mother taught me before she passed. I took it up afterwards. Haven't really had a lot of time recently."

I nod, understanding what he means. "High school is pretty time-consuming, and for at least the past week, you've been *slightly* preoccupied. You know, with your typical falling off a fifty-foot wall and living to tell about it, hiding from Law Enforcement, spending a few days in the hospital, and pretending to be someone you're not and all."

Jacob grins in response, enjoying my humor. "If your dad still has his guitar, do you think he'd let me play it?"

"Definitely," I smile, taking a right turn. "Dad will be ecstatic to have someone playing music again."

"Nice! If you want, I could teach you."

I look over at him as we pull up to a stop sign. Aaron's voice enters my head. *'Say yes.'* I smile, having already known my answer before he interjected. "That'd be amazing. Thank you."

"Of course. You're doing so much for me, it's the least I can do." I pull into the driveway after turning onto our street. "Why am I so nervous?" he frowns.

"Why am I?" I retort. He laughs, smiling a perfect smile that even beats Chris's. The smile that convinced me I did the right thing by saving him. "Okay, ready?"

"As ready as I'll ever be."

I open the door, helping him through. "Welcome to your new home."

Mom and Dad are in the kitchen talking when they notice Jacob. Lily is on the couch when she bounces up and runs over, carefully wrapping her arms around Jacob, wary of his hidden bandage.

"Oh, um… okay," he chuckles. Lily steps back and introduces herself.

"I'm Lily, Madrona's sister," she explains. "Sorry, I am just really excited! We needed a change around here."

"It's all good. I've heard so much about you. You're the star of the softball team, right?" I'm glad I told him that because she beams in pride and hugs him again.

"Lily, let's give him a chance to get in the door," Mom chuckles. "Welcome, Jacob. For as long as you need or want, this will be your home."

"Hey," Dad greets him. "Finally, I won't be the only man in the house. Living in a house of women can get at you." They laugh and shake hands, even though they've already met. "Seriously, though. I'm glad there's another guy," he murmurs loudly, and we all laugh harder.

"Thank you for allowing me to stay here. I am eternally grateful."

"Of course. Just remember Jacob, you don't need to be so formal," Dad chuckles.

"That's a relief. Thanks, man."

Dad laughs. "No, thank you. As Lily said, we needed a change. We've all been stuck in a rut recently, and we're hoping you'll help us out," he confesses. "Which reminds me, Lily and Madrona set up your room in the attic. Girls, why don't you show him where he'll be staying?"

Lily beams in response. "Follow me!" She probably wants to grab his arm and drag him up the stairs, but the crutches save him.

He struggles to get up the steps at first but soon gets the hang of it. I follow behind them, ready to steady if needed. Lily opens the door at the end of the hall, and Jacob enters the room illuminated by the lamp and ceiling lights. He stops for a moment, takes in the room, then sits down on the bed, resting his leg.

"I thought I'd be in a dusty, cramped attic, but this is amazing! Thank you."

"You can change it if you don't like it. Rearrange, pull stuff out, add stuff in, whatever you like. This is your space," I explain, knowing he probably hates the light since he's Erebus.

I expect him to return with something like, 'I might do that,' but instead he says, "Why would I do that? This is perfect. I love it." He flashes his smile at Lily, and she looks like the happiest person in the world. She's right; he's already caused a subtle, positive shift in the atmosphere here. *But for how long?* My smile slowly fades. *No, don't think about that. This is a happy moment.*

"She loves you already," I smile. "She's always wanted an older brother."

"I'll do my best to be as close to an older brother as I can," he says. "What about you? What do you think about all this?"

"I'm not sure yet. I'm glad Lily's happy, but it'll break her heart when you leave. She gets attached very quickly," I agonize, imagining her face when he leaves. She'll be devastated.

He stares at the ground for a moment. "Do you believe in fate?" he murmurs.

Before I can open my mouth to reply, Lily runs in. "Mom wants to know if you need anything."

I look at Jacob, who shakes his head. "I think we're good. Thank you."

"Oh, and she also said you should get started on your homework," she informs me. Mom's hidden message to let Jacob rest.

"Okay," I sigh. "Thanks." She runs back down the small flight and into the hall. "That's my cue. Feel free to catch up on some rest, and let me know if you need anything. I'm the first door on the left." He nods as I walk out the door and head into my room, looking at my stack of homework. I sigh again and sit down with my music.

I pick up my homework then hesitate before beginning. I stand and reach under my bed, pulling out a box. There are multiple items inside it. I pick up the one on top and look at the picture.

My face smiles back at me, laughing. Standing close by my side, a guy with curly dark brown hair. It was shorter when this picture was taken, over a year ago. He had been growing out his hair when the photo was taken, just before he started chemotherapy and had to cut it all off, so it's strange seeing him like this. We're both smiling, and my arms are wrapped around his torso. Aaron. I remember this moment. And I want to remember it all the time. A happy memory to chase out the sad ones. I place it on my desk and get to work, and for the first time, look at the photo without crying, but instead smiling.

FIVE

    Boom. An explosion goes off. Screaming and cries of help come from the door at the end of the hall. The door opens and she enters, revealing piles of bodies beneath stone, fallen from the ceiling. More bodies are scattered around the room, against walls and coated in a layer of dry blood. She flinches slightly, as she recognizes a face on one of the fallen.

    The building continues to shake, releasing more stone from higher levels. Screams tear through her ears, until they're suddenly silenced. And yet, the quiet is worse. Her line of sight moves, and suddenly, she's in another building. A girl screams as rocks fall, about to crush her. A young man jumps out to save her, moving her out of the way. They crash on the other side of the room just as the falling concrete smashes into the ground where the girl would have been.

    Terror rips through her as she realizes who these people are. She tries to scream at them, but nothing comes out. 'Jacob! Get Lily out of here,' she tries to yell, but no sound leaves her mouth, and she's not in control of her body.

    "We have to get out of here!" he yells over the sound of the falling pieces of the building.

    "No! We have to get it!"

    "Leave it!"

    "No, we must protect it!"

    "Then I'll get it. You get out of here!" he says, then runs deeper into the building as Lily begins to make her way

out. Her vision shifts, following him, watching him hurdle the debris, making his way through the building.

He enters a lab and snags a vial off a counter bordering the room. Shoving it in his pocket, he starts running, trying to get out as fast as possible. The floor begins to crumble, and he runs to the nearest support beam.

Outside, a cable hangs down from the building, all the way to the ground, six stories below him. The floor beneath him starts to give out as he launches himself out towards the cable. He grabs it and yells in pain as it burns into his hand, trying to slow his fall. His grip isn't enough to stop him, but it slows his speed and he's about to put his feet on the ground...

. ~ ∘ ✦ ☾ ∘ ☼ ∘ ☽ ✦ ∘ ~ .

I open my eyes and jerk into a sitting position. My face is all wet, dammit. I wipe away my tears and sweat, trying to calm myself down. This is new, this variation of the dream. I've never seen anyone I know. This time I recognized three people: Lily, Jacob, and... Ivy, the face among the fallen. Dead. My eyes start tearing up again. *No, stop crying. Stop crying. It wasn't real.* But my tears don't stop flowing, frustratingly. I stand up and grab my sweatshirt, also replacing my sleep shorts with jeans, and head down the stairs. I need air. I head out the front door and embrace the cool morning air.

I don't know what time it is, but it's clearly before seven, as the sun is not fully up yet. The sky is dark to the west, and orange and pink streaks color the sky to the east where the rising sun is waking the birds. I stand here for a moment, then sit on the porch steps, trying to slow my breathing.

"Calm down. It's just a dream," I assure myself. But it didn't feel like a dream. It felt so real. As it always does. I can still feel the sensation of hopelessness, the feeling of my voice being muffled. The feeling of loss when I saw Ivy's body. My tears begin to slow, but they don't stop. My chest hurts and my eyes are sore from crying. The cold air feels good on my warm face, and it slowly calms me.

Behind me, I hear a creaking sound and turn to see who it is, then go back to wiping my tears away. I don't want to cry in front of him. After a struggle of getting down the steps, he lays his crutches to his left and sits down next to me.

"What are you doing up this early?" he asks.

"What are *you* doing up this early?" I counter.

He's quiet for a moment before answering. "I've always been an early riser. The saying, 'The early bird gets the worm,' is taken very seriously where I'm from." He's looking out at the sunrise, slowly turning from red and orange to pink and yellow. "Lily said you punched the last guy who tried to comfort you, so I guess I'm asking permission first," he chuckles, making me smile.

"I promise not to punch you," I smile, still fighting my tears.

"Tell me," his voice is soft and quiet, giving me the sense that I'm not alone. Literally, but also mentally. My breathing slowly settles, and I speak.

"Some nights, I get these nightmares. Always the same place, a collapsing city. Destruction, buildings crushing people beneath them, almost as if a huge shockwave went off, followed by multiple explosions. Every time I see it from a different point of view. It feels so... real," I shudder. "I remember everything as if I were there."

He frowns before answering. "What... What color are the buildings?"

"The windows are tinted gray. Concrete is painted-" I glance around to make sure no one else is listening, "b-black," I murmur, hearing myself mention the forbidden color. "I've never seen the city before, but somehow I know every corner of it in my dream."

"Strange," he whispers to himself.

"What is it?"

"Nothing," he answers quickly. "Are you going to be alright?"

"Yes," I claim. Then reconsider for a moment. "No. But not because of the nightmare." Warily, he slowly puts his arm around me. He's warm in the cold morning air. Carefully, I rest my head on his shoulder. The birds are singing joyful tunes as the sun rises above the horizon, throwing bursts of warm colors in every direction.

He's cozy, like a fireplace after being away from home. Comforting, safe, peaceful. Well, probably the opposite of peaceful, but still. We sit in silence for a moment before he speaks again. "...So, you punched someone."

I chuckle. "Yeah..."

"How hard was it?"

"He's had a massive bruise on his face all week," I smirk. "All green and purple."

Jacob laughs before saying, "Damn, it must have been a good one. Did he deserve it?"

"At the moment I thought so. Not so sure anymore," I falter. "He said all the wrong things. He followed me to my safe spot, away from everyone."

"Well, that's his mistake."

"I feel bad about it."

"Don't," Jacob replies. "He shouldn't have been there in the first place." I nod because he's right, but I still feel bad.

"Thank you. For being here."

"Anytime," he smiles.

My tears have finally stopped, but my face is still wet, so I wipe the remaining drops away for the last time. The sun is just above the distant mountains now, and the color is slowly fading. The rays of sunlight illuminate the morning mist, making the whole world turn yellow. The empty streets, clear sky, and thin layer of frost give a feeling of peace. Everyone around us is still asleep, making the world quiet. I try to imagine this street bursting with playing children and the occasional car, as it will be in just under an hour. The cold bites at my hands and nose, but Jacob's comforting arm around me diminishes even that small discomfort.

Suddenly I have a memory of the last time I felt safe and secure like this, held and comforted like this. My smile fades and memories of Aaron flood into my head. It was the day before he started feeling poorly, just over a year ago. We were at the bleachers of the football field. Our spot on the fourth row. He was telling me about the previous morning. The two of us together, alone. The field was empty, everything out in the open. He was upset about his brother, and I was helping him through it. Afterwards we laughed about something completely random. It was the last time we were together at our spot.

Jacob looks at me, sensing the change in my mood. "If you want me to leave, you just have to say so." I shake my head ever so slightly, and he pulls me into a hug. I sigh into his chest, suddenly feeling a wave of assurance coming over me. His arms are comforting, and I know I don't want to cry right now. Not anymore. I stuff it deep into myself for later and take a deep breath. It's okay. *I'm* okay. His embrace is cozy, but I know it's time to get up now that I've recovered.

"I need to get ready for school," I tell him, shaking off the sudden humiliation of crying in front of him. He nods and releases me. Suddenly I feel cold without his heat. "Thank you."

"Again, anytime."

I nod, helping him up and inside. Luckily, no one woke up while we were on the porch. I throw toast in the toaster for him and head upstairs to get dressed. When I come back down, he's already buttered it and begun eating. Once we've both eaten, Lily comes down and greets us.

"Are you going to school too?" she asks Jacob.

"No, I think your parents said my first day is next Friday. They don't want me to rip my stitches carrying a heavy backpack or getting in a fight with the locals," he chuckles and shoots her a wink.

I'm grabbing my bag, as Ivy knocks on the door. I open it for her, and she bursts inside the threshold, almost knocking me over. "Hello!" she shouts past me to Jacob. He waves back, acknowledging her with one of his perfect smiles.

"One moment, please," I say to her and forcibly push her back outside, closing the door behind me.

"One, don't ask about his relationship status. Better yet, don't mention dating in general. Two, his parents just died, so be *very* nice," I tell her.

She nods, practically shaking. "He's huge! You didn't tell me he was *that* fit! And he's so handsome!" Ivy sways then freezes, staring off into the distance as if in a trance.

I violently shake her out of it. "What did I say?"

"Don't mention girlfriends and be nice."

"Good," I open the door again. "Ivy, meet Jacob. Jacob, this is my friend, Ivy."

"*Best* friend," she corrects.

He holds out his hand. "Nice to meet you."

Ivy eagerly shakes it and answers, "Nice to meet you also."

"Well, we better get going," I rush, trying to vocally push her out the door.

"But I just got here!"

I start pushing her, and she gives in. "Bye," she waves at Jacob.

"Have a good day," Jacob calls as I succeed in shoving her through the door.

"You too," I reply. "Lily, don't forget to remind Mom and Dad to take you." She nods and I close the door.

The click of the door opens my friend's floodgates, as Ivy pelts me with questions. "Why can't I ask whether he has a girlfriend or not? Oooh, I guess you already know if you don't want me to ask. What happened with his last girlfriend? Are they still together? Did they have a bad break up? Is she dead?"

Ivy winces, but continues on, undeterred. "Was he close to his parents? Any siblings? Are they still alive? Where are they? Tell me all about every moment since he showed up. And go!" she orders.

I get started, answering what I can, but skipping all the so-called juicy parts I know she'd want to hear, because I don't want the idea of us dating in her head. And this morning, he was only being a friend anyway.

'Oh, definitely,' Aaron's voice chuckles, entering my mind.

Shut up! He obeys.

Besides, Jacob could very well have a girlfriend back home. And while that thought might make my heart twinge a bit, no one else needs to know it.

When I get home from school I walk upstairs and fall face first on my bed. "Ugh," I grunt into the mattress.

Jacob appears in my doorway. "How was school?"

"Great," I smile as sarcastically as possible.

"Do you want to talk about it?"

I sigh. "It was fine. It's just that Chris was acting weird. He's Ivy's brother, the one I punched. He walked with us to school and apologized to me for encroaching the other day. Next thing I know everyone starts asking, 'Are you and Chris together?' I know it wasn't intentional on his part, but the whole day I had a difficult time not walking up to him and punching him *again*," I grumble.

"Why would that question upset you so much?"

"Because Aaron only died six months ago. Every time I think of having someone replace his spot, I feel like I'm forgetting him, but either way, I don't want to even risk going through that agony again." A drop falls from my eyes, free falling one moment, and in a million bits the next as it lands, impacting my jeans.

"You can't let Aaron's death stop you from loving another person ever again. The chances of your next boyfriend dying are basically below zero percent. Besides, I doubt Aaron would want that kind of life for you. A life without love is no life at all," Jacob replies.

I sigh, thinking he might have a *small* point. "Maybe... I don't want to think about school anymore. Tell me something about you. It can be a vent session if you need, you know, to even the slate."

"Are you asking me to tell you about my life?"

"Sure. I just need to think about something other than all the ways I could punch Chris."

"Alright," he chuckles. "On the day you found me, I was walking through the woods, on my side of the wall obviously. I was trying to burn off some steam, as I was seriously pissed. I had just walked in on my girlfriend kissing another guy. Instead of confronting her right away, I was trying to calm down, so I didn't do anything stupid like break the other guy's legs. I wasn't paying a lot of attention to the path I was taking, but I ended up near the wall next to a few guards.

"We see them all the time, and we've all been a guard at some point. The job rotates around the community. I nodded a greeting and turned away as I wanted to be alone, and they attacked me from behind. I lost most of what little was in my pockets as they beat me and dragged me to the wall. One of them held a keycard up to a scanner and opened a door into the wall itself. As they dragged me up a set of internal stairs, I fought them, but one managed to stab me when we reached the top. I fell off the wall and hit a few branches on my way to the ground. I think that's the only reason I survived the impact. Right before I fell, I was wrestling with one guard when a piece of paper fell out of his pocket. It was a note with our representative's signature and my picture. The words 'next target' were written beneath it.

"I don't know why I was a target, why I was forced over here, but I have to find out," he claims.

"They just grabbed you and pushed you over? No words said?"

"Nope. They didn't speak a word."

"And the note said, '*Next* target'?"

"Yes, it did," he frowns.

"Then clearly you aren't the only one. Maybe there are other Erebus hiding here," I suggest.

He thinks for a moment. "Others who survived the fall? I doubt there'll be many. But if there are, I know how we can reach them," he grins.

"How?" I ask.

"Simple. Midnight on a full moon," he explains. "In the middle of the night, we gather in the streets. It's a celebration of sorts, that there will always be light in the darkness. If there are other Erebus here, they'll be out then."

"The next full moon is a week from Saturday," I note.

"We don't have long to wait then, do we? Maybe we can get some information from them. If not, we should at least be able to get an Erebus phone. I lost mine when I lost my bag, but maybe someone else was wearing theirs when they fell," he explains.

I think about that for a moment. *Other* Erebus living here? What if there are hundreds who are living in secret? We thought it was rare to find one, since they are usually killed shortly thereafter. But more living here without us knowing? Is it even possible? Then I remember what he said about his girlfriend.

"She cheated on you?" I ask softly after a moment of silence.

"Yes. She did."

"I can't imagine what that felt like," I empathize. "It must have been horrible."

"It was. It hurt a lot. And I had no idea, either. It was so out of the blue…" he trails off, a pained look working its way onto his face. He clearly hasn't had time to process it yet if it happened the day we met.

I don't know what to do. Should I try to comfort him? I remember how angry I was when Chris kept talking. I decide to simply mimic Jacob's steps earlier. Slowly and carefully, I wrap my arms around him. He hugs me back. His embrace is just as comforting as it was before, and I know it's my turn to be supporting him.

"We'll find them, the other Erebus," I whisper. "We'll figure this out." His arms are around me and mine around him. For a moment I close my eyes and breathe. He smells like cinnamon. I've always liked cinnamon. In his embrace I feel safe and protected. Cared for, just as I did with Aaron.

'You like him,' Aaron's voice taunts me. Maybe. There's definitely something there. *'Just admit it.'*

No, I can't. It's too soon.

'It's there, whether or not you're ready to admit it,' his voice murmurs and disappears, leaving Jacob and I alone together, keeping each other from falling apart.

Jacob and I spend our Saturday preparing for our Erebus meet up.

"Preparing?" I ask when he brings up the idea. "What is there to prepare?"

"You, assuming you're coming," he smirks. "You have been teaching me your ways, now it's time for me to teach you mine."

I smile. This could be interesting. I've always wondered about the Erebus. He hasn't told me much about them, and I haven't asked.

"Well, get talking then." I sit down next to him on his mattress. The sun is peeking through the clouds, shining directly through his attic window and fills the room with a yellow, calming, and happy glow.

"First, things are very different in Erebus territory. *Very* different. Aether live in comfort here, but most of our people live in poverty. Many can't afford food and must steal to survive. This is how most of us feed our families. Stealing from those few who can afford food. And because of this, because of the fact we either steal successfully, or spend a few weeks in jail while our families starve, we've gotten very good at it.

"If there are other Erebus out there, they will likely try to steal from you. So, empty your pockets and only bring what is necessary," he orders.

I nod. I always thought the Erebus had much more money than we did or lived in a communist community or something, so this fact is stunning. I try to picture Jacob stealing to survive... sadness fills me before I can crush the thought under my foot.

"Second, they'll freak out when they first see you. They'll know on-sight you aren't an Erebus pretending to be Aether, just from the way you carry yourself. Even if you try to walk and squawk like us, they'll have been trained to know you're different. So... they'll probably try to kill you, thinking if they don't, you'll likely run away and tell the night guards they're out. It may be worse if the Erebus here have found each other already and formed alliances, then they may group attack," Jacob frowns.

I feel a whisper of fear push its way through my thoughts and onto my face. Oh, great. Everyone seems to want to kill me, whether they know it yet or not. The Aether will kill any who help hide Erebus, and the Erebus will kill Aether for fear of being found and sentenced to death.

"So... how do I avoid being attacked?" I ask.

"You don't. There's no way we can make you look like an Erebus, since that means cutting your hair, and afterwards you'll need to look Aether again," he ponders. "You'll just have to stay alive long enough for me to convince them to not kill you. I'll try to stop them, but I'm obviously handicapped," he gestures to his cast and crutches. "These people will likely be experienced, so I'll just have to give you fighting lessons that will keep you alive for a few seconds until I can get them to stop." He looks me over for a moment, as if scanning a blank canvas for scratches, marks, or dents. I feel myself shrink back under his gaze and hope he doesn't notice.

"So, I have to fight an Erebus," I state, not as a question, but more as a fact. A fact I can't easily believe.

"Just until I can convince them you're with me. But that might take a second, since they won't stop fighting to talk to me, so it'll probably be more of a one-sided conversation," he sighs.

I shudder. "Even better."

"Yeah, I'm still working on that part. But you will be fine. I'll be there to help, or to try my best. Either way, if any Aether had to fight an Erebus, I'd probably put my money on you.

I feel a swell of pride when I hear the truth in his words. "Still, I have to fight an Erebus," I repeat. This could be ugly. Extremely ugly.

"You can stay home. I can go by myself."

"That's definitely not happening."

"Well, on the bright side, we already know you have a hard punch. We just have to work on where to put it. Based on your structure I can tell you're fast, and you're clearly not heavy, so you should have a speed advantage as well," Jacob points out. "That speed will come in handy when you need to dodge a fist coming towards you."

"Okay. You can give me the How-To-Stay-Alive-Against-An-Erebus 101 when we finish here," I say. He laughs, and the joy and humor that emits from it almost puts me in a trance.

"Sounds good," he nods after a moment. "If I were them, I'd think we were coming to kill them, to finish off the job, the one the guards didn't. We'll have to gain their trust, prove we're on their side."

"How are we going to do that?"

There's a pause. "I'll figure that out later." He moves on quickly. "We should bring a flashlight for starters. A weapon would be nice, but it'd provoke them...

"We should bring them food if they're starving. I doubt they were as lucky as me to have someone help them out," he thinks aloud, "but I doubt they'd accept it unless I found a way to make them trust us. They'd think it was poisoned," he explains. "Besides, it'll just be another thing to carry, another thing to have them attempt to steal before we can talk. Then again, if they're alive now, they'll have found a source of food already."

"Anything else we need to go over?"

He shakes his head. "I don't think so. Ready for How-To-Stay-Alive-Against-An-Erebus 101?"

I smile at his continuation of my joke. "I think so."

"Well, obviously I can't fight you and help you get a sense of what it'll be like, but I can give pointers and get you something to hit. Stand up and show me how you'd stand during a fight."

I stand up and plant my bare feet on the rug a couple feet away from the bed, facing Jacob, with my shoulders back, my left hand outstretched in front of me as if I'm holding off an opponent, and my right curled into a tight fist as I swing my arm in circles. My legs are close together, and I sway with the lack of balance.

He looks at me and bursts out laughing. "Okay, what is that?"

I frown, dropping the pose. "My position."

He continues laughing. "Holy stars, I can't unsee that." He waves his hand at me. "You look like... nevermind. Let's just pretend you never did that, okay?"

"Did what?" I smile, playing along.

"I forgot you all outlawed violence, and therefore don't know what any of this looks like," he chuckles. "Alright. Spread your feet for balance but keep them under your shoulders. Are you right-handed?" He continues after I nod the affirmative. "Ok, then place your nondominant, left leg slightly in front of you, pointing towards your opponent. You never want to face an opponent directly. You can minimize the area they have to attack if you face them angled. Try to balance on the balls of your feet, so you have flexibility of movement and can react quickly. Swinging power comes from your lower body, so you need a strong stance to get the most from each punch."

I obey his instructions.

Jacob looks me over for a moment. "Good. Now, you aren't heavy or big, and women are typically faster than they are strong…" I glare at him. "What? It's true, and in this case, it will keep you alive," he defends. I sigh and nod my head. He's right. Though it might be sexist, it'll keep me alive.

"Now, you want your base stance to have your hands up; one, to protect your head, and two, to be ready to deliver that punch. Bend your elbows and tuck your right hand against your chin." Jacob demonstrates holding his own fist close to his face, his elbow tucked in close to his ribs. I copy him, and he nods approvingly. "Great. Now your other hand, bend at the elbow and put it at the same level as your right hand but slightly farther out from your face. In a fight, your left hand will act as your first line of defense when it comes to blocking an incoming punch.

"Now, your hands. You have two options: an open palm or a fist. Clenched fists with your fingers covering your thumb equal broken thumbs. Your thumb has to go on the outside of your fist. Or curl your knuckles, but keep your palm open," he instructs. I curl my open hands into fists, and he reaches out and opens them. "No, like this." He stretches open his own hand, then folds his knuckles out of the way, pulling them back and pushing his palm forward, keeping his fingers clear of his palm.

I mimic the form of his hand.

"Keep your hands open and your knuckles out of the way, so you don't break them when you punch. The other option is to wrap your thumb on top of your other fingers. Keep your wrist straight when striking your opponent, never bend it during contact."

I adapt my position to his instructions and await his next pointer. He gets up and slowly moves in a circle around me. He taps my leg with a crutch. "Keep a slight bend in your knees. It's more comfortable and allows for a faster transfer of energy up to your fists." I slightly adjust as he continues in his circle, stopping in front of me. "Plus, it makes it harder for you to be knocked over if the attacker happens to land a punch.

"Body angled, shoulders slightly forward, and head facing your target but protected behind your hands," he tells me, carefully tilting my head up slightly to face him instead of his feet.

His height strikes me for the first time as he makes corrections to my stance. I already knew he was around six-two or three, but now I'm looking up at him while standing for the first time. He's a whole foot taller than me - yes, I know I'm short - and even with the crutches stopping him from standing up straight, he still towers over me. For a moment we stare into each other's eyes, then both break away simultaneously. He backs away and avoids eye contact, almost embarrassed.

Suddenly I'm wishing he hadn't moved. A small part of me almost wants to… *No! Not going to even think that. There's no way. He's super hot and you are not, so-*

"You look good. Now show me how you hit," he still avoids eye contact but holds up an open hand about chest level. Thankful for his interruption of my thoughts, I hold up my strangely positioned hands and throw my right one into his waiting palm. I slightly pull back at the last second, not wanting to hurt him. In the brief second that our hands touch, I can feel the rough skin of his palm under the heel of my hand.

He shakes his head as I fall back into the position. "No, no, no. When you throw a cross punch, you want to use your whole body. Pivot your back foot, keeping the ball of your foot on the ground, to turn towards your target. The power of a cross punch starts with the legs, and that pivot is generating torque for your upper body. This punch will be the most powerful in your arsenal.

"Your attack should travel *through* the target, not *to* the target. If you want the hit to cause any damage, you must aim for a foot *behind* your target. This causes more damage. Follow the punch with your shoulder. That puts even more force behind it. You want to push my hand away. Don't hold back; you won't hurt me." He backs away and nods for me to try again.

I throw my hand, swinging my arm so it doesn't stop at his hand, but allows the momentum to continue through it, forcing it backwards. "Much better. Back to the ready position." I obey, waiting for his next command. "One, you need to keep tension in your core, here." He places his hand on my stomach. I inhale sharply, shooting my eyes up to look at him, and he pulls away almost instantly, face flushing bright red for a moment before he cleans it up and goes back to normal. "Two, you're used to looking down. Your head is always bent down. Here, you need to keep it up so you can see what's coming at you, so you can keep your balance, and because it just looks badass and threatening." He smirks as he takes my face in his hand and carefully tilts it upward again. "I know it's hard to do, but if we don't do this correctly, your family might be grieving for you. We don't want to do that to them, do we?"

I slightly shake my head in agreement. I don't want to look at him when I'm feeling so raw and exposed, but I know that is what he's waiting for, so I look deep into his eyes and see more than I'd ever seen before. A hint of hurt and grief hides behind the strength he shows. But alongside that, worry takes a part. *Is he worried for me?* A warm feeling erupts through my body, making me want to make him proud, a feeling I've only had a few times before…

I gather my courage. "Okay." Tightening my core muscles and keeping my head up, I shift so my hands are up, and my feet are ready. My hands form a fist in front of me, ready for an oncoming attack.

"I think you've got it," he smiles. "Show me a few more times before we move on." I throw a few punches, but it only takes one for me to realize it's harder than it looks to do everything at once. I instinctively want to close my fist, and I automatically aim to impact the target, not drive my hand through it. Finally, after multiple hits, I eventually succeed, my hand driving through Jacob's, and he smiles.

"Alright. On to phase two of How-To-Stay-Alive-etcetera, etcetera. Let's get you something to hit," Jacob grins.

It takes us a while to find something for me to punch out of view of the neighbors, since I can't be seen punching anything, as fighting is still illegal, just as it was yesterday, and the day before, and the day before that… Finally, we grab a thick blanket and pillow to tie around a tree deep in the woods.

Building a makeshift punching bag proves to be the easy part. Getting Jacob through the thick forest on crutches is much harder. It's slow going as he navigates carefully over rocks and tree roots. I help where I can by lifting and holding tree limbs out of his way. Luckily, thanks to a thick forest, it doesn't take long to get out of view of the house and road.

The birds chirp happily to no specific tune, yet somehow seem to blend together their own song of joy heralding the end of winter and the beginning of spring. It's almost mid-day, and the sun is directly overhead, though the cover of the forest roof saves us a place in the shade. Beams of light shine down from the places in the branches where the sun can leak through. Wildflowers are forming buds, and small creatures are running around the undergrowth. I smile and stand for a moment as we find a small clearing, closing my eyes and soaking up the sun, the warmth cutting through the chilly air, and the sounds of life, the smell of the forest…

I feel a pair of eyes on me while I stand facing away from him, and I turn to see him smiling.

"What?" I shrink back, slightly embarrassed, though I don't know why.

"Nothing," he answers quickly, then moves his eyes away from me and to the surrounding forest. He sighs. "It's so nice here. Calm, peaceful, quiet… Well, not quiet. The birds make sure of that."

I smile at his words. "They sure do, don't they," I reply, listening to the new direction to their disorganized, yet perfectly planned tune.

"On the other side of the wall, we don't have a lot of forests. It's really just the one near the wall. Our previous representatives cut down most of the trees for logging and more land. Now we're going through great efforts to replace them. The birds don't sing in many places, and all the deer are hunted, as many of our people are starving," he frowns, looking down. My smile fades as he says this. Having lived next to a forest my whole life, this is hard to imagine. But the words 'wasteland', 'desert', and 'lifeless' enter my head.

A look of sorrow enters his face, then is quickly wiped away. "Let's get back to the task at hand. Show me the ready position," Jacob changes the subject.

I nod and obey, taking a few steps back from the tree and moving into my stance. I prepare to attack the tree and look to him for permission to start. He nods, and I follow the steps he taught me. My right foot pivots as I begin my swing. My fist collides with the tree. A sharp instant pain shoots up my arm but disperses after a split second. I start to fall to the right, and my instincts tell me to back off, but I know backing off in this way will just get me killed, so I follow through and place my right foot, saving my balance and moving around the tree.

"Holy shit, that hurts!" I wince.

"Sharp, split-second pain?" he asks.

"Yeah."

"Ouch. It means your wrist wasn't straight when it hit. You risk a wrist sprain if you don't keep it straight at impact." Jacob rubs my stinging wrist, the skin under his rough hands tingles, then he sets it into the correct position. "Firm up. Good. Now don't let it leave this position all the way through the punch."

I nod and throw a few light punches to get used to the positioning, then start slowly hitting harder. I get my wrist straight and for the first time I can feel the energy reverberate from my fist to the tree in the split second where contact is held. The feeling sends a jolt through me, almost like pure excitement. I'm learning to fight. And if someone finds out, I'm dead. But instead of feeling scared, I smile, as the defiance, the opportunity to right a wrong, brings a rush. I'm breaking the rules, but it's for a good reason.

Now that I know what it feels like to land a punch correctly, I want to feel it again and again. The energy charge flows through me as each hit lands the right way. My fist begins to hurt from the repetitive force, but I keep hitting. I hit for all the things I'm angry about. Aaron's death, Chris taking advantage of my weakness, the horrible things some representatives do, and it slowly relieves stress. After almost a full hour, I sit down next to Jacob on a log a few feet from my tree, my knuckles slightly bloody.

"You feel it?" he asks, grabbing a wet rag I didn't notice before. "I do. And it feels amazing," I chuckle. He nods, smiling as he gently dabs the wet towel against my knuckles. I wince at the slight pain, but it's almost comforting.

"It does." His perfect smile. The one that reminds me why I'm doing this. The one that almost hurts to watch fade. He continues caring for my destroyed knuckles as we sit in silence for a moment. His rough calloused hands brush against mine as we listen to the birds.

SIX

Sunday dawns crisp and cool. The sun is hidden from view by a thick layer of clouds, so Jacob and I bundle up against the chill before heading back into the woods for another lesson. He does a quick examination of my knuckles to ensure they have healed enough since yesterday to continue. His touch causes my heart to twitch in my chest, and I mourn the loss when he deems them good and lets go.

We run through a quick review of the things we covered yesterday: proper fighting stance, protective hand placement, and the powerful straight punch. Satisfied, I remembered the motions, Jacob moves on to the next subject. "The jab. The jab is all about speed. While less powerful than a cross punch, a quick jab can stun your opponent long enough to either allow you to get away or give you time to land a powerful cross. Remember, your advantage is going to be speed, so this punch is exactly in your wheelhouse.

"You'll also be hitting with your left fist this time, so it'll provide a good relief to your right knuckles when sore from that cross punch.

"You'll start from the same basic fighting stance, left foot forward, just as before. Good, now you're going to extend the left arm, using your first two knuckles as a guide. Without overextending your elbow, jab straight ahead, then quickly bring your fist back up to guard your face." He demonstrates the move, throwing out a lightning quick jab, so fast I can barely register it. "Jabs are meant to be faster rather than harder."

I follow the steps and take a couple attempts at it, punching the air. It's awkward at first, using my nondominant hand. But eventually, I get the hang of it, moving quicker and quicker.

"The key thing to remember is to bring your hand back quickly to its defensive position. That looks good. Now try a double-jab, a quick pop-pop."

I reset my stance and throw out a quick one-two. Then repeat. Once Jacob is satisfied with my mechanics, we head back over to the punching tree. I practice jabbing in singles and doubles for a while until Jacob halts me and has me start mixing it up with the occasional cross power punch. He catches me wincing as my right knuckles complain about a second day of abuse.

He holds up a hand to have me stop. "In any true fight, you are going to get hurt. You need to be prepared to take damage when you enter a fight. Accept that you will get hurt and keep going. Throwing punches hurts. Being punched hurts. But you have to accept it and keep moving."

Accept it and keep moving. I'm still thinking about those words later in the day as Lily and I lounge on the living room sofa later that afternoon. She's watching a show on TV, but I'm barely paying attention to it as I reflect on this morning's training session. Gnawing a little on the inside of my cheek, I turn those words over in my head. How they echo Aaron's messages, how I need to accept his death and keep moving, keep living. Deep in the recesses of my own mind, I don't realize Lily has paused her show until she speaks.

"Thanks for making a change around here," she says. "I think we all needed something different."

"What do you mean?"

"I mean bringing Jacob home. Getting Mom and Dad to let him stay with us. You've been happier since he showed up. Less... zombie-like." She holds up her arms straight in front of her and gives a blank expression that makes me laugh. Becoming serious again, she continues, "His coming here has changed you, and seeing you like this again is saving us. He seems to have pulled you out of your depression, but something tells me you're pulling him out of his pain too."

I think about that for a moment. Am I? I know Lily means pain from the crash, but his parents didn't actually die in a crash. His mother *did* die of cancer five years ago, but shouldn't he have moved on by now? And again, I'm back to the 'accept it, and keep moving' concept.

Maybe Jacob does have a hidden pain. His eyes always have a sad look to them, even when he is smiling or laughing. It's a different pain than the one reflected while he was injured. Some scars aren't visible on the outside.

Am I helping him get over something that's punching him in the heart, just like he is for me? I doubt it. Erebus are supposed to be cold-hearted people who believe in suffering for happiness. But... Jacob isn't cold-hearted. He's a nice person, always showing his gratitude and empathy.

Then I remember the first part of what Lily said, about him pulling me out of my pain, about me being happier after he showed up. Is he making me happier? Do I like him? *No! He's just distracting me from my pain, which means I'm happier. No, I don't like him like that.* I will never love again.

"He hasn't pulled me out of my grief," I protest. Even while I say this, I hear the obvious lie. "He just manages to distract me from it."

Lily rolls her eyes, probably seeing the truth on my face. "Then... stay distracted. It's nice to see you happy again."

I'm still distracted walking to school by myself Tuesday morning, otherwise I would have realized Chris was about to ambush me.

"How's the hand?" He doesn't hesitate to reach out and take my hand for a quick look. He frowns slightly as he takes in the swollen knuckles. "Wow, you really did a number on it."

Yanking my hand back, I shake my head. I can't tell him it wasn't hurt from punching him. I wince as I see his face for the first time that morning. The bruise has grown in size and color. His upper eyelid is a deep purple, then expands out to greens and yellows.

"I am so sorry about your eye. It looks really painful."

"You know how you can make it up to me?" *No. Don't do it.* I shake my head, silently begging him not to speak his next words. "There's a movie theater a few blocks from the hospital. I was wondering if you'd want to go with me tomorrow evening. You don't have to, of course, if it's too soon, but if you did, I would accept your apology."

Well, shit. Now I feel like I have to. Great. I know what he's doing. He's hoping to get me to go once, and he's hoping I'll have a good time, so I'll go again, and there goes my plan to never date again.

Wait. *Oh, yes. Yes, yes, yes. Lightbulb.*

"As friends," I demand. Bomb dropped. Mind blown. The crowd goes *wild* at my brilliance! He hesitates for a moment before replying. *Haha!* I think. *No way he can recover from that. Hopefully.*

"Okay. So... Wednesday night? Seven-thirty?"

And... he just ignores it. The crowd sighs in disappointment.

"Sure," I wince, knowing I'm going to regret that word for a while.

Who knows, maybe this will be good for me. Maybe his plan will work. One small part of me wants it to, but the rest of me doesn't. Though, of all the guys to have asked me out, Chris is probably one of the best. *No. He's not, Aaron was.* Memories flood into me. How could I have done that? Why did I? By doing so, I'm killing his memory. Regret enters my system, and I excuse myself, rushing into the school and heading straight to the bathroom. I sit in a stall for a moment, trying not to cry when Aaron comes.

"What do you want?" I whisper, knowing he's there.

'To let you know I'm proud,' Aaron's voice admits. My mind isn't letting him be visible to me right now, but his voice is enough.

"Why would you be proud?"

'Because you're finally trying to move on. You have two guys who care for you, and one's asked you out. I know you don't care for Chris the same way he does for you, but maybe you will one day. And the other, Jacob, ... Well, I know you feel something for him. I live in your head.'

"You're wrong. I don't care for him. I'm only trying to save his family from what you're putting me through. As for Chris, I can't. He was already strictly on the friend list."

Aaron's silent for a moment. *'It's still a possibility.'*

"Why?" I inquire. "Why am I all but hallucinating you, and if you're from my mind, why are you disagreeing with me? Why are you trying to get me a new guy this early? Why am I hearing you in the first place?"

He sighs, then answers. *'My death has made you depressed. Over the past six months, that depression is slowly driving you insane. You are going crazy. Do you hear me? You need someone you can trust, someone who trusts you. Someone who can comfort you, help you through this. And a friend isn't going to get you there. You need a reason to live. I'm here to help you, to get you on the right track. As soon as you're there, someone else will take over. You'll move on, and I will no longer be needed. You must move on, Madrona.'*

I let one tear loose then hear the first bell. Time to get to class. I nod and suck it up, taking a deep breath. I can do this. Jacob's words echo in my head. "Accept it and keep moving."

'You can,' Aaron whispers. *'You will.'*

My mind gives me a quick glimpse of him, smiling, then he's gone.

Okay, time to go. I move out into the hall and become another body in the growing crowd.

"So…" Ivy begins, as we walk home together, "you're going out with my brother tomorrow."

I groan before answering. "I'm not going out with him. It's just a movie. It's *not* a date," I growl.

"Well, *he* seems to think it is. He's told all his friends it is. He told *me* it is."

I groan. "Great. Well, it's not. I'm making up for punching him. That's the only reason I'm going. So he'll accept my apology and leave me alone."

"Okay."

I almost stop mid-step. She never makes it that easy. "Wait, really? No, 'you're lying' or 'tell me another one' or anything?"

"Nope. I won't bother you about this. But when you *do* go a second time, I'm going to get to say, 'I told you so.'"

"Alright, fine. *If* I do, which I *won't*, you can say 'I told you so.'"

Ivy and Chris are waiting to walk home from school with me after class on Wednesday. Jacob opens the door to my house as we walk up the front sidewalk, having seen us approaching.

"Who's this?" Chris questions, his face displaying outrage, but his eyes showing distress.

"I'm Jacob," he introduces himself, holding out his hand. It's taking all my self-control - assuming I have any left - to not laugh at Chris, who quickly wipes the concern out of his eyes.

"Nice to meet you, Jacob. I'm Chris," he responds, accepting Jacob's hand and shaking it forcefully. "Don't think I know you. Did you just move here?"

"Yes, I did." Neither of them has stopped shaking each other's hands. They're giving each other death stares, and unsurprisingly, Jacob wins in the end. "I've been staying with Madrona." Chris looks like he's going to go nuclear.

"Good, good. Madrona's a nice girl," he glares.

"Yes, she is."

"How long have you been staying with her?"

"Two weeks, I believe." Yep, Chris is definitely going to explode.

"Are you still up for tonight?" Chris abruptly asks me.

Ah, he wants to make Jacob jealous that I'm 'going out' with him. Jacob's not going to care though; he knows I don't want to go anyway. I told him all about yesterday's ambush when I got home from school yesterday.

"Am I allowed to cancel?" I ask, in a friendly voice, trying not to sound rude. "I'm not feeling great." That's not a complete lie.

Chris looks me over. "You're fine," he concludes. "We're going out tonight," he brags to Jacob.

"I know."

Chris is hit with a wave of shock but wipes it from his face almost instantly. "You know?"

"Yeah."

"She told you?"

"Yeah."

"And you aren't angry about it?"

"I'm not mad at her."

"At her...?"

"I'm a little frustrated with you, to be honest."

"Can't say that I don't feel the same way about you."

"She doesn't *want* to go."

I can feel the tension rising. They're both alpha males trying to fight for dominance. And worst of all, they're fighting for dominance over me.

Chris opens his mouth to say more. "Okay. Quit it, will you?" I intervene. If I don't interfere a fight could break out, and there goes Jacob's cover. "We are going as friends; we are not dating," I remind Chris. "And *you*," I turn to Jacob, "Need to keep your cool." I stare intensely at him so he gets the meaning. *Don't expose yourself. Aether don't typically put up a big fight.*

Jacob glances pointedly at Chris. I shake my head, and Jacob tilts his in acknowledgement.

Chris gives a grunt of annoyance, but Lily and my mother pull up in the car and approach us.

"Jacob!" Lily yells and runs over to give him a hug.

He smiles and hugs her back. "Hey! How was school?"

"It was okay," she responds, then sees who's standing on the sidewalk. "Oh, hey, Chris." It comes out almost as an afterthought. She completely ignores him after that and races off inside the house. *Ouch, the poor guy.*

"Hello, Chris," Mom steps up on the porch. "How are you? Don't think I've seen you recently."

"I'm doing great, Dr. Carter," he replies. Oh... Now they're competing for my mom's approval. Well, Chris is going to win this one. "How are you?" He flashes a smile to rival Jacob's. Too bad I only find it annoying and suspicious now.

"I'm doing well, also," she answers. "Thank you for asking."

"Well, I have homework to do, so… bye Chris, bye Ivy!" I push Jacob in the door before he can say or do anything.

"See you tonight," Chris grins and grabs my forearm, pulling me away from Jacob in a tight embrace, trapping me against him. My arms are at my sides as he hugs me, his hand at the back of my head forcing my face into his chest. He smells like sweat. *Ugh. Okay, I want out.*

I break away from his hug. "Sure, see you tonight," I fume, then continue pushing Jacob inside.

"Wear something nice!" he shouts before I practically slam the door in his face.

The door shuts, and Jacob bursts out laughing. "You looked so disgusted when he hugged you."

"Well, I was!"

"Madrona, be nice to Chris. He clearly cares about you a lot. Maybe you should give him a chance," Mom suggests. Dammit, she's taken his side. Though to be fair, she has known Chris longer than Jacob.

"No, Mom. I have no intention of being Chris's girlfriend. There are hundreds of girls at our school; he can pick someone else."

"Well, he's handsome, and he's nice-" she begins, trying to convince me.

I silence her with a motion. "No, Mom. Just no. Tonight's outing is a one-and-done kind of thing. I just want to put the punching incident behind me, and this is the only way to do it."

It's seven o'clock. I have maybe twenty minutes before Chris comes by, early of course, so he can make a good impression on my parents. While Chris has won over my mother, Jacob won over my father the moment he asked to play the guitar. My father has always appreciated music like I have and actually *cried* when he first heard Jacob play. I had been doing my homework and sadly missed the moment, but Lily told me all about it afterwards. My mother can be swayed away from Chris, but it'll just take time.

"You ready?" Jacob queries through my closed door, as I debate what to wear. I was going to wear a typical sweatshirt as always, despite what Chris said, but Mom's told me I have to wear a dress.

"No," I admit. "Definitely not ready." Ugh. I hate dresses. They make me look stupid and always seem to make guys stare at my ass. I finally select a deep blue sweater dress and throw it on over a pair of black leggings. Aaron once commented on how it accentuated my blue eyes and wearing it now almost feels like a betrayal. Wearing a memory of him going out with a guy I don't even like.

'I'm fine with it,' his voice is supportive.

Not now. Talk to me later.

He sighs. *'Fine. Good luck,'* his voice replies, chuckling, and goes away.

I open the door and see Jacob still waiting for me in the hallway. "Woah," Jacob is taken aback. "You look… amazing."

"I hate dresses," I scowl.

"Why? You look *stunning*," he reassures.

I know he expects me to smile, but I'm too busy being self-conscious. I don't like being the center of attention, and that means I can't look *too* good. "Because of that!" I justify.

Jacob rolls his eyes. "You look nice," he compliments. "I like the necklace."

My mom put makeup on me, which I wasn't happy about, but also had me put on a necklace. No, *the* necklace. She dug it out from my not-so-secret bin under my bed. It's the only piece of jewelry I ever wear. A cheap charm I got at the market when I was seven. A charm of a spearhead. A charm that represented my courage and strength, my tendency to run at things head-on. I stopped wearing it recently, as I didn't see myself fit to wear it after Aaron died, when I lost my courage. But now it's back.

"Thanks," I smile.

"Head up," he tells me, tilting my face up slightly, "and shoulders back. Don't want to be slouching, do we?"

I laugh and reply, "I'll probably slouch on purpose, doing all the things I can to make him quit liking me."

"Fine. Just don't slouch until you're out the door, then. Don't want to be a bad example for Lily."

I smirk at him. "Okay."

He moves behind me. "Are you doing your hair?" he questions.

"I wasn't planning to."

He shakes his head and has me sit in my desk chair. He digs a brush out of my drawer and sets to work.

"You know how to do a girl's hair?" I smile.

"I had a sister," he reminds me. "I got lots of practice once my mother passed." I begin to nod, but he stops me, "Don't move your head."

I can feel Jacob carefully run the brush through my red hair. "Your hair's beautiful. Have I ever told you that?"

"No," I answer truthfully. I don't normally think much of it, anyway.

"Very, very few people have red hair now. Of a hundred people, one *might* have red hair. It's rare," he tells me. "Your eyes contrast it perfectly."

"I didn't know you paid attention to my eyes."

"Those beautiful blue eyes, how could someone *not* notice them?" he smiles. His praise is giving me butterflies. I smile, trying to hide my blush but failing. The curse of pale skin. "Your hair compliments your dress, making you look almost explosive. Fierce, but attractive."

"Stop complimenting me!" I finally give in, laughing.

"Why?" he asks, separating my hair as he sets to work.

"You're making me blush," I admit. He stops his work and looks at my bright face, then bursts out laughing.

"You look like a lobster!"

"I know!" I laugh with him.

"But you still look amazing," Jacob replies. I smile back at him when I see his mouth form that perfect smile. Not like Chris's, which seems to be more calculated. Jacob's smile isn't pure happiness either. Oftentimes there's a hint of regret or sadness in it. Proof that he isn't perfect, that he's been shattered to a thousand pieces, just like me, and taped back together. But he is still able to smile. It's slightly scarred with memories of the past, but it shows that he still cares. That he still loves. That he has and will continue to, even after what he's been through.

His hands move through my hair with swiftness, showing he's done this a thousand times. When he asks, I hand him a hair tie or clip. When he finishes, he helps me stand and walk over to a mirror. I gasp when I see his work.

"How did you learn to-" I begin but can't seem to finish. My red hair is pulled into a bun with four braids, two on each side that merge into one and form a hold around the rest of my hair.

"I loved my sister," he shrugs. He walks with me down the stairs and my mother gasps at me when she sees.

"Oh, my word… you look absolutely beautiful," she swoons, her expression telling me that she's proud, proud of who I've become. "Jacob, did you…?"

He nods, smiling with pride.

"Where'd you learn to do that?" she asks

"My mother taught me," he answers truthfully.

"It's amazing," Mom says in awe. Maybe she'll be swayed faster than I thought.

"Well, I had to help Madrona look her best," he chuckles, smiling. I smile back, filling my expression with gratitude. My mother clearly notices this, but I don't care. His blue eyes have caught mine for the moment.

Mom pulls me off to the side when our glance finally breaks and whispers, "We're going to talk about this later." She's smiling, so it shouldn't be bad, and I won't need to worry. She wants to talk to me about boys. I think she now knows why I don't want to go out with Chris. Along with that, I think she might have turned to support Jacob. Either way, I sigh when I hear a knock on the door.

I open it to see Chris in nice pants and a button-down shirt. His mouth hangs open when he sees me, and I smile. Not because he thinks I look good, or because I'm happy to see him, but because of how silly it makes him look, almost like a large-mouth bass.

"You look... *particularly* beautiful tonight," he stammers.

"Thank you," I falsely smile, annoyance over this whole evening still rushing through me. "Jacob did my hair for me." Chris's expression instantly falls, and he turns to glare at Jacob, who smiles, waving. I struggle not to laugh.

Chris holds out his arm, and I look at my mother. She's giving me the 'be nice' look. I sigh and reluctantly take his arm. It's going to be a long night.

"Have fun," Jacob says. "Be safe." He stares down Chris with a glance that claims *I will kill you if you let her get in any harm*, but it softens after a few seconds.

My mother waves goodbye as I sit in the passenger seat of his car, and our non-date is officially underway.

We arrive at the movie theater quickly, as it's not far from my house. I laugh when I see the movie. It's one of my favorites, a high school romantic comedy.

"Popcorn?" he offers, and I shake my head. Mainly because I don't want to share with him and give him any ideas, but also because I'm just not hungry. He shrugs as we take our seats, not seeming to care.

"You alright?" he frets.

No. "Yes."

"You sure?"

No. "Yes."

The commercials begin streaming, and we sit in silence with the strong aroma of butter and salt. He's being good and keeping his distance, not trying to make contact.

'Can I talk now?' Aaron's voice asks, entering my mind.

As long as no one's talking to me, and I can fully pay attention to you.

He cheers and is suddenly seated next to me. His smile fades to a frown, and I feel concern hanging in my gut. I know that expression. *'I'm not going to be visible to you for much longer.'*

The movie finally starts. Why not?

'Because you no longer need to see me.' I have nothing to answer with. He's probably right. I need to stop hallucinating.

Will I still hear you?

'Only for a little longer. My time to leave you is fast approaching.'

Don't... don't leave me. Not yet. I'm not ready. I feel my eyes growing slightly wet, but I shove it down before anyone notices. I don't want anyone to know about my mental conversation with my dead boyfriend whom I'm hallucinating. Don't think I'll get a good reputation from that.

'I won't leave yet,' he comforts. *'But I will soon. You aren't alone anymore, so you have no need of me to keep you company. But yes, I will stay for now and help you let go.'*

After glancing at the screen, I look back at the empty seat next to me. My eyes tell me there's no one there, but my heart says otherwise. I choose to see with my heart, and Aaron's face appears, smiling at me. *'I should probably leave you to your... date,'* he smirks.

I'm going to strangle you. He starts laughing, then slowly fades away, and the chair is empty once again.

I look up at the large screen. The two characters run into each other in the hall, the typical high school romance movie boy-meets-girl scene. The girl drops her project, and the guy offers to help her fix it, feeling bad about having broken it.

I start to remember when Aaron and I first met on the bleachers at the game. We had seen each other before, but it was the first time we'd spoken, the first time we'd been next to each other, since we only had one class together that year.

A small cluster of tears escapes at the memory, the two of us standing and cheering with the rest of the crowd as our team scores a touchdown. Afterwards Aaron and I started sitting together at every game, and I found myself always looking forward to them. One day he finally asked me out, and I still remember the feeling I got when he did. It felt like every piece of my world and my future was coming together, like I had met my other half, one I didn't know was missing until that moment.

I hope Chris is not staring at me. He doesn't have my permission to see me cry. I almost ask Aaron to come back and help me pull myself together, but I remember what he said. I need to move on without him. He'll be here for me when I really need him, but I do need to let him go, let him rest in peace.

More tears follow. I stand up and head towards the restrooms, quietly walking away.

"Madrona?"

"I'll be back in a second," I assure him, not turning to face him. I enter the restroom, the only place he can't follow me, and hide in one of the stalls. I can't stop the tears now. I should have just said no to Chris at the beginning and dealt with the guilt. Right now, the only person I care about is someone who understands my pain… Jacob.

I hear a knock on the bathroom door. "Hey, Madrona, you alright?"
I need to pull myself together. I pull a hand up to my necklace and find comfort in the cold metal, keeping me grounded. Not here. I wipe my tears and struggle to fix the makeup my mother did for me. I take a breath. A deep breath.

Okay. In and out. Calm down, Madrona. It's alright. You are going to exit this room and be happy. Maybe slightly irritated and perhaps slightly annoyed, but happy. You will not ruin tonight.

"Are you alright?" Chris repeats from outside the door.

No, but I'll be fine for now. Walking over to the door, I quietly open it and see Chris standing there, frowning.

"Sorry," I smile. "Just needed a minute."

"You need to talk about it?"

"No." *End of that.*

"Do you need a hug?"

"No."

"Do you need anything?"

"N-" I'm silent for a moment while I think about it. "Is there a possibility of ice cream after the movie?" I smile and raise an eyebrow jokingly.

He laughs. "There is *always* a possibility for ice cream."

Back in our seats, the characters are on their first date, at the girl's favorite band's concert. Chris puts his arm around me. It takes all my willpower not to throw his arm off and move over a few seats. Friends are allowed to put their arms around each other. I am aiming for friends. Not lovers, not enemies. Friends, like we were before.

Still, I go stiff when his arm touches me. When he tries to pull me closer, I resist, and he stops. I'm trying not to look at him, using false interest in the movie to not meet his gaze. I take another breath. *Calm down, Madrona.* I know why Chris picked this movie. Not just because it's my favorite, but because he wants to prove he cares and remembers the small things.

He waits another minute before attempting to pull me closer again, despite the seat's armrest that blocks him from me like a protective shield, but I don't let him. This is close enough, and it's already making me a little uncomfortable. I can feel him staring at me, his breath on my arm. I try to steady my heartbeat, and it slowly starts working. I want to appear calm, not completely enveloped in chaos like my mind really is.

"Are you sure you're okay?"

"Yes, I'm fine," I try to convince him calmly, though I'm freaking out beneath the surface. Calm, appear calm. I think my heart stops as I wait.

"You don't seem fine."

I turn and stare at Chris. "I'm fine," I snap, and turn back to the movie. I sigh quietly, making sure not to let him hear.

Chris reaches for my hand and holds it in his. I try to pull away, but realize he's squinting in the dark, inspecting it. I look at my hand and can barely make out the small cuts speckling my knuckles on top of slight bruising from fighting practice. They're scabbing over now, but still there. I turn away.

"What's going on?" he asks.

I don't answer, staring directly at the screen even though I'm not truly paying attention to what's going on.

"What the hell happened?" he repeats. "These cuts are on the opposite hand that you hit me with. And they look new."

I can't tell him the whole truth, but I can trust him enough with small details. I sigh like I'm giving in and finally speak. "I was punching some trees."

"That's violence, Madrona! You'll get yourself in trouble!"

"I'm sorry, I'm just... I'm just so... angry. I had to get it out."

"What was making you angry?" he pokes.

"I don't want to talk about it."

"Please."

I allow a long pause before answering. "I'm just stressed. Aaron is dead, Chris. He's dead, and people are pushing me, telling me to get over it. You are trying to start a relationship with me, and all I want is to be friends. I need time, and people aren't letting me have it. Then you throw Jacob into this mess, and it's...complicated," I pretend to burst, selling a lie woven of half-truths.

"Jacob..." he muses. "What... what do you think of him?" He's jealous, so I should have expected this question.

"Despite what you seem to think of him, he understands my pain. He understands that it changes you, that it makes you into a different person than you were before. That grief isn't something you move past or get over. It must be accepted before you can keep moving. But it comes with you, wherever you go, as it becomes a part of you forever. It helps...having someone around who truly understands."

Chris nods. He knows he's lost, and I can see the hurt on his face. He's silent after that but pulls me into a hug with such force I can't fight back, so I give up. The only thing separating us is the armrest.

For once, I'm grateful he's here. Just telling him I'm not the same has released a lot of my stress. I've been trying to be the same Madrona I was before, but it just hasn't been working. It's been easier to let Jacob and all that's going on distract me from this truth.

"I'm always here for you; you should know that," he says, and suddenly it's different. I can almost feel the air shift, almost feel the change in him. Suddenly it's like it was before, and we're friends. Just like we were when we jammed out with Ivy at the middle school dances, like we were when the three of us went to movies on Friday nights and slept in until two the next afternoon.

Finally, I let him hug me for real, completely ignoring the movie in the background. He walked in here expecting to come out with me on his arm, and he did. But not in the way he'd hoped. I walked in here wanting to end this dating nonsense, though I wasn't expecting to succeed, and I did. I smile and slowly release him.

He pats me on the back, and we turn back to the movie. Finally, just friends. I was expecting him to be angry, to fight back against me trying to let him go, but he didn't. For once he understood.

We turn back to the movie as friends, and for the first time in a few weeks, I enjoy being around him. He just needed to stand in my shoes.

Chris drives me home. I thank him, then turn to go walk inside, but he speaks.

"Have a good time?"

I consider it for a moment. "I did," I smile. That was an honest answer. I'd expected to have the worst night of my life, but since the moment when it all went back to how it was before, I've had a great time.

He chuckles and nods. "If you ever need anything, just… let me know."

I nod, smiling. I'm about to walk in the door when he comes up from behind me and pulls me into a hug. I hug him back. He releases me with a "good night," and I enter my house.

The moment the door is closed, I walk over to the living room couch and sit in the dark. After the movie, we went and got ice cream and the taste of it lingers in my mouth.

I'm exhausted from the emotional upheaval. I wouldn't have noticed if it weren't for the loose floorboard at the bottom of the stairs, but someone makes their way quietly towards me and a familiar scent envelopes me. I keep my eyes closed when Jacob sits beside me.

"Hey."

"Hey," I answer.

"How was it?"

"Not bad. I finally got him to let go of the whole 'I think I'm in love with you' act. He's back to being a friend now."

He smiles. "Good. How did you do it?"

"I told him the truth; that I'm not the same as I was before. I told him how hard it's been trying to pretend to be my old self when I'm someone entirely new. That you were teaching me how to accept my grief, fold it carefully in my heart, and keep moving forward."

"Do you believe in fate?"

"Not really."

"I didn't either. But now I'm starting to. Think about it. We helped each other. We were the right people, in the right place, at the right time, for the right reason. I don't think chance played a part."

"Maybe. Whatever brought you here, I'm grateful. I think you saved my life, not the reverse. Aaron's death drove me deep into depression. I know I was worrying my family, but I just couldn't work up the energy to do anything about it. I was suffering alone, and it was slowly killing me. I started hallucinating. To be honest, I still am, but it's getting better," I answer, the truth to my words stunning me.

"What do you see when you hallucinate?"

"Him. Aaron. He talks to me. Telling me what to do and what not to do. He was there when I found you. He helped me decide to help you," I admit.

"Before I passed out, I heard you talking. I'm assuming you were talking to him?" he asks.

"Yes. I still hear him. Today, yesterday, every day before. But he's coming less and less. Saying less and less. I think it's because of you."

"You saved me first, so it only seems fair to be able to return the favor."

Jacob squeezes my hand, and we sit in a comfortable silence, each lost in our own thoughts, until it's time for bed.

SEVEN

Friday morning, and Jacob's first day of school, dawns cool and cloudy. A low fog lingers just above ground and plays peek-a-boo with the forest trees out back. Ivy stops by the house to walk with us. She attempts to question me about my date with her brother, but Jacob saves my ass by distracting her with questions about her classes. She begins telling him about all her teachers and the classes she enjoys. I send Jacob an appreciative smile, and he shoots me a small one back with a wink.

"Spanish with Mr. Brenton, and history with Mr. Wills? Physics with Mrs. Presli?" I ask, joining their conversation, and he nods. "We have three classes together!"

When we get to school, of course Chris has to make an appearance.

"Hey, Madrona!"

"Morning."

"Jacob."

"Hey."

"First day, huh?"

"Yep."

"Looks like you are causing a stir already," Chris grins. "We don't get a lot of fresh meat around here."

It's only after Chris points it out that I see he's right. Students are talking with their heads together, taking repeated quick glances over at our small group. The guys seem to be sizing Jacob up as either competition or a potential teammate, while the girls are mostly smiling coyly and ogling him beneath their eyelashes. I shouldn't be surprised; I know how attractive Jacob is, but I still feel a surge of anger at their behavior. It takes a minute for me to recognize the feeling as jealousy.

"Well, have a good first day," Chris finishes up, and I jerk back to my friends realizing they've been carrying on a conversation around me. I'm still a little stunned Chris has been cordial to Jacob.

"Have a good day to you as well," Jacob replies.

They stare at each other for a moment more, shaking each other's hands, when Chris finally breaks off and runs off to his group.

"Woah," I turn to Jacob. "What just happened?"

"They were having a non-verbal conversation. Chris was letting Jacob know that while he may have lost out on having you as anything more than a friend, he won't let anything bad happen to you, so Jacob better be careful." Ivy doesn't seem to notice Jacob's slight discomfort.

"Wow. Uh, okay," is my only answer to her explanation.

"Well, we should be getting to class," Ivy finally realizes the awkwardness of the situation and changes the subject. I nod in agreement, and we take off towards Spanish.

We walk through the halls until we reach our first classroom, entering the large and organized room, with small tables in columns of four.

"Madrona, Jacob will be your new partner, since your previous one changed periods," Mr. Brenton announces. Jacob takes a seat next to me at my desk, smiling. *How lucky am I?*

The whole day is pretty normal. In every class I have with Jacob, the teacher introduces him and goes on like there's nothing different, which he seems happy about. At lunch a few senior guys start picking on him. All he has to do is stand, and they shut up, since he towers over all of them.

After school, we escape back to the forest. The fog has dissipated, but the skies remain overcast. There's a damp chill in the air.

After a quick warm up, we run through a short review session of power punches and jabs before Jacob launches into today's lesson.

"Remember, there are no rules in street fighting. Anything and everything goes. It's about survival, not fairness. If you need to fight dirty to stay alive, then fight dirty. If you are looking to stun your opponent so you can make your escape, target the crotch, knees, eyes, nose, or solar plexus," Jacob points to the soft spot between the bottom of his sternum and the top of his stomach. "A strong kick or punch to this point can easily knock the wind out of someone. If you go for the knee, try to hit it from the side. The ligaments aren't strong enough to withstand a sharp lateral movement. This disables your attacker and prevents him from chasing you down. Attacks to the eyes and nose trigger a person's tear ducts, causing disorientation and temporary blindness. Pain from a broken nose can also distract your attacker, so take advantage and run.

"Now, if your intent is to knock out or potentially kill your opponent, you need to aim for the base of the throat, the base of the skull, the temple, the chin, or the side of the neck. These points should be saved for a life-or-death situation. Killing someone, even an enemy, should not be taken lightly. Usually, it is better to incapacitate than terminate."

I almost flinch. I hadn't stopped to consider that I might need to kill someone. It's a sobering thought. *Do I even have it in me to take a life?* I envision my parents and Lily's faces. If threatened, yes, I absolutely could if it meant protecting those I love. Resolve reinforced, I return my attention to Jacob.

We spend the next two hours working through techniques to target the vulnerable spots on an attacker and how to keep my balance and recover from strategically placed kicks. It's a bit tricky to practice since I can't actually do the true hits and kicks on Jacob, but I think I get the rough concepts by the end of the lesson.

We sit on the forest floor and catch our breath. "Thank you," I whisper, confused on why it came out so quiet.

"Of course," he answers, smiling again. "Thank *you*. For taking such a big risk to help me."

I speak quickly before I lose my courage. "You have the most amazing smile," I tell him. "You probably get whatever you want with that."

"Not everything. It gets me pretty far, but some things need more convincing."

The deepest part of my mind wonders if he's talking about me.

'He is, obviously,' Aaron's voice laughs in my mind.

Shut up! It was just a stray thought!

"You know you have the most fantastic laugh?" Jacob asks.

Aaron laughs in my mind. *'And he leans over… and slobbers all over her face.'*

Shut up! Aaron's chuckle slowly fades, and I know he's gone for the moment.

"My laugh is horrible," I reply truthfully. I've always hated my laugh.

"No, it isn't. You can say whatever you want about it, but I love it," Jacob argues. I smile, and he flashes that perfect smile again. He may be an Erebus, but he's amazing. Not perfect, scarred and in need of some fine-tuning, but he's the only one who's been able to make me laugh in the last six months.

"Why did you save me?" he questions. "Honestly."

"I-I don't know. I just felt a… I don't know, a connection, a tug. It wouldn't let me leave you…" I trail off at a loss for how to explain that feeling, that pull. I saved him because I saw something in him. Felt some kind of tether to him. So I just give a small shrug and change the subject. "When all this is over, will you go home?"

A shadow passes over his face. "I don't know," he replies. For a moment my heart lifts, then I realize the true meaning of what he said.

"What? Isn't that why we're doing this, to get you home to your family?"

He's quiet for a moment, and I see him hit with a wave of something… sorrow, pain, grief. It slaps me in the face. How did I not see this before? It was right in front of me, and I missed it.

The lie he shaped, the story he built, it wasn't a complete lie. It was based on the truth.

"I wasn't fully honest with you," he gulps.

Oh no. Don't say it. Don't say what I'm thinking. Don't say it.

"I had just gotten home. My girlfriend had cheated on me two days before, not the day I met you. I was still getting over it, frequently taking walks around town to keep myself occupied. On the day we met, I walked in the front door… and…," a tear rolls down his face, and I realize this is the first time I've seen him cry.

My own eyes start shedding tears in response. "No…" I whisper.

"I have no family to go back to," he whispers. "They're all dead."

EIGHT

I wrap my arms around him, and he quietly cries into my shoulder. Slowly he wraps his arms around me.

"Shh," I comfort, trying to calm him. His family is dead. I tilt his head forward, and his eyes are obscured by tears. I take my sleeve and slowly wipe away his tears.

"Isn't that my job?" he asks.

"Not right now it isn't," I smile. "At the moment, it's mine." We sit in silence for a moment before he speaks again.

"I've had time since coming here to think about it. My guess is that they came to kill me," he explains. "But I wasn't there, so they… they killed my family. My father, my brother and sister…." The tears start to fall faster, but I wipe them away before they can go anywhere. "This is why I have to know. I have to know what's going on, so I can avenge my family," he tells me and raises his head to look at me. "I shouldn't have lied to you."

"No, I understand. You needed time," I say gently.

"But you deserved to know."

"No, I didn't."

"You deserve so much more."

I shake my head. "No, I don't," I answer truthfully. "I deserve much less than I already have."

"You deserve way more. You didn't deserve to go through the pain you did."

"Neither did you." I am crying tears on his behalf even though his own have stopped. My arms are still around him.

He's warm, and his cinnamon scent fills my senses. He moves his hand, and I feel him drawing his thumb across my wet cheeks.

"Now it's my job."

I smile and shake my head, but I don't stop him. He keeps putting me first, even though it should be me comforting him. He just lost his family. The tears slow to a stop, and we stare into each other's eyes.

"You saved me twice," he confesses. "Once when I was dying, and the second time you gave me a will to live, the moment I first saw you."

"So did you," I reveal. "Again and again, every day." He gives his perfect smile and I laugh. I know what I just said. I did the thing Aaron wanted all along. I admitted it. And so did he.

He leans toward me slowly, carefully, giving me a chance to stop him. I can feel his breath on my cheek as he moves closer and carefully presses his lips to mine. His cinnamon smell, his warmth, the feel of his arms around me overwhelm my senses. The birds continue chirping, the light breeze stirs the trees, the small animals play in the brush, but I don't notice any of it. All I know is the feel of his lips on mine. They are soft as they brush up against my own. His hand comes up to caress the side of my face, and I feel loved, cherished.

A surge of warmth flows through me. I missed this feeling, no matter how much I tried to avoid it. One cannot hide from life, no matter how hard she might try. One cannot deny or avoid love. Fate isn't quite the right word. More like destiny, no matter how stupid it sounds.

And in this moment, I believe everything will work out. As long as we're together, we'll make it. We'll find out what's going on with the Erebus. We'll find out why Jacob's family was killed and stop the parties responsible from doing it to any more families. I will keep living, and loving, after Aaron's death. He'll never leave me, but it won't stop me from living my life. Just as Aaron wanted.

Jacob saved me from my grief, just as I saved him from his. He's here for me, as I'm here for him. He pulls away and says, "I've wanted to do that for a while now."

"So have I," I reply truthfully. I tried to deny it, but it's true. We kiss again, free of our worries for this short time.

Later, as we head home, I remember back to the moment when I helped him up in the forest to walk to my house for the first time. Rising together. Fighting gravity together. We will do this together; we will rise out of this dark and cold pit, together. *Together, together, together.* The word ricochets in my mind. We will rise together, even if the world tries to stop us.

·〜 · ✦ ☾ · ☀ · ☽ · ✦ · 〜·

Once we enter the door, Lily runs over to squeeze the living daylights out of us. I can't breathe for a moment while she hugs me as tight as possible, then moves on to Jacob and hardly touches him.

"Hey," she greets us.

"Hey," I reply.

"Mom and Dad just left for work," Lily informs us. "They said we have to get our chores and homework done before we go anywhere." Of course they said that.

I groan. "Ugh. Don't they know it's Friday, and we have all weekend?"

Lily just gives me a look.

"What?"

"Homework," she demands. "Get it done, soldier!" I laugh and salute, while Jacob gives her a quick bow before we exit to our respective rooms. She can't go anywhere until we all get our stuff done, so I guess she is waiting on us.

I sit down at my desk and see the picture of Aaron and me. Smiling. Happy. My heart aches as I realize what just happened. I just kissed another guy. I just did exactly what I said I'd never do again. Fall in love. And this time, I fell in love with an Erebus. *Great. Amazing job, Madrona.* The sarcasm is thick, even in the recesses of my mind.

One day Jacob's going to leave or die, and I'll be left in pieces again. Or we'll both die, and my family will be the ones in pieces. I've made myself vulnerable.

Aaron's voice enters my head again. *'No, you haven't,'* he persuades me. *'You are stronger now than you have ever been. And love is always worth it.'*

I shake my head. "I just betrayed you or at least your memory!"

'No, you didn't.'

"Yes, I did! I just kissed another guy! Someone I hardly know! And on top of that, he's an Erebus!"

He shakes his head and looks at the picture of us on my desk. *'I remember that day,'* Aaron smiles, his hands settle on my shoulders. But I can't feel them, no matter how much I want to. No matter how much I *need* to.

"Me too," I admit. "We were at the market, and you bumped into a pallet of apples."

He laughs as he continues, *'They went everywhere! It was such a mess. And the guy was yelling at me in French.'*

"You were trying to apologize, but he would not have any of it. I still don't know what he was saying," I chuckle.

'Maybe, something like, "El stupido, you make shit pile of manzanas."'

I'm laughing now. "That's Spanish, but I bet it's still pretty close."

He smiles, *'We had to pick all of them up and clean them so there wasn't a spot of dirt on them, even though they were covered in dirt to begin with.'*

"Ugh. Don't remind me."

'Dang, that took forever.'

I nod. "You felt so bad. And all you did was lightly bump the pile while walking by."

'Afterwards you were trying to tell me it wasn't my fault and made a comment on how the apples knocked themselves over.'

"You asked how that was possible, and I was searching my mind for a valid response," I give a small chuckle.

'You were like, "Uh… they grew legs and moved over three feet, of course."' I nod. The picture was taken at that moment by a nearby photographer while we were trying to imagine apples growing legs. *'This is why.'*

"Why what?"

'Why you need to move on. So you can have more moments like that one. Well, maybe not exactly like that one. Hopefully you don't have to pick up more than a thousand apples, clean and stack them neatly again, but still.'

I smile, but it fades as doubts start creeping in.

'Don't do that. Don't second guess yourself. Don't spend your life mourning me. Live it to the fullest, just as I did. Make the most of every moment you have; enjoy the time you have with the people around you because nothing lasts forever. Trust yourself. Trust your gut feelings. Your heart will expand to fit more love inside. It is your capacity for love that makes you strong.'

I consider his words for a moment. He's right. My feelings for Jacob don't diminish what I had with Aaron. I can honor Aaron's memory by moving forward, by continuing to live. I nod, "Okay, I'll try. Just… don't leave me. I'm not ready to fully say goodbye."

He smiles and answers. *'I haven't yet, have I?'*

I pull out my homework and put in my earbuds and glance behind me to make sure he's still there. Aaron smiles at me, and I smile back. My music starts, and I begin my work, occasionally glancing at the picture of us that day at the market. After a few minutes I turn around, and he's gone.

'Not gone. Just concealed.'

That's good enough for me.

I finish my latest homework over the next hour or two, and by that time, Lily comes up to tell me to make dinner.

"Why don't you make it yourself?" I ask, then realize how that sounded. "Sorry, I don't mean to be rude."

She smiles. Lily's always been great at understanding the true meaning behind people's words. "It tastes better when you make it," she admits. I glow with pride. My expertise in cooking is basically nonexistent, so I'm glad she enjoys what little I can throw together.

"I'll be right down," I reply. She's getting ice cream today. She gives a smile that claims she's the happiest person in the world and bounces downstairs. I close my binder and take one last glance at the picture before following her.

She and Jacob are talking on the couch when I enter the room.

"Hey."

"Hey."

"Lily was telling me about-"

"The new horror movie that's out!" she interrupts. Lily is obsessed with scary movies. I'm not. I prefer not to watch them. Why? Because they do what they're supposed to. They scare me.

I glance at Jacob because she interrupted him too fast to be normal, and her tone said she was stopping him from saying something. I raise my eyebrow at her, and she ignores it. "There's a new one out. It's supposed to be really good, and it's in theaters today."

Jacob rolls his eyes and mouths, *I'll tell you later.* I nod and sigh, "You know I don't really watch horror movies."

"It could be fun," Jacob argues. "What, are you scared?"

"Yes!"

"You weren't supposed to admit it," he laughs. "Come on. I won't let the scary monsters get you."

"You like horror movies?" I ask.

"Yeah," he replies. Of course the Erebus likes horror movies. Why am I surprised? "It might be fun. We could all go out and see it this evening."

Please no…. Okay, Madrona, be brave. He won't let them get you. You'll be fine. It's okay. Just try it… once.

"Okay, fine." I'm going to regret this. "But we're getting ice cream afterwards." Lily cheers. At least I can look forward to something.

"Best… day… ever!" she yells, jumping on the couch cushions. Yep, she's very mature. Well, now that I think about it, she does do a pretty good job of being mature when it's needed.

One hour later, after I've made us dinner, we pile into my car and head to the movie theater. We are walking up to the building when I see the sign showing the movie we're about to see. My heart nearly stops when I see what's on the cover. An old, beheaded doll. Why? Of course, it had to be dolls! The one time I watch a horror movie, it has to be about dolls.

"I can't do this," I stop walking. Jacob turns and lightly taps me with one of his crutches.

"Come on, it can't be that bad."

I look back at the cover. Yes, it's *that* bad.

"I… I can't. I just can't."

"Why?" he asks. I glance at the sign again. Lily realizes we've stopped and knows why instantly.

"Dolls," she explains. "She's terrified of them."

"You didn't tell me it was all about dolls!" I almost yell, though my voice cracks on the last word.

"Of course, I didn't! I knew you'd never go."

"Alright. Lily, go on in, and we'll be right behind you," Jacob says. *Dolls. Dolls. Why did it have to be dolls?* He looks at me with his eyebrows raised. "Seriously? Dolls?"

"When I was four, I came down the stairs for a glass of water," I explain. "My father was watching a horror movie on dolls with a friend. I was terrified. Didn't sleep that night. Hardly slept the next. After that, when I was seven and was finally getting over the fear. I was going through our attic and saw an old doll. It didn't have any eyes, and there were spiders living inside it. Red chalk had fallen next to it, and it looked like blood. There went another night's sleep, and so much for getting over the fear. After that, I was twelve when a friend pranked me with another doll…" He gets the point. A childhood fear I've never gotten over.

He sighs and thinks about it for a moment. "Okay. Let's go on in and find Lily, and I'll be right by your side. I'll protect you from the dolls," he comforts. I feel like a child being told there's no reason to be afraid of the dark. "We're going to do this for Lily. You can bury your head in my shoulder during any scary parts."

We're going to do this. There's no reason to be afraid if he's there, right?

He struggles to balance on one crutch and holds out his hand. "Ready?"

I step forward and he puts his arm around me, using my stiff body to gain his balance, holding his second crutch in his left hand with the first.

"Yeah," I nod. He's warm, and his cinnamon smell is comforting. It'll be alright. It's just a movie about *dolls*. Dolls. I should be panicking, but I feel his arm around me and take a breath as we enter the doors. We slowly work our way through the building until we find Lily with a box of popcorn, placing a sweatshirt over two seats.

"Nevermind then. Didn't know how long you guys would be," she says, putting her sweatshirt back on. I glance up at the huge screen. Commercials. The movie will start in a few minutes. *Dolls. Stupid dolls. Why is everything always about dolls?*

"Okay. Why don't we sit down?" Jacob asks.

I help Jacob into the seat to my left, putting Lily on my right. Even though it makes it much harder for him, he keeps his arm around me the whole time, comforting me and letting me know it's alright.

I glance up at the screen just as the commercials end. Oh no. It's starting. The screen goes black, and a small beat-up doll grows in the darkness. The camera zooms in on its face. Its eyes are closed, and someone gave this doll *way* too much blush. The eyes burst open, and centipedes crawl out of their empty sockets. A shiver goes through me as I remember that day in the attic. The opening credits scroll for a moment, then the movie truly starts.

I burrow myself into Jacob's side and his arm goes around me. For once, I don't care who sees or what they think. I'm safe in his embrace. Safe from the millions of live dolls that are hiding in the warehouse the dumbass characters are about to enter.

I close my eyes almost the whole movie. Every time they show a doll that doesn't look right, my eyes close. Jacob plants a kiss on my forehead, and it's a nice, but all too brief, distraction from the millions of dolls on the huge screen. Dolls, dolls, dolls. Why is it always dolls? Terrifying, horrible dolls?

Jacob carefully gives me a light squeeze, and I remember he's there. His warmth, his cinnamon smell, the sense of safety. He's here to protect me. He'll be here tomorrow when the Erebus try to kill me... Suddenly the dolls are wiped from my mind. I have to fight an Erebus! And *not* die! The dolls instantly become a minor problem.

I press my nose into Jacob's chest. He's wearing a green sweater that's soft against my cheek. The coziness, the safety... He's here with me now. I will live. He's going to be here with me tomorrow. I will live. I won't be afraid. Slowly, I look up at the screen and see the dolls. Another shiver goes through me, but soon I realize the whole movie is just scenes of dolls attacking people, those people running then coming back to try to get rid of dolls and failing, on repeat.

I take a breath and look over at Lily. I see why she likes these movies. The excitement and suspense, but most of all, I know she likes to laugh at how stupid the characters are. At some point in the movie, I finally stop focusing on the dolls and follow Lily's example of focusing on the stupid characters. Why would you choose a candle over a handheld searchlight to see in a dark room full of live dolls? It's not like they're reacting to the light.

I glance up at Jacob and find him looking back. "You seem to have calmed down," he whispers over someone's scream as a doll tries to suffocate them.

"Found a pattern. And noticed how stupid the characters are."

He laughs quietly. "Yeah, that's pretty usual for horror films. The dolls aren't bothering you?"

"Oh, they're bothering me. I just think it helps… that you're here," I whisper slowly.

Soon the movie ends, and we exit the building after I help Jacob up and we struggle to get through the seats together.

"So…" Lily starts. "What did you think?"

I consider my answer for a moment. "I still hate dolls, but I'm no longer fully against horror movies. Still against them, but I'll go, if you really want me too," I glance at Jacob and know I don't have to add the words, *as long as he's there.*

She cheers. She's always wanted to get me to like horror movies, so I'd go with her.

"Alright. Let's go get some ice cream," I smile. I earned it. She did too. Jacob earned it also, but he just deserves it with all he's been through the last few weeks.

"Yay!" Lily yells, and Jacob and I laugh. Then she asks something I wasn't ready for. "Do you two like each other? Madrona was like clinging to you the whole time, and you were comforting her and all…" I'm not fully surprised she noticed. We weren't exactly being secretive about it…

Jacob slips me a questioning look, and I shrug in response. "Kind of," he admits. *Good answer.* "Well, yes. I guess so," he smiles at me. I smile back. *It's official.*

I nod. She already knows anyway. Lily's grinning in excitement. I'm not worried about her telling anyone. It's not like her to gossip. It's nice since I can vent to her and know no one will hear about it if I ask it of her.

The ice cream stand is only a block away, so we don't bother moving the car. Just as we reach the stand, a brief moment of static comes before the speakers turn on. Everyone on the street stops and stares at the nearest loudspeaker, on the street corner next to the crosswalk.

"Fellow Aether. Your representative, Janice Spade, has an important message for you," the male voice says.

A deep, but strictly female voice booms overhead. "Hello, fellow Aether. It is with a heavy heart that I must tell you our fair land is on the precipice of destruction. Erebus have breached our defenses and invaded our homeland. I am proud of our Law Enforcement who have worked around the clock to apprehend these criminals and submit them to swift justice. In light of this violation, today I signed Executive Order 1L4B into effect, thereby postponing our current elections and declaring a state of emergency. I will remain your representative during this uncertain time. Also, effective immediately will be the suspension of Erebus trials. Erebus violating Aether land will be subject to execution without trial. Any aiding or abetting an Erebus will promptly receive the same punishment.

"In two months, I will be accompanied by guards into the Place of Truce, where I will speak with the Erebus representative directly and put a stop to this invasion once and for all. In the meantime, my priority as your leader will be to increase wall security to protect us from the dreaded Erebus."

"Thank you, Miss Spade. Aether, remember to keep a close eye out for Erebus. Do not panic, as we have doubled the guards on the wall. Again, if you see an Erebus, immediately run the other way and report to the nearest Law Enforcement agent. I don't think I need to remind you how dangerous they are. May you find happiness if you deserve it, and if you do not, may you work to earn it," the voice finishes and is followed by a brief static before the speakers shut off.

The streets grow loud with conversation. Some people are most definitely panicking. I glance at Jacob, and he nods. There have been more. The Erebus guards are throwing people over the wall, knowing they'll be sentenced to death. But why? What do they all have in common, or are they all just random people?

NINE

"What do we do?" Jacob whispers his question into my ear.

"Pretend to be worried, don't stop talking about it and how afraid you are. We'll do as planned and head back after getting her ice cream," I whisper under my breath, so Lily doesn't overhear. He nods.

"My tattoo is still covered, right?" His voice is barely a whisper.

I carefully move behind him and glance at his neck. "Yes. Might need to recoat though. It's hard to see, but I'm starting to make out the edges when I look long enough."

We follow Lily into line for ice cream and mimic everyone else on the street.

"Should we be worried? I mean, more Erebus are coming over. How many more? Is it even safe to be outside anymore?" Jacob's eyes widen, turning fearful as he speaks, and it is utterly convincing. Perhaps it's because the emotion isn't completely faked.

"Of course, we should be worried!" I answer, listening to others' conversations and noticing all are of a similar manner. "The Erebus are evil and dangerous. Before, it was rare to see them, and we still needed to stay vigilant. Now, it's bad enough to warrant a state of emergency! I've never heard of a representative canceling an election before. Clearly there is more going on than they are telling us. How many Erebus have they caught? How can they be confident they found them all?" I gulp, continuing the charade.

"What are we going to do?" That hint in the corner of his right eye tells me he's secretly asking about something else.

"It sounds like everyone else is going to stay inside at night and keep away from isolated places. I think that's a good idea," I look into his eyes, so he knows I mean the opposite. *We're going according to plan.*

"There's more Erebus crossing?" Lily shudders, having found a place in line.

"That's what they're saying," I reply as a person in front of us glances back, obviously listening to our conversation.

I was hoping Lily would ignore the message, but of course she wouldn't. Even if she had ignored it, she'd have still noticed the panic around the street.

"That's not good," she shakes. I glance at Jacob and hope she doesn't mention anything that'd hurt him. I can see he's just now realizing how wide the fear and propaganda of his culture has spread. I can also see the hurt behind his eyes at Lily's unknowing fear of his people.

"No, it's not. But it's nothing we need to worry about," I comfort. "Law Enforcement is handling it. They will keep us safe." She nods, and I know she'll have more to say about this later. She always does.

We're in front of the line now, and the person eavesdropping on us has left. Lily picks out her usual flavor; she's obsessed with caramel. Jacob picks strawberry, and I go with plain old vanilla, trying to make it quick and not spend twenty minutes deciding.

I throw ten bucks on the counter, and we head back to the car. Mom and Dad should be off work by now. They'll have heard the announcement and want us back to the house to make sure we're safe. Hopefully, the news won't send them straight into panic mode, leading to overprotectiveness and strict rules, causing potential problems for tomorrow night.

I pull into the driveway and, sure enough, my parents' car is sitting there. Hopefully this will be quick because Jacob and I need to talk.

Mom opens the door as we approach, obviously waiting for our arrival. She embraces each of us tightly. "Oh, you scared us! We heard the announcement and were worried-"

"Where were you?" Dad interrupts her.

"We went to see a movie and then got ice cream," I explain as Lily wanders up to her room.

"There's something going on at the hospital, so we just wanted to make sure you're alright," Mom sighs.

Jacob frowns. "What's going on?"

"It's… nothing for you to be concerned about. Just a few false rumors flying around," Mom smiles reassuringly.

"More of a nuisance, really." Dad shakes his head, as if dismissing a thought. "Anyway, we just came to make sure you're okay."

"All good here," I confirm before Jacob and I head upstairs. Just as we round the corner to head up the stairs, Jacob grabs my arm and holds a finger to his lips.

"What?" I whisper, and he motions in the direction of my parents. Gesturing for me to stay put, he noisily climbs the stairs, heads toward my door, opening and shutting it without entering before soundlessly returning to my side. An impressive feat, especially with a broken leg and crutches.

"Listen," he mouths, and I finally understand that he wants us to eavesdrop on my parents' conversation.

Mom sighs loudly, and I hear a chair scraping against the wood floor.

"I can't believe he's gone," she murmurs. "It was Law Enforcement, wasn't it?"

"It must have been. They're the ones who control the cameras, and it'd make sense that they don't want people knowing about their operation, much less questioning it."

My heart is racing in my chest, and I struggle to keep my breathing quiet.

"He was just trying to help those people, figure out where they came from, so he could send them home," she sniffles. I look pointedly at Jacob, opening my mouth to ask what he thinks they mean, but he shakes his head, nodding again at my parents around the corner.

"They were trying to make an example of him. They don't want people asking questions, only following orders. They're trying to keep it under wraps," Dad tells her. "We have to be careful, lest we end up like him."

There's a slight pause in their conversation before Dad deliberately starts talking about something random with the house. Jacob tugs my arm, and we sneak up the stairs to my room, where he cups the doorknob in his hands, opening the well-oiled door without making a sound and closing it behind us.

"What was that?" I ask him.

A corner of his mouth perks up. "I was going to ask you the same thing," he says as he lowers himself to sit on the edge of my bed, propping his crutches up next to his side.

"It sounds like Law Enforcement is doing something at the hospital," I say, running the facts through my head again and again. "Something they want to be kept a secret."

"Do you think this could be related to the announcement earlier tonight?"

"I don't know," Jacob grunts in frustration, running his hand through his hair in agitation.

So many pieces, but no clear picture. I sigh and glance at the picture on my desk. Aaron is smiling back from his silver frame, and I hear a whisper. My eyebrows knit together, and he whispers it louder. *'Remember,'* he murmurs in the back of my mind. *'Remember what I said.'* I shake my head, confused. My eyes travel to my backpack, and the grass stains on the bottom from all the times I'd thrown it on the ground, running up to him on the bleachers.

Then it all clicks into place.

·〜 ∘ ✦ ☾ ∘ ☼ ∘ ☽ ✦ ∘ 〜·

"Madrona?" Aaron whispered, his arms around me as I cried into him. His shirt was soaked from tears and sweat, because it took more energy than it should for him to climb the metal steps. But he did it for me.

I looked up at him, and he carefully slid his thumb across my cheeks, ridding me of my tears. His face is pale and thin, almost ghostly compared to the way it was before, bright and alive.

"Shh…" he put his finger to my lips, and I buried my head into his chest, hugging him tighter, as if doing so will stop the inevitable.

He carefully and gently runs his calloused hand through my hair.

"Hey," he murmurs. I tilt my head up to look at him, and his lips press softly against mine. "Don't cry. Let's enjoy these moments while they last." He kisses me again, then once more cleanses me of my tears. I nod, he's right.

"Talk about something. Anything," I beg.

He sighs.

"At night, I walk around the hospital when I can't sleep, and insomnia has me caught in its clutches. The nurses are too busy with the other more immediate patients, so I mosey around like I own the place.

"The hospital has all these interesting nooks and crannies; the basement levels, in particular, are a giant labyrinth. A couple of weeks ago, I discovered a room at the back of the hospital, somewhere I'd never been before. I opened the door and found people lying on small cots, all wounded or dying. It was eerily quiet, so I'm guessing their IVs were filled with sedatives. They had signs of trauma, cuts and broken limbs and open wounds, some in various stages of healing. And there were a bunch of them. Like, a whole lot of them. I counted to thirty-seven before I saw something move out of the corner of my eye. When I turned, I realized it was one of the patients raising a hand, waving, trying to get my attention.

"I walked over to see him and asked what was going on. He mumbled about a lot of strange things that didn't make any sense: 'We were forced to come here,' and 'please, help us,' and 'we just want to go home.' I figured they were criminals preparing for execution, so I asked what crime they committed. He looked up at me and said, 'We still were breathing.'

"I heard footsteps from another hallway on the other side of the room, so I ran back the way I came. The next night I returned, but the man was gone, so I never got more of an explanation. A few of the others I'd seen were also gone. But in their places, new people filled the beds."

I frowned. "Have you been back since?"

"No, I was afraid I stumbled over something Law Enforcement was trying to keep under wraps, so I left, not wanting to get in trouble," he answers.

"What does it mean?"

"I don't know," he replied. "I don't know."

I gasp and jerk out of my trance.

"What?" Jacob lifts his head and looks at me with a worried expression.

"Oh my god," I shake my head. "It all makes sense."

"What does?"

"The Aether have known about Erebus coming over the wall for months. You weren't the first to be forced over," I tell him, explaining what Aaron had said when he was still alive.

"Law Enforcement has been trying to keep it a secret, trying so hard, that they're getting rid of Aether who find out or question orders…"

"That must be what your parents were talking about!" Jacob's hands rush to the sides of his head, and I watch as it all clicks into place for him too. "This has been happening for far longer than we thought! The Aether knew about it, but couldn't keep it under wraps forever, so just now the cat's creeping out of the bag."

"This changes everything. We didn't know the Aether were actively looking for you before. If Law Enforcement is so deeply involved, I'm surprised we haven't been caught yet. We were solely relying on the hope that they *wouldn't* be looking for you, but now that they are, it's going to be much harder to conceal you."

Jacob nods but chooses to look at the positive. "But it also proves that there *are* other Erebus here. If so many have been caught, I would imagine an equal amount must have escaped or remained hidden."

"You're right, there has to be others."

Jacob smiles, "I'm not alone."

"You were never alone," I tell him.

His dark eyes meet mine, and he wraps an arm around my torso, pulling me close. I breathe in his scent, and he sighs. "I need to get some things done. I have homework."

I nod, and he stands, leaving me to stare at the picture of Aaron and me. A crushing weight enters my chest, but I push it off. I have things to get done, too.

Jacob knocks on my door an hour later. "Madrona?" He asks, then sees me in my small place in the closet. "Hey, you alright?"

"I don't know," I choke out, half laugh, half cry. "I think I'm kind of freaking out. One, there's a kill order for both of us. Two, Aether Law Enforcement is killing people for asking questions, for putting the pieces together. Three, my parents could be on their list. Four, I'm probably going to have to fight an Erebus tomorrow. An Erebus. Someone who's probably had years and years of training, and I've had a week. Five, I kissed an Erebus I hardly know. Six… I can continue, but I don't think you want to hear it."

"I would sit next to you, but I don't think I can fit there. I don't think I'd be able to get back up either," he smiles gently. He holds his arms out, and I stand and walk over to him, letting them wrap around me. Holding me safely within his embrace.

"I'm sorry. I'm just so… stressed. I imagine you are too." I hastily try to clear the tears from my face.

"We have a lot going on right now, don't we?" He gives his handsome smile. Just seeing it lightens my mood slightly. "I can't do anything about most of the things you said, but I can fix one thing. Ask me something. Anything you want, so you can feel like you know me."

We sit down on the edge of my bed, and I think for a moment, grateful for the distraction. "The scar on your right hand. How'd you get it?" I had completely forgotten about it, as it didn't seem important, but suddenly I have a burning curiosity.

He sighs, but speaks. "I was eleven, just learning to fight. A friend cut me there, and it left a scar, even after it healed." I look into his eyes and wonder if his words mean more than they seem to. It's true that wounds from friends are the ones that linger. "Alright, my turn. I hardly know anything about you either. Just a lot about your family."

I glance at him, awaiting the question.

"What's your favorite color?"

I laugh. "I was waiting for something harder," I explain. "Gray, but not just any gray. The kind that reflects a stormy sky off a lake. Bluish gray."

"Why?" he asks.

I think for a moment. "It's the color of the sky before it rains. I've always loved the rain. It gives life to the world, and nothing would live without it. Yet, everyone often grumbles when it arrives... Okay, my turn. What's *your* favorite color?"

He pauses for a moment. "I... I don't know."

"Can't pick one?" I ask.

"I guess white then since it contains all the colors."

"Wow. A surprising choice for an Erebus. I thought for sure you'd pick black."

"People's origins shouldn't define them for a lifetime."

I contemplate his words. They contradict Erebus and Aether ideals, but I can't help but think he's right.

He asks the next question. "What's your favorite thing to do?"

"On warm nights, I like to sit on the front porch after everyone's asleep and stare at the stars. I'll just sit and... exist.

Watching the stars and the moon illuminate the grass. I've always found the stars interesting, but I don't know why. Maybe the distance and empty space fascinates me. The fact that we're so small and inconsequential. When I make a decision I deeply regret, the stars remind me I can only do so much damage, and that no matter what I do, the rest of the universe will always be there, not even noticing me because I'm so small."

He stares at me for a moment, and finally I say, "What?"

"I can't believe you aren't Erebus," he laughs.

I smile briefly before it fades, "We're going to have to be more careful. Law Enforcement was already a concern, but with more guards, it's twice as bad."

"We'll stick to the plan. Tomorrow night we'll search for other Erebus, see what they know, and figure out what to do after that. Everything's bigger than we thought. The Aether seem to know something of the Erebus's condition, while the Erebus are still confused themselves."

"With the Erebus sending more and more people over here, the Aether have clearly noticed. I'm sure they're also looking into why, so we need to find out before they do. Who knows what our Law Enforcement will do, if they're already killing our own people?"

"We'll find out before they do," he promises. His lips meet mine, filling me with warmth as he kisses me before exiting the room, though his scent lingers long after he leaves.

I spend the night stressing about the next day, so I don't get much sleep. When I wake up in the morning, I feel like I was hit by a train. I glance at the clock and force myself up. I need to make Jacob and Lily breakfast.

Lily tells me I look like a zombie again, but I'm deprived of sleep instead of life. Heavy bags hang under my eyes as I begin to make the three of us breakfast, when Jacob tells me to go back to bed and that he'll take care of Lily. I obey and drag myself back up the stairs, crashing on my bed in seconds.

The next time I wake up, I grunt at whoever's shaking me awake. They are saying something, but I can't hear them. A sleep-induced fog is blurring out my vision and hearing. Slowly they come back, and I open my eyes to see the clock reading two in the afternoon. I slept in until two. Two, wow! I never sleep in.

Shit!

I burst into a sitting position and see Jacob staring at me. I slept in until two! My brain finally re-engages, and I catch a few words from Jacob, "--to wake up. You must have been tired. When was the last time you had a full night's sleep? Or at least half of it?"

"Never," I smile, and he flashes one back. I'm squinting in the light through my windows. He must have opened the blinds. I groan and force myself out of bed. My legs nearly buckle as I take a step, but he catches me, despite the crutches. I glance up at him. "Thanks."

I continue to the bathroom where I fill the sink with cold water. *Ugh. This is going to suck for five seconds.* I dunk my head in the sink and hold it there for a moment. Icy water shoots up my neck, sending a jolt through my body.

"Damn!" I shout, yanking it out quickly with a start. I dry my face and drain the sink, walking back over to Jacob. "Okay, sorry. I'm here. Thanks for waking me up."

"Sure. That's a harsh way to wake yourself, though."

"It works," I snort, wiping the sleep from my eyes. "Sorry. I shouldn't have slept in."

"You needed the rest."

True, I did. I really, really needed the rest.

"Alright, I'll be down in a second," I tell him, then shoo him out the door. I swear I'm blushing while I push him out of my room.

"Report to training in ten," he laughs. I smile then close the door in his face.

I'm downstairs in three minutes, changed and looking as if I've been awake for hours. A sandwich sits on a plate in front of me with apple slices arranged on the side.

"Made you lunch."

Suddenly I realize how hungry I am and devour it. "Thank you," I continue inhaling the food. "Dang, this is good." It's far more flavorful than my plain everyday sandwiches.

"Finish up, and let's get started as soon as possible." I glance around the room to make sure there is no one home to hear his words. "Lily's at a friend's house, and your parents are working, so we've got all afternoon to get ready."

"Okay."

As I eat, Jacob sits down on the couch, and I realize he has my father's guitar out. His left hand meets the neck of the guitar, fingers making odd shapes as they press the strings, changing the sound released. His right hand strums loosely. My father holds the guitar like it's a beast to be tamed. Jacob holds it like an old friend, cradling it as a tune comes through.

I close my eyes as I listen to him play. It's a soft song, calming and comforting. He doesn't strum hard, but delicate and light. He starts humming along with the tune and seems to enter a trance, closing his eyes and letting the music flow. It starts off light and positive, but soon grows sad, as if it's saying goodbye to a loved one. The tune seamlessly morphs into another one, bringing forth many different emotions. Worry as it speeds, sadness as it slows, anger as it gets louder, happiness as it bounces from note to note with small bursts of energy.

When he stops, he looks up at me to see I'm smiling. "What?" he asks.

"That was beautiful," I praise. "I didn't realize you could play that well."

He smiles and shrugs, "I don't know if I'm all that good, but I love it. Playing... has always been an escape for me."

"How long have you played?"

"I believe I mentioned my mother taught me before she died, but I was eight when she first handed me a guitar. I had been begging her to teach me for months. I remember her laughing at my facial expression. She said I stared at it like I'd found priceless treasure. I've played ever since. I briefly stopped when she entered the hospital but slowly took it up again a few months after she died."

I understand why he cradles it now. This instrument was a part of his childhood, his family, his home. It takes him back to those memories. The tune he played must reflect emotions from his childhood as he remembered those moments.

"You'll have to teach me," I blurt out. He flashes an extremely handsome smile, and I'm filled with a strange emotion. Is it joy, pride, love, or something else? Or perhaps all of the above?

"I promise I will. We can start after you spend some time defeating that poor tree," he chuckles. "I kind of feel bad. It's become a punching bag."

"Well, maybe we can find a different tree and give that one a break."

We head outside with the blanket and pillow once more. It's still difficult to get Jacob's crutches through the forest, but he's grown obviously stronger over the last week, and he's relying on the crutches less and less. My parents are optimistic he'll be able to transition to a walking cast in another week or so.

I brace the pillow up against the tree and tie the blanket around them both before stretching my arms. I did wake up only thirty minutes ago.

Jacob resumes his position on the log. "How about some light hits?" I go through the same motions as before. The sting from my fist's impact with the tree is jarring at first, but I keep going, throwing a few combination punches…jab, jab, power punch.

After half an hour, I stop. Hitting is exhausting, and I don't want to overdo it before tonight. I sit next to Jacob on the log, who has been quiet almost the full time, observing me as I beat the poor tree.

"You're quiet," I notice.

"Just watching."

"Just watching me punch or just watching me? It kind of felt like the latter," I grin, and his face turns to a bright, cherry red. I laugh at his blushing, and he smiles.

"Maybe it was," he smirks, going back to his normal color, "Maybe not." I stare at him, giving him an unsure look and he returns it. We have a moment of exchanging strange faces before we both burst out laughing.

"Let's call it a wrap. I don't want to tire you out before tonight. You should be fine. You've been a quick study. You know how to hold your own, and you look good from this angle. Not that you look bad from any angle…"

I blush as I untie the blanket, and we head back to the house.

With some time to kill before dinner, I demand my first guitar lesson as soon as we sit back down in the living room. Jacob chuckles and hands me the guitar. It's smooth and curved. It's truly a beautiful instrument. I'm sitting next to him as he explains the parts of the guitar. Head, neck, body. Just like a person. Head has the knobs which tune the strings.

"Don't touch those yet," he warns before continuing. "You change the sound the guitar emits by changing the tension of the strings. You use your fingers to hold the string against the fret," he points at a small, short metal piece across the neck. There are many, all evenly spaced at the head, but growing closer, the nearer to the body. "By pushing the string behind the fret, the fret changes the length of the string able to vibrate, changing the sound.

"Your left hand stays on the neck while your right hand rests above the strings, your arm bent across the guitar's body," I follow his instructions and wait for the next thing. "Um… place your middle finger on the top string, third fret. The third space between metal pieces. Yep, like that. Now put your pointer finger on the second fret and second string. Exactly that way," he says as I arrange my fingers in the way he tells me. "Now, put your last finger on the lowest string on the third fret. Okay, keep that shape. This is one way to make the 'G' chord, one of the most common chords."

Guitar lesson one lasts for an hour as he teaches me chords, how to strum, and has me practice them. Occasionally he demonstrates what it is supposed to look or sound like so I can compare. Every time I strum the strings, they give off this horrible buzzing sound called 'fret buzz.' Jacob tells me this is normal, and I'm either not pushing hard enough, or my fingers aren't lined up with the strings. I just need to practice more to make it go away.

By the end of the lesson, I can play four chords: C, G, D, and E minor. He shows me a bunch of songs you can play with only these chords. All require three fingers, except for E minor, which only needs two. It gives a low sound that echoes in a cool way and is easy to play. This is the first chord I master and eliminate all fret buzz from. The tips of my fingers have purple indents across them, showing where I was pressing against the strings. My hands are tired from the work and hurt from the strings.

"After two weeks your fingers will build calluses, and they won't get the indents as they adapt to playing. And the hand ache just means your hands don't have much strength in their outer muscles," he explains. "You sounded good though. I've never known anyone to do as good as you on their first day." I feel a swell of pride, but don't want it to show, so I dull it down.

"Thank you, for showing me this much. Can you give me another lesson tomorrow?" There's something about the guitar that feels right. Like I've played it before and just don't remember.

"Of course," he smiles. "Are you tired?"

"Not really," I admit.

"Good, because you're going to need energy tonight," he sighs. I look at the clock. It's almost six. My parents should be home soon, picking up Lily on their way.

"We have maybe half an hour to burn before my family gets back. What do you want to do?" He thinks for a moment.

"Want to play a game?"

I smile. "Sure."

TEN

Lily and my parents went to bed two hours ago. I simply lie on my bed and stare at the ceiling and wait, as does Jacob in his room. The clock slowly ticks towards eleven-thirty, the time we had planned to head out. Both of us open our doors simultaneously as the minute hand clicks into place.

"Ready?" Jacob mouths. It's hard for me to see his lips in the dark, but I can just barely make out his question.

"Think so," I mouth back. We try to be as quiet as possible. I have no idea what I would say to my parents should they wake up and catch us.

Jacob and I silently make our way down the hallway to the front door. Grabbing our jackets, we step outside and embrace the chilly air.

We work our way down the empty street, sticking to the shadows. We journey a few blocks through the darkness, and I ask, "Do we know where we're going to see them?"

"Nope," he says, watching the full moon disappear behind a cloud. We continue walking the streets for half an hour before I speak again, as we're trying to be quiet. Jacob has no clue where they'd meet, so we're just wandering around until we hopefully find someone.

"Should we have seen them by now?" I whisper my question.

"Maybe, maybe not. I don't know how many survived the wall and Law Enforcement capture."

We take another left, followed by a right when I see a shadow dart across the street where there aren't any lights to illuminate it.

"There!" I point, but Jacob's already seen it. We run after it, or rather I run, while Jacob hobbles as fast as he can with his crutches. I pull ahead of him but no longer see the figure among the darkness. I slow down to wait for Jacob to catch up, turning to watch him approach, and shrug my shoulders at him to indicate I don't know where the figure went.

Everything happens so fast. A figure bursts out of the dark alleyway to my left with a knife, a hood pulled overhead, throwing his face into complete darkness. I manage to sidestep this initial attack and automatically fall into my fighting stance. I register the Erebus appears to be male and fit, a lean fighting build, similar to Jacob's. I use my speed to dodge another strike and even manage to throw a hit, landing it in his gut, but missing his solar plexus. He's quite a bit taller than me, so striking his head seems daunting. He takes another swing and a searing pain tears through me. He caught my leg with his knife; it's a deep cut, and I feel blood oozing down my leg. A wave of nausea hits me, but I focus my mind and ignore it.

Then I stop thinking and just react. I ignore everything, gaze narrowing to focus only on my attacker, as I dodge his next strike and land a hit on his wrist, causing the knife to go flying.

"Wait! We're on your side!" a voice yells, but I hardly notice. It sounds so far away. My world has contracted to a six-foot radius.

The Erebus punches my injured leg with force, and it buckles under the sharp and intense pain that shoots up my spine. I catch myself before completely going down, pivot sharply off my good leg, and manage to sneak a kidney punch in his side as I rise. He gasps. I manage a smile. Weak spot. He stands quickly and throws another attack at my leg but misses as I'm anticipating that attack point, and I retaliate with two quick jabs at his exposed side. He lets out a pained yell and stumbles backwards, then rebounds. My body is positively humming as it gears up to block his next blow.

"Wait! We're unarmed!" Jacob calls out again, and the figure finally pauses in his attack as he notices Jacob.

"She's Aether. She'll notify Law Enforcement!" the figure counters, a deep male voice echoing down the alley.

"She's the reason I'm alive! We just want to talk."

The figure steps into the light and pulls down his hood. He has long hair just like Jacob did before I cut it but looks as if he's recently shaved and doesn't have a beard. He's blond and bears a scar across his right cheek. He looks older than us, maybe in his early thirties.

Jacob's eyes widen as he steps into the light also, hobbling with his crutches.

"L26? What the hell are you doing here?"

"M93!" Jacob exclaims, embracing the man. "I got thrown over the wall after they attacked me."

"Same story here," the blond chuckles. "But still, what the hell is she doing here? And I thought Aether didn't fight? This one clearly knows what she's doing!"

"This is Madrona. I basically landed on her when I fell over the wall. She saved me instead of leaving me for the

Aether guards. Kept me alive for a bit until she could help me look Aether and get me to a hospital. I've been staying with her family, who don't know I'm Erebus," Jacob explains the situation. "As for her fighting, I gave her a couple brief lessons over the past week, but that's it. Guess she's just a natural." Jacob looks proud of me, and I flush slightly under his praise.

"You two know each other?" My adrenaline rush is fading, making my vision slightly blurry, and my leg throbs making me light-headed as I watch my blood continue to seep down my leg.

"Madrona, this is M93, my trainer. He's the one who taught me to fight," Jacob introduces us.

"Why am I alive, then?" I wince at the pain.

"You're quick, and I'm hurt. I had a rough landing coming over the wall. Where did you learn those evasion techniques?"

"Like L26 said," I use his Erebus name, "he taught me how to punch correctly. Everything else, I just… did. It felt right, which scares me, if I'm being honest. Aethers are not supposed to support violence."

"Huh, strange," he glances at Jacob, who is busy looking at me like he's trying to solve a puzzle. M93's eyebrows knit, then return to normal as he moves on. "Sorry about your leg."

"I'm fine," I quickly answer. The dim light hides the extent of the damage, but I can feel the wetness of my pant leg.

"Are you hurt?" Jacob comes over to inspect it, but I swat him away.

"Sorry about your side," I wince again, in part feeling horrible about hitting M93 and the rest for the searing pain in my leg. "How'd you survive the fall?" I manage to ask through gritted teeth.

"I also landed in the forest, maybe a week ago. Got caught in a few branches ten feet above the ground. While they likely helped me survive by slowing my impact with the ground, they still majorly bruised my ribs on the way down. May have cracked one or two, not a hundred percent sure since I couldn't go to a hospital." He exchanges another glance with Jacob. I have a feeling I'm missing an entire unspoken conversation.

"Well, you were luckier than I was," Jacob frowns, looking down at his leg encased in a cast.

I glance at my own leg. I need to do something to stop the bleeding and keep it from getting infected, but I'm starting to have difficulty thinking, my mind swimming in the burning pain. M93 searches for his knife along the empty street, then stuffs it back into his belt.

"Have you seen any others? Other Erebus who survived the fall and didn't get caught by Law Enforcement?" I question.

"Not yet," he sighs. "But we can't be the only ones who made it. I've been watching the wall, keeping track of everyone they've thrown over since I fell. It was initially at fifteen a day, but the numbers are slowing. Now, it's closer to ten a day. Sadly, the ones I saw all died on impact."

"We were hoping to find out why they're tossing Erebus over the wall, and how they decide who goes over. That's why we risked coming out tonight," I explain.

"All we know is A70 is the one giving out the orders to his guards," Jacob follows.

"A70?" M93 curses under his breath. "But why?"

"We don't know."

"How do you know he's behind this?"

"I was fighting the ones trying to toss me over. A paper with my photo and the words 'next target' fell out of one of their jackets. His name was signed on the bottom," Jacob explains.

"Well, I'm not surprised he's the one behind this, but again, why?"

"That's why we're here. Trying to get as much information as we can. Maybe piecing together what each survivor knows will give us the big picture."

"Well, it's just past midnight, so hopefully we'll start to see some more faces." He looks at me. "Though, your friend here might be a problem. They'll try to kill her, just like I did, for fear she'll run off and report us." Exactly what Jacob said.

"She's staying," Jacob defends me. I smile my thanks. "If you heard the loudspeaker announcement yesterday, she's also dead if the Aether find out she helped me, and I won't risk sending her back alone."

M93 pulls him aside and murmurs something so quietly I can't hear. Jacob answers and M93 says something else before coming back over to where I'm standing. I'm too light-headed to care, the pain keeping my mind occupied from wondering why.

"We should get moving and see if we can find anyone else," M93 suggests.

We all start walking, but when I take a step pain bursts up my leg. I inhale quickly, trying to keep from screaming.

"You alright?" Jacob asks as I look at my wound. He kneels by my side and inspects it, curses under his breath before tearing a strip from his shirt. "That's a deep cut. Maybe we should go back…"

"I'm fine. Let's keep going," I lie.

"Okay," he says, tying the cloth around my leg. I gasp as he tightens it, then helps me up. It's better, but every step is painful. The knife must have cut into my muscle, as the bleeding continues. *Great. Stitches for me.* Jacob glances at me worriedly as the blood slowly soaks the cloth but moves on. He knows I can handle it. Or at least, I hope he does.

"Sorry again," M93 says.

"It's fine. I expected worse."

We continue down the street, searching for more Erebus. We're almost to the library, I realize. We've been walking for a few more minutes when another shadow sprints across the street, followed by three more. A group. We hurry after them, walking fast down the block after M93, who's sprinting. My leg is still bleeding, and if anything, it's quickening, making the light-headedness worse. M93 rounds the corner and continues after the other group. I follow, my leg screaming and burning as I take each step to round the corner after him. I hear a whistling sound and a whack, then my vision is enveloped in darkness as I crumble to the pavement.

When I wake, my eyes don't open, and I'm greeted with a massive headache. I groan at the pain, which seems to radiate from everywhere, when I hear voices.

"She's alive!" someone cheers. "I was starting to worry I killed her."

"Well, she's Aether, so she'd have deserved it," a female voice scoffs.

"She never did anything to you or anyone else to deserve to be killed!" Jacob's voice. *He's here.* A wave of warmth comforts me with this knowledge. "She's on our side! She saved my life, despite the fact I wasn't Aether."

"You may have told us your story, but we need to hear her side. It's suspicious that she helped you without expecting something in return," a deeper, more mature voice speaks over the argument, a man, perhaps in his late thirties or early forties.

I slowly open my eyes, but shut them quickly, as I'm blinded by light.

"What the hell?" I mumble and hear the flashlight get turned off.

"Keep that off. We're too exposed for any light here," M93 orders.

I open my eyes again and see a strange male face inches from mine. I reflexively jerk back, and the headache flares again with the sudden movement. My eyes shut, and I groan again at the new wave of pain.

"I guess we don't need to give her mouth-to-mouth," the face chuckles. He has fair skin with his dirty-blond hair pulled back in a mullet and a thin scar across one cheek. I feel the sudden urge to slap him.

"She was still breathing, idiot!" the female voice from earlier snaps at the young man.

I try to sit up so I can see my surroundings, but finally realize my arms are tied behind my back. I try to move my legs, but they are tied too, and the attempt makes me gasp at the next wave of burning pain as my earlier injury overrides the headache pain.

"What's wrong with her?"

"What do you mean what's wrong with her?! You whacked her in the head with a plank of wood! She probably has a killer headache. Throw in the knife wound on her leg and some blood loss, and I'm sure she feels just peachy!" There are a few chuckles in the group.

"You alright?" Jacob quietly asks me.

"I'll recover," I reply testily.

"You said that after getting a deep knife wound, even as you slowly bleed out."

"I'm fine," I snap, then shrink back in surprise at my tone. "Sorry, that was overly harsh. What did I miss?"

"Well, after you blacked out, M93 and I had to convince them not to kill you, while one almost gave you mouth to mouth," he pauses to glare something evil at the blond guy, "We told them our story, but they insisted on tying you up just in case."

"You didn't get restrained?"

"No," he sighs.

"Why not? They're so amazing," I follow up with an artificial chuckle. "Best thing ever."

I hear a few people burst out laughing, Jacob included.

"She's harmless," Jacob tells the group. "You can untie her."

"You said she fought M93," the female voice points out grumpily.

"She's Aether. I gave her a couple lessons, so she'd survive tonight," he argues.

I'm not sure if I should be thanking him or shouting at him for arguing for my uselessness.

"Madrona, will you attack them or run off to tell someone they're here?"

"Don't be ridiculous," I respond. "If I turn you in, I'm turning myself in, which means I get to join you in the shooting range. I have no interest in being used for target practice, plus Jacob, L26, is my… friend. We're simply asking for help to find out what's going on, so he can safely return home."

"Just untie her already. It's not like she can run anyway," M93 helpfully points out.

I feel someone cut my feet and hand restraints. I stretch my arms and unwounded leg, being slightly stiff from the uncomfortable position. I can finally get my eyes to stay open, glance around and drag myself over to a wall, propping myself upright. We appear to be inside a dark warehouse of some kind. I can't make out the machinery in the dark, but there are stacks of boxes along the wall near me. Surrounding me is Jacob, M93, a girl with dark pixie hair shorter than the Aether limit, and three guys, one being the jerk from earlier sporting the mullet. There's another tall one with a buzz cut about the same age. Lastly, a slightly older guy and the owner of the deeper voice. All appear to be Erebus.

"What's your story?" the tall one asks me.

"My boyfriend died recently. I was walking through the woods grieving privately and saw Ja-" *Right. He doesn't go by that here.* "-L26 fall off the wall. I… I couldn't leave him there to die. I knew I needed to leave, to run, but I couldn't. I couldn't save my boyfriend, but I could save *him*," pointing at Jacob. "I cared for his knife wound and made a makeshift cast after resetting his broken leg.

"I came back the next day with food, water, and medicine. I cut his hair, and he picked a name; he's called Jacob here. We also crafted a story to explain his injuries before I got him to a hospital where they cared for him correctly. Every day we'd have 'how-to-pretend-to-be-an-Aether' lessons, so he could learn to blend in.

"Once he recovered enough to be discharged from the hospital, my family invited him to stay, since our story was that his parents were killed in a car crash…" I look at him and see a brief hint of pain, before it goes away almost instantly, "…and he's been staying with us, pretending to be Aether, while we try to figure out what the hell is going on."

I pause briefly and look at Jacob, who gives me a go-ahead nod.

"We recently discovered our hospitals have been receiving Erebus patients before they are killed. We don't know why they bother to heal them before killing them. Any Aether who's verbally wondered why there have been so many knife or bullet wounds has ended up missing or dead. Aether Law Enforcement has supposedly killed everyone asking questions on why there are so many Erebus coming over the wall. It's bigger than we thought. Something is going on with the Erebus *and* the Aether, and we believe if we find out why you're being thrown over the wall, we'll find out what's going on here. They have to be connected in some way."

Everyone is silent after hearing the news about the recent Aether disappearances and deaths.

"Why 'supposedly killed'?" M93 asks.

"Aether are just disappearing. Here one day, gone the next. We're assuming they are being terminated and not just imprisoned, but there's no proof."

There's a long, drawn-out pause. "The story fits," the female in the group finally decides. "I'm I32. This is Y17, N87 and Q08." The numbers and letters confuse my brain, but best I can figure, Y17 is the tall guy, N87 the smartass with the mullet, and Q08 the older guy.

"How do you keep track of these names?" I ask Jacob quietly. He shrugs and says, "You get used to it," he smiles. I smile back, but it's nowhere near as flashy.

I try to stand to fully join the group but struggle as my blood loss has made me weak. M93 helps support me until I can manage on my own. I nod a brief thanks to him.

"How long have you been here?" I ask the group.

"Two weeks," the one called Y17 replies.

"How have you stayed alive and hidden?"

"Similar story, pretending to be Aether," he smiles, and they step into a thin beam of dim light. I can finally see them well enough to note they all have Aether haircuts and clothes.

"How'd you know what we look like?"

"We hid in the shadows and copied haircuts using our knives. Grabbed some clothes from a bin labeled 'For Homeless'." I nod. I'm impressed with their ingenuity.

"Where've you been staying?" M93 asks them.

"Traded the few things we had for sleeping bags or blankets. Each night we find cover and build up a tent with the blankets and lay out the sleeping bags. We found each other in the woods. Erebus recognizes Erebus," Y17 replies.

"Did you all survive the drop because something broke your fall?" Jacob asks. They all nod in response. "So, at least six of us made it. Six out of over a hundred survived… Do any of you still have your phones?"

N87 steps forward. "I do, but I have it turned off, so no one can track me and know I survived the fall." He glances at me and says, "Can we talk without the Aether listening for a moment?"

Understanding the threat I pose, I nod and hobble across the road without complaint until I'm out of hearing range, my leg spiking sharply with each step. I watch them talk for a moment. Large hand gestures are shown. They must be frustrated about something. Q08 points at me and raises his hands in the air. Jacob calmly replies with something that makes them all shake their heads. M93 steps forward and speaks. N87 picks up his phone and hands it to him. There's a moment when no one's moving and M93 nods, handing N87 his phone back. He speaks again, and Jacob motions for me to come back.

I hobble back over and ask, "Something wrong?"

Jacob's the first to reply. "No. Just… something they don't want you to know." I glance at them. What wouldn't they want me to know? *Anything. For infinite good reasons.* Okay. Probably not important anyway.

"Okay." I trust Jacob would tell me if it's really important.

"Dang. I was expecting you to lecture us on why you should know," I32, the female, smirks.

"They don't know anything about why they're throwing us over the wall," Jacob changes the subject.

"You know what that means, right? No one who's been thrown over will know anything," Q08 replies. "We have to find other sources." He trades looks with each member of his group. Clearly, they were already trying to find the answer themselves before our run-in.

"Is it even possible?" I32 mumbles.

What are they thinking? Is what possible?

"Maybe," Y17 muses.

"No, we can't. It'll be too well guarded," Jacob protests, having caught on.

Oh shit. This does not sound good.

"It's the only way we'll get some answers," M93 notes. "They're right about that. But it's a suicide mission."

"If we get caught, we'll be *lucky* to be killed," Jacob argues.

"So, we won't get caught," N87 chuckles.

I can't believe the next words spoken.

"We're breaking into the POT. We're breaking in and spying on the representatives. They're the only ones who know what's truly going on."

·∽· ✦ ☾ · ☼ · ☽ · ✦ ·∽·

Oh, no. No.

"L26's right. It isn't possible," I protest.

"Q08 has a little thing to tell you," I32 grins along with the trio making up her group.

Man, she's annoying. Something tells me we won't be best buds.

Q08 steps forward, looking a bit smug. "It's been done before. You can break into the POT. I've done it."

"How?" I ask.

"What? When?" M93 follows.

"You can't do that alone," Jacob counters. "Who else was there?"

Q08 smiles when he realizes he's grabbed our attention. "A year or two ago, a few buddies and I were drunk and betting on random things. I bet we could break into the POT and get out unscathed. I won," he's grinning something evil as he finishes speaking. "We planned it out and succeeded.

"We had an inside source who got me the building blueprints, and we used the vents and external airways to enter."

So. It is possible. It's been done, and by these people, that we happen to run into.

"We'll need a distraction for the exterior guards while others slip into the building's air vents. The vents allow access to all rooms in the POT, even the soundproof inner sanctuary where the two representatives meet face-to-face. The sound proofing works both directions; the representatives can't hear anything from the outside while in that room. The getaway is a bit harder, as the distraction will likely have the guards on high alert by the time we're ready to exit. Someone will need to be on the outside, car idling, ready to start driving, and get us the hell out of there!"

"And if anyone's caught by the Aether guards, they're dead after being tortured. L26 was right about that. However, if we're lucky and the Erebus catch us, we get to skip the torture step and go straight to death," I32 notes.

"What time is it?" Jacob asks me abruptly, in a surprising subject change.

I glance at my watch. I hate wearing it, but it's handy. "One-thirty. Law Enforcement patrol starts in half an hour."

"Shit, we have to leave," Jacob starts. "Let's meet outside the library at sunset to finish this conversation. You know where that is, right? Not far from here." They all nod. "Good. Get out of here before the guards come. Don't get caught, and try to stay inconspicuous. See you soon."

"Nice to meet you, L26," N87 shakes his hand.

"You as well," he replies, and the four of them head out, disappearing into the darkness. "You should leave too," he turns to M93, who nods in response.

"I'm glad you made it," he replies. "And I'm grateful this one is here to help you." He's looking at me, accepting me, despite my Aether origins. "You're very lucky, L26."

"I am," Jacob acknowledges with a smile, before sadness and pain enter his eyes.

"What is it?" M93 inquires concerned, seeing the change come over his friend.

"They tried to get me twice. The first time they found my family instead of me, and..." he chokes on his next few words. "They killed my father and siblings. They're all dead. A70's men only found me after I came home to discover their bodies," he gulps down a tear.

"No," M93 shakes his head in disbelief. "They didn't."

"They did," Jacob replies. "Anyway, I just wanted to let you know that if we get back, they won't be there." M93 nods, his own eyes growing red as he fights off his own tears.

"I'm sorry, L26. They were great people and did not deserve their fates." He pauses, taking a moment to mourn them. "I must go," he says after a moment.

"Goodbye. May the moon be with you, M93," Jacob bows as best he can with the crutches.

"With you as well, L26. Until sunset." He takes off, running down the street, leaving Jacob and me to start walking home.

"How am I going to explain this mess to my parents?" I ask, motioning at my leg, which is matted with dried and fresh blood. The blood loss is really starting to affect me, and I'm swaying more than I was before, as I continue to keep my vision from fading, fighting away the darkness, for each step towards home.

"Don't forget the large bruise on your face and big knot on the back of your head," he teases me as we walk back. "Maybe you could say you fell down the stairs."

I laugh. "Am I that clumsy?"

"Maybe," he chuckles. "I don't know."

Our return trip is much faster since we walk directly home, as opposed to our wandering routing the previous direction. When we walk in the door, I grab our first aid kit and a towel to keep the mess minimal. Each step home was excruciatingly painful, and I'm relieved to be back. I feel only half present, and I know I'll pass out in the near future. Hopefully, I can take care of the task at hand before I do.

I spread the towel out on the long coffee table before I sit down on it, pulling my injured leg to lay out in front of me before my legs buckle. Gasping at the sharp pain, I cut open the already ruined pant leg with a pair of scissors, so I can reach the cut easier. Removing Jacob's makeshift bandage restarts the bleeding, as it takes the clotted scabs with it. I grab the gauze pads, putting pressure on the wound. My other hand uses clean, damp pads to wipe away the dried blood on my leg, so I can better see the full injury. The world is slowly spinning, making the task more challenging.

"Oh, great." *Shit.* "Need the... disinfectant," I tell Jacob, as I lose the battle against the darkness splashing across my vision.

"Madrona?" is the last thing I hear, as I fall into unconsciousness.

· ~ · ✦ ☾ · ☼ · ☽ ✦ · ~ ·

I groan. Everything hurts. Ugh. I feel something soft. Where am I? I open my eyes to see my room, then sigh in relief. It must have been a vivid dream. Wait a second...

I sit up fast and look around, instantly regretting it as twin flashes of pain shoot up my leg and back of my head. *Nope, definitely not a dream.*

But I'm in my room. The clock reads six-thirty in the morning, so everyone's still asleep. Outside my window, the sun is slightly above the horizon. I almost flinch when I turn to see a dark figure passed out in my chair. Taking a deep breath, I calm down, realizing it's just Jacob.

How did I get up here? I look around the room for answers and see Jacob's crutches lying against my bed. How did he get across the room to the chair without them? And how did he get me up the stairs? I look down at my leg, carefully pull back the clean bandage affixed to it, and find over twenty-five stitches, perfectly spaced and beautifully done. *Oh shit.* Did he wake up one of my parents to help tend my injury and put me to bed?

Jacob stirs and opens his eyes.

"Good morning," he smiles. There are deep purple bags under his eyes.

"Morning," I reply. "What happened after I passed out?"

"I finished cleaning your wound and placed the stitches. Iced your bruise and put disinfectant on all your cuts, like you said. Then I got you to bed, so you could rest more comfortably."

I look at him. He took care of me while I was out, not my parents. "Thanks," I'm a little breathy in relief that my parents don't know what happened. I freeze. *Unless...* "How'd I get up here?"

"I carried you."

"Your leg is broken. You can't carry me and maneuver your crutches."

"It was."

Jacob sits calmly in the chair, just looking at me. *Wait. Was, as in past tense. What the hell?*

"It can't heal that fast." I shake my head.

"Long story," he replies.

It's not possible. You can't heal that fast. No one can.

"It's not possible," I voice my thoughts. "Besides, you could hardly walk yesterday." He gives me a look that says a thousand words, summarized in only four. He was faking it. *It's not possible, though. He must be messing with me.*

He just shakes his head, then stands, walking over to my side. Walking. Without the crutches.

"Don't!" I cry out, trying to stop him before he injures himself.

"What?" he asks, standing up with his cast still on his leg. He's in a slightly awkward stance as the cast makes one leg longer than the other, but he still stands there, calmly, without any outward signs of pain.

"You weren't kidding." I blink a few times, realizing he spoke the truth. "When did it heal?"

He shrugs. "Only a few days ago. The cast makes running awkward, so you were able to sprint ahead of me last night. I was about to dive in and stop your fight with M93 when he finally heard me and stopped. As for when we met I32's group, it was too late for me to do anything, since they got the jump on us and took you down immediately."

I wait before continuing, still trying to comprehend. "How is this possible?" I ask. He's silent for a moment.

"I can't tell you. It's not just my secret to share, and the others from last night don't want it getting out yet. For now, I feel I need to respect their wishes."

I nod. "I get it." I've been in that spot before.

"I'll tell you when I can."

I nod again. I don't know if I'd believe it anyway, so I'm not worried. I realize I've never seen him walk normally before until now. Though, even now he's dragging a cast along with him. His posture is perfectly straight, and he looks confident, strong, and of course, handsome.

"Just… don't tell anyone."

I smile. "I'll add it to the long list of secrets."

He grabs an icepack off my nightstand and places it on my forehead. I wince as I realize how sore it is. "You have a massive bruise," he sighs. "You took a beating last night."

"Yeah, I guess I did." I chuckle, remembering the plank of wood. "Ugh. I have to make my parents believe I fell down the stairs." Jacob chuckles. "Is that how they survived, the others? Do they heal quickly also?"

"That's our belief. The four of them were dropped relatively close to each other. They were able to crawl far enough for cover, then sat for a day or two before they were healed enough to move out to find food."

I try to imagine sitting for days, suffering and being unable to die. "Everyone else who died, could they not…"

"We believe some of them could heal faster, but not most. It's a very rare thing, and we aren't even fully sure how it came about," he frowns. "We have a guess though."

"You said you wouldn't tell me because they wanted it to stay secret."

"I'm not telling you. That is something else," he says.

I nod, not pushing any further because I'm still trying to wrap my head around all this. *It's crazy! No, I'm crazy. Aaron said it himself. I'm going crazy. This isn't real…. Stop it!* I tell myself. *There's a scientific answer to this. You know that. That's what they're hiding from you, due to distrust.*

Back in control of my runaway thoughts, I try to get up, and pain shoots through my leg causing me to let out a large gasp. Don't think I'm going to be walking today. Should be better by tomorrow, but today's out of the question. Jacob gently pushes me back down with a hand on my shoulder.

"Not a good idea," he insists.

There's no point in fighting him. He's right. If I try to move, I'll just make it worse.

"How much sleep did you get last night?" I ask as he holds the ice pack back up to my forehead.

"Don't worry about me," he smiles.

If he's refusing to tell me, it's clearly not much. "You were up that long, taking care of me? You should get some rest," I tell him after he tilts his head slightly to acknowledge the time was significant but not wanting me to feel badly about it.

"I'll be fine," he answers, smiling at me. "Besides, I wouldn't sleep well anyway."

I suddenly feel a twinge of guilt. I hadn't intended to wake him, but he'd woken anyway. He must have only gotten an hour of sleep, if even that. "No, you really need to rest," I insist.

"As I said, I wouldn't rest even if I slept," he rubs his eyes.

I know he's expecting the question. "Why?"

He's silent for a moment. "I haven't slept soundly in a long time. Not since the day…" I know what he's talking about, and he knows I know. The day his family died. "...Since then, I've been having these recurring dreams. Of a city."

I frown, and he locks eyes with me. "Wait, like, *the* city?" I ask.

"Yes."

Oh my god. That's not possible, is it?

"The same one. It's an Erebus city I've only been to once. I only saw one corner of it, and yet somehow, I know the whole thing, every block and tunnel and even every sewer. Just as you do, except you've never even seen it."

"How…" I start, then realize he doesn't know either.

"That's the question I've been trying to answer. How is all this possible?" he waves his arms. "The morning I found you on the porch, I had also dreamt of it. I'd just woken up and was going to take a walk, but I heard you walk out the door."

"Last time… did you see Lily?" He nods. *Oh my god.*

"And Ivy," he says. I feel faint, remembering the image of her body lying lifelessly in the rubble. "The building was crashing down, and I was just watching as my body ran through the debris, trying to get something. I woke up just as I got out of the building by sliding down a rope."

"That's exactly what I saw," I shake my head. This isn't possible. It's *not* possible. Except it is. It's happening. But why and how, I have no explanation for it.

Another question without an answer. "Either way, you need to sleep. I'll be fine for a bit, as I'm clearly not going anywhere."

He flashes me a smile, then it fades, and he nods, knowing I'm right. "Okay," he says, then plants a kiss on my forehead and sets down the ice pack. As soon as he reaches the chair, he passes out. Only seconds later, I do, too.

ELEVEN

She knows what is happening before she can see, but she can feel Jacob next to her. Buildings crash down around them, explosions taking out the foundation of each building, causing them to crumble. Fire, blood, and screams. The smell of burnt flesh. Buildings of black concrete crush people as they fall. Another shockwave goes off, and the few remaining buildings that were holding together crack and collapse. The whole city is being destroyed.

Her view changes, and she sees Lily running, trying to get out of the building. Lily finds a set of stairs and almost gets to the bottom when the stairs start giving away and fall beneath her. Turning quickly, she opens the nearest door and finds herself three stories off the ground. A chain hangs from somewhere high up. Lily grabs it and gives it a tug, finding it's secure. Slowly, she climbs down. When she's only ten feet off the ground, the chain snaps and she falls, landing on her arm. Lily lets out a cry of pain, and suddenly Madrona's view changes again. She's no longer just a spectator but an active participant as she runs toward Lily, screaming her name. She grabs Lily's unbroken arm, helping her up and away from the building.

"Jacob's still in there!" Lily yells. Madrona feels her expression change, "Stay here!" she yells at Lily and sprints back towards the building. She sees Jacob sliding down a rope, trying to slow his fall, his hands bleeding as it burns into them. She runs over to stand beneath him, so when he slips and falls *the remaining five feet, she catches him, causing them both to go to the ground, but protecting him from a harder landing. The breath is knocked out of her lungs as he lands on her.*

They both scramble to their feet, and Madrona yells, "What were you doing?"

"I had to get the vial! Lily wouldn't leave without it," he explains, then runs over to where Lily is waiting, picking her up and carrying her away from the buildings. "Come on! We need to hurry!"

They need to reach the bunker. She wants to yell at Jacob for taking unnecessary risks, to ask what is happening, but she isn't in control of this dream, and nothing comes out of her mouth.

They run down the street, avoiding the falling debris, nearly getting crushed beneath thick stone multiple times. She realizes her dream-self is limping; she must have injured her leg.

They turn around a corner and see the street slope down into an underground bunker whose doors are closing.

"Wait!" Jacob yells. The people closing the door are not Aether. They both have tattoos on their bare arms, the Erebus moon. They hear his call and motion for him to hurry. They run harder than ever, Madrona struggling not to trip with her limping leg, as she's half dragging it now. They've almost made it into the bunker when her vision goes black.

I jolt awake into a sitting position. My leg instantly gives a painful protest, and I fall back to my pillow. Jacob wakes up at the same time I did. Our eyes meet across the room, and I know he saw the same things I did. I try to slow my rapid breathing and notice he's doing the same, trying to calm down. His hand jerks to his pant pocket where his dream-self had hidden what he called 'the vial.' Jacob sighs in relief to find it empty and leans back in his chair. The bags under his eyes are gone, so he's gotten some rest, despite the dream.

"You saw that, right?" he asks.

I nod. "The vial? What's in the vial?"

"I don't know. There was some kind of lab in that building, and if I was willing to risk my life, if Lily was willing to risk hers, then it must be something important," he says.

He's silent for a moment, and I know he's not telling me something. Something important. Perhaps it's the same thing he's not allowed to tell me. I decide not to question it and move on, for now.

I glance at the clock and realize what time it is. Ten in the morning. Everyone should be awake now, but the house is so quiet, I'm wondering if everyone's out for the day. I check my phone and sure enough, my parents are at the hospital and Lily's with a friend.

Clearly not wanting to talk about the dream anymore, Jacob yawns, "Well, if no one's home, I guess that means I won't have to use those," motioning to the crutches. "Looks like you might need them instead, so it works out."

I feel restless. I need to move. I've never been one to sit around. I attempt to stand again, but my leg sends sharp agony up my spine. The cut must have gone into my muscle because every time I tense it, it retaliates by sending another wave of pain. I gasp again but fight against it. My instincts tell me to stop, but my mind tells me to keep moving.

Jacob stands up quickly. "What are you doing?"

"I need to move," I grit my teeth at the spikes of bright and burning pain. "I can't just sit in this bed all day." He nods, and I let out a small squeal in surprise as he scoops me up like I weigh nothing. My leg is in agony. I'm getting spots all over my vision as I bite down on my lip and do all I can not to scream. A slight coppery taste enters my mouth as my lip starts to bleed. My headache multiplies all over again, and I'm lightheaded, but I feel Jacob's warmth and use it as an anchor, and the worst of the pain ebbs away.

His strong arms are holding me as he carries me carefully down the stairs, trying to jar my leg as little as possible. He's stronger than I thought. He carries me into the living room where he sets me down on a chair, pulling up an ottoman so I can elevate my leg.

"There," he says, lightly chuckling. "Better?" I join in, and soon we're both laughing. Not for any specific reason. Just because we are able, and we're enjoying this moment while we can. I sit in my chair while he makes us lunch, this time throwing some noodles in a pot over the stove, crafting spaghetti complete with homemade tomato sauce.

"It's amazing you know how to cook so well," I break the silence.

He smiles and explains, "I like to eat, so I figured it was in my own best interest to learn how to cook. Plus, I figured it made sense to learn skills that might come in handy later in life. Skills other than how to kill a person. I don't find glory in killing or hurting. Very few of us do. We must all learn to fight, but that doesn't mean we like to use our skills."

I think there's a deeper meaning behind his words, almost like he's using reality as a metaphor that can be applied elsewhere. Another thing I like about him. Aside from being a handsome badass, he's clever, talented, and sometimes philosophical.

I thank him as he hands me a plate and takes the seat across from me. At first I eat slowly, trying to be polite, but my hungry stomach growls at me like a beast, so I eat a little faster. I try to remember the last time I had spaghetti and realize it was over six months ago, when Aaron was in the hospital. I push the thought from my mind. Not going there today. Today's going to be a good day.

After we finish eating, we pull out a deck of cards and play a few rounds, in which I dominate, but when we pull out the board games, Jacob annihilates me. Once we get bored of games, Jacob pulls up a movie, not horror, luckily.

I get cozy and lean into him. His warmth, the cinnamon smell, his strength... How lucky am I to have Jacob here to take care of me? *Very. Very lucky.*

I must have passed out shortly after the beginning of the movie because I wake to see the end and Jacob smiling down at me. "Good morning," he chuckles, grinning, even though it's afternoon. I smile back, and he runs his fingers through my hair. *I'm safe*. Those words never seemed to ring true since Aaron died. Not until Jacob showed up.

Just catching the end of the movie and still half asleep, I sit snuggled up against Jacob. He begins to talk to me. About his family. His father had been a teacher, his mother a doctor - a healer - which is apparently what they call doctors over there. His older brother had worked at the farm near their home. His younger sister was fourteen, while his brother was almost twenty.

He describes the land around his home. "Huge round hills, almost like waves in the ocean," he explains, painting an image in my mind. "Each night we'd go to the top of the highest one we could find and watch the sunset until we saw the stars." He tells me about the dog they had when he was a child, that passed away when he was seven, killed by a mountain cat that had been stalking them in the trees of a nearby forest. His father tracked down the large cat and hung his skin in their home.

"I hated looking at it," he sighs, a wave of sadness passing over him. "It reminded me that we are all the same deep down. All we want is to survive, and many will do whatever is necessary to do so."

He goes silent, and I decide it's my turn. I tell him about the cat that used to roam the neighborhood before the night guard killed it, thinking it was a raccoon. I tell him about how each night a family would take it in and give it a place to sleep, along with some food and water. I tell him about the day we took him in, and how Lily fell in love with that cat. I also tell him about how her heart was crushed when the neighbor's kids found its body on the road.

I tell him about some of the key moments in my life, since he already knows about my family. The day I planted the tree that grows in our front yard when I was four that now stands over ten feet tall. The first time I saw what my parents really did in the hospital, since at the time I was six and thought they just put band-aids on everyone's scraped knees. The day I sprained my ankle and couldn't walk for over a week. My first school dance. The day with Aaron in the market and the day he died.

Jacob kisses me, and his cinnamon scent enfolds me in a safe embrace. Next thing I know, he's snoring. I quietly chuckle and attempt to drape a blanket over him. I get cozy myself and let my exhaustion take over.

When I wake, I'm greeted with his scent. My head is resting on his shoulder, rising and falling with each of his breaths. His hand is slowly running through my hair. I can hear his heartbeat, slow and calm. Content, happy and strong.

My head is throbbing a bit, so I close my eyes again and grimace at the pain. My leg thinks it must be a competition as it also starts screaming at me. I try to push the pain aside and focus on the gentle strokes I feel Jacob making on my head.

"What time is it?"

He's silent for a moment before answering, "Just after three. Lily should be home in a few minutes." *It's time to get up.* I unwrap my arms from Jacob's torso, glancing at the gash across my thigh. This will hurt, but I need to walk. To the bathroom at the very least.

Slowly, I stand and shift my weight onto the injured leg. It shrieks as expected, but the screaming is muted by Jacob's hand on my shoulder. He stands next of me, ready in case I fall. Carefully, I hold his arm and take a step. It sends agony through me anyway, begging me to stop. But I'm in control, not it. I take a step and pain screeches up my body. I take another step and my leg buckles. Jacob quickly lunges, catching me before I hit the ground.

"Don't push it too hard," he warns. "You need to heal."

"I need to walk," I respond. He doesn't say anything because he knows he can't stop me. I look at the stairs and nearly faint.

"Need some help?" he asks. I consider it for a moment, then sigh. *Yeah, I'm going to need some help.* I nod, and he scoops me up again like I weigh nothing, climbs the stairs, and sets me down on my strong leg at the top of the stairs. I hobble over to the bathroom, then after relieving myself, head to my desk chair, take a seat, and pull out my homework.

He laughs. "You're doing homework?"

I nod. "Need to get it done. My essay is due tomorrow." I pull out my paper and history book, working on my notes for the next part of the essay while Jacob sits on my bed watching. It takes a moment before I remember what else is happening today. "Oh, that's right! We're supposed to meet them at the library tonight!"

"Are you sure you can come?" He glances at my wound.

I turn dead serious. "I'm going." End of sentence, not going to be changed. "I'll be fine."

He sighs, knowing he can't convince me otherwise. "Okay," he replies doubtfully.

I turn back to my homework. His answer worries me. What does he think will happen tonight? Is he just worried about me, or does he want to keep me out of this? My mind is racing with these questions while I'm absent-mindedly taking notes.

"What are we doing tonight, anyway? Are we building a plan or something, because if we are, I could be useful."

"Your usefulness isn't what I'm worried about. Last night you were pretty beat up. What if we have to run or something, and you aren't able to? By talking to us, by simply *not* turning us in, you will be killed. I'm worried about you. The other night when you were knocked unconscious, it scared the hell out of me. I nearly beat the shit out of the guy who hit you. Then when you passed out from blood loss, it scared me even more," he admits.

I'm silent. I want to say something but don't know what to say. When I finally find the words, I speak. "After Aaron died, I made a decision. No one else I love or care for will die. I will do whatever is necessary to make sure no harm comes to my family... or to you. And if it's something I can't stop again, like cancer, I don't... I don't think I'd be able to..." memories flood into my head. The last time I saw him...

I'm in Aaron's hospital room, and he's asleep again. He slept most of last month since his body is exhausted from fighting the sickness. We know he won't make it, so I'm spending every waking moment with him.

His eyes are closed, and he rests against a pillow. He would look peaceful, were it not for all the tubes, the IV and heart monitor. One moment he is breathing, resting, and the next... there's a blaring sound.

The heart monitor is erupting, crying out to all who will hear that his heartbeat has stalled, a long straight line running across the screen. A nurse hurries into the room, gently pushing me to the side to silence the machine, as I grab Aaron's hand. The alarm stops, and the sudden quiet is jarring, my cries mingling with those of his family's now the only sound.

The nurse quietly moves about checking for a pulse, signs of breathing. She softly shakes her head, notes the time, hugs Aaron's mom, and leaves us to mourn in peace.

I feel my chest caving in. He's gone. In a matter of seconds. But I was there, as I promised him. I was there until the end.

· ᵕ ॰ ✦ ☾ ॰ ☼ ॰ ☽ ✦ ॰ ᵕ ·

A tear rolls down my face as the memory leaves my mind. Jacob must know what I'm thinking about, what the last words to my sentence were. I don't know if I'd be able to handle it. Not if someone died now, so soon after Aaron did. I might break, I might shatter to the point of no return.

I wipe away my tear as I hear the front door open and Lily shouts, "I'm home!" She doesn't need to see me cry. I'm the strong older sister who helps her be strong too.

"Hey Lily," Jacob greets her, quickly grabbing his crutches from my bedside, as he'd left them there this morning. "How was your day?" She quickly launches into a tale of how all three of her crushes got into an argument at the local burger joint and two were eventually kicked out. He talks with her while I continue working on my essay, listening and sometimes chiming into the conversation. I smile as he and Lily continue talking about her day and the other exciting things that happened. He's exactly what Lily wanted: an older brother. And he's exactly what I want. Someone to help, someone to trust, someone to love.

My parents return at the same time as Lily, and after she and Jacob leave my room, I quickly put on an unruined pair of pants to hide the long gash and my whooping twenty-seven stitches. A blanket hid them from Lily, but it would not do since I couldn't sit in my chair all day. It is extremely painful to put the pants on, but it is necessary. Knowing about my injury would lead to questions, and questions would lead to deadly truths. Sometimes you have to lie to people to protect them.

By the time we've eaten dinner a few hours later, it's almost sunset. Both my parents and Lily had winced at the sight of my bruised face. But I just laughed and made up a hilarious story about my clumsiness. My discoordination is well known, so they had no trouble believing I was capable of such a debacle. I hobble out the door, doing as much as possible to hide my limp from them, but when they notice, I just say I twisted my ankle in the same spill and that it's fine.

Finally, Jacob and I are out the door. The library's two miles away, and I don't want to - fine, I'll admit it, *can't* - walk that far, so we climb ungracefully into my car and drive the three minutes to our meeting place. We stand outside the car as the sun slowly goes down, erupting in an explosion of color and light, just before it finds the darkness and the streetlamps light up, becoming our only source of light.

M93 and the group show up right on time.

"Greetings," M93 smiles, as we turn and walk into the library. We can immediately tell he's made an effort to blend in better with the Aether with freshly cut hair and new clothes. "How is your leg?"

"Twenty-seven stitches," Jacob frowns.

M93's eyebrows rise, and his hands cover his face. "I'm so sorry. Have you been able to walk?"

"Yes," I assure him. "Not well, but I can move." He nods and steps back as I32's group steps forward to lead us into a private conference room.

Jacob's the only one to greet them, but his tone is unenthusiastic. "Hi."

"Cut the chit-chat. We need to get to work," I32 orders, scowling. *What is her deal?*

"We have three weeks until the representatives meet in the POT. Three weeks to build our plan, gather the things we need to complete it, and to train. And in your case, three weeks to heal," Q08 motions to me. He seems to be our expert here. He leads us over to the conference table and lays out the basics, the things we need to start planning.

"First, we need blueprints of the building. The design, the floors, everything. I know someone on the other side who can bring those to us, so we'll just have to go get them as he throws them over the wall-" he's interrupted by Y17.

"Wait, why are we doing all this when we can just scale the wall with rope and a hook? Why go into the POT in the first place?"

"Because if we go back over, we'll be dead in minutes, and this time they'll make sure we don't survive by putting a bullet through our brains," N87 gives a false smile, talking slowly like he would to a child as if to say, 'You are so stupid.' "We have to find out why they're doing this, and *then* we can evaluate from there."

"Anyway..." Q08 moves on having regained the floor, "We first need blueprints, which I can have in a day or two. Then we'll need to know all the guard rotations and numbers. We'll need a map of the area and planned escape routes to allow for a faster getaway in case we're chased down afterwards. And before all of this, the most important thing I need... is a bag of cheesy-poofs."

"What?" I'm not sure I heard him correctly.

"Cheesy-poofs? Seriously?" Jacob follows.

"They are critical to breaking in. In fact, we may need more than one bag," Q08 grins. I look at his group, and they stand there like this request was expected.

"Okay," I sigh. "Fine, I'll get you your cheesy-poofs."

"Again, that is the *first* and *most important* thing on the list."

"Okay," I chuckle. "I will protect them with my life." But as soon as he turns away, I roll my eyes and his group loses their grip on seriousness and bursts out laughing, well everyone except I32 that is.

"Alright. One, cheesy-poofs. Two, blueprints. Three, guard rotations and numbers. Four, map of area. Five, I need a computer," he finalizes.

"I can get you the guard rotations and area map," I answer, grinning when they look skeptical. My uncle was a guard and loves to talk about his old job. But they don't need to know that.

Q08 finally nods at me in confirmation. "I'll get the blueprints from my pal, but I'll need a computer strong enough to hack the POT system."

"I can get you that," M93 volunteers.

"Good. Three weeks to plan a breaking and entering of the POT. That is not a lot of time. People spend their entire lives planning this and fail. We would use my old plan, since it was successful, but a lot has changed in five years, so we can't trust that anything is the same as it was before," Q08 explains.

"In two days, we will meet back here at sunset again. Let's try to have everything by then. With that information, we'll be able to plan what we need to actually break in.

"Good luck, and may the moon be with you all. Well, all except you," he notes, looking at me. I roll my eyes at him, and he continues, M93 chuckling in the background, "Good luck. And you," he looks at me again, and I'm growing slightly agitated, "get me those cheesy-poofs. Make it three bags."

"Okay," I sigh. *What is it with him and cheesy-poofs?*

"May the moon be with you as well," M93 says, followed by Jacob.

We get back in the car as the five of them disperse to wherever they came from. The meeting wasn't very long, so it's just after sunset. My parents aren't in the main room when we enter the house, so Jacob and I sneak inside without being detected.

Lying to them is slowly tearing me apart. But I have to stay together.

I struggle to climb the stairs to my room, using only one foot and a hand to climb them, hopping from step to step. As soon as I reach my bed, I'm pushed into a careful sleep, my healing wound massively draining my energy.

TWELVE

The next day, Jacob walks with us to school. The two of us hobble along with our injuries, well, Jacob's false injury and my real injury that shoots pain up my leg every time I take a step.

Ivy wants to know all about what happened over the weekend, so we start talking quietly, and I finally confess to her that Jacob and I kissed. She explodes, letting loose, "I told you so!"

"We aren't dating, though. We saw a movie with Lily, but that's all," I defend. Ivy screams in excitement, completely ignoring what I just said.

"Where's my five bucks?"

I sigh and pull a five-dollar bill out of my backpack. While I didn't technically agree to the bet in the first place, I also didn't tell her no. She waves it in my face, but I'm smiling. Honestly, I'm glad I lost. Because it means there's someone there for me.

"Not only are you half-dating, but you are happy about it!" Ivy beams.

It jolts me a little to realize she's right. I am happy.

My mom greets us when we get home after school. We give her a quick rundown of our day which was largely uneventful. I wince as I climb the stairs slowly, trying not to make a big deal of my injury while my mother's watching. Once we're out of view, Jacob stops using his crutches and carries me over to a chair. I sigh in relief since my leg has been killing me from using it all day.

After resting for a moment, I head into the bathroom to inspect my wound in private and see that it's slowly healing. The stitches should be ready to come out in a week, so that's good. It doesn't hurt as much to walk, but my muscle is still torn and will need time to heal. Still, I consider myself lucky. The knife didn't go in too deeply; it could have been much worse.

"It's looking better," I tell him after splashing water on my face, trying to wipe the exhaustion and pain from my face. "Thank you for taking care of me, again." Jacob smiles.

"This morning your parents gave me an old phone to use, since mine was… *crushed in the car crash-*" he winks at me, "-I want you to have my number, so you can call me if something ever happens. Well, I mean, you should have my number anyway, but you get the point."

I chuckle, nodding. "Okay." I appreciate his concern.

I enter the number into my phone, then find myself looking at the picture of Aaron and me.

"That's Aaron?" Jacob asks, studying the picture. I nod. "You look happy."

"It was a good day."

Jacob nods, and I feel his hand on my shoulder. I stand and lean into his hug. He knows my sense of loss. In fact, he knows it better than I do. I lost one person I loved. He lost his whole family. I cry into his shoulder. For Aaron, for his family who I haven't spoken to in weeks, too afraid I'll fall apart in front of them. For Jacob, for his family and his loss. For all the lost Erebus out there who are dying. For all the Aether who are being killed for asking questions. For everyone who has suffered and for everyone who has cried.

I eventually realize Jacob's tearing up too, which doesn't happen often. But when it does, I never judge him, as he never judges me. We have earned the right to our tears. His warmth and scent are comforting, so I try my best to comfort him. My arms are around him and his around me when I kiss him. It's a sad kiss. A kiss of loss and grief, but also of understanding and hope. Undying hope, a flame that doesn't go out in the rain or under all the water in the world. It may dim to only a spark, but it soon recovers and grows back to a bonfire. A flame that is eternal, no matter what happens.

"You said you could get the guard rotations?" he asks, later that night after everyone else has gone to bed.

"Yeah. I think I mentioned it to you before, but my uncle worked in the POT for some time. He's always telling us stories of all the people he's caught and the various ways they'd try to get in," I yawn, exhausted.

"You might be more helpful than I realized," Jacob smiles. "Don't worry, I knew you'd be pretty helpful already."

"Thank you." I hesitate, then turn more serious. "What do you think would happen if my parents found out? About you, I mean."

"I... don't know. Maybe they'd freak out, which is the likely option, but I think with everything going on, they'd ask further questions and decide from there," he pauses. "You have pretty awesome parents. Remember that."

I always will.

Screaming, crying, shouting. It's all the same. But... different. It's dark. She can't see the people around her, but knows they're there as bodies bump into her, stuffed inside the dark bunker.

"What now?" Lily's voice asks. Jacob's been carrying her and hasn't set her down yet, so he can buffer her broken arm from being jostled.

"We wait out the attack," he answers.

"Why would they do this?" Madrona watches her dream-self whisper the question.

"You know why," Jacob replies, as they push through the crowd to get to the back of the bunker. There's a light towards the back, and they move towards the source. She can start to make out his shape as they move closer.

"They're destroying the whole city for that?" Madrona says under her breath.

'What is it?' her true self tries to yell, but nothing escapes her mouth. She's trapped, only here to watch.

"That's my guess. This is our salvation. It's the only thing that can stop them from taking over," he answers quietly. Madrona watches herself nod in understanding.

'What's going on?' her true self tries to yell again but can't. It's like yelling underwater.

"We have to get it to the General."

Jacob nods, pushing through the crowd until they reach the medical stations. He lays Lily down on a stretcher where the doctors come over to help. He immediately checks and rechecks his pocket, making sure the vial is still there.

Jacob leads Madrona over to a wall where they can watch Lily, where they can run to her if she needs help, but far enough out of the way to allow the doctors to work unimpeded. All around them are stretchers lying on the ground, filled with people. Some patients are bleeding out and missing limbs, while others are dying from the blow of impact, still alive, but begging to die. A young girl, five or six years old, lies on a stretcher.

Madrona's face fills with anguish as she sees the poor girl's body. She's missing an arm and has a small pipe sticking through her stomach. She's crying, and she's dying. They can't help her. Nothing they do can save the girl. Her dream-self walks over to the crying girl and smooths her hair with one hand, holding the girl's hand in her other.

"It hurts," the girl whispers in between sobs.

"Shh... I know. I know it hurts," her dream-self replies, and starts humming loudly so the girl can hear. It's a gentle, happy tune. She switches to singing, and the girl slowly calms down.

"I'm scared."

"I know. There's no reason to be scared. Of this world or any other. When we die, we simply return to our family, those who have passed before us." The girl knows she's dying, *so there's no point in hiding it from her.* "Close your eyes and see them in your head."

She continues singing softly, as the girl's breathing slows. "Thank you," *the girl murmurs just before her breathing stops altogether. The girl is dead. She is no longer in pain.*

Madrona was never religious, but she prays anyway. For the girl to have a safe trip to the afterlife, if there is one. For her to return to her family. She prays in case there is some being out there to hear it.

She turns to Jacob, who holds her in a tight embrace as tears stream like a river down her face.

I wake to find myself crying. By the time I sit up in my bed, Jacob is at my door wiping a tell-tale tear from his own face. I take a breath and try to calm down. Jacob pulls me into a hug, and I cry into his shoulder. It may have been a dream, but it couldn't have been a normal one. It felt real. I could remember every emotion and every feeling that my dream-self felt. The memory sticks as if I had actually been there, rather than fading away as a dream normally would.

"Did you see… all the people…?"

He nods. My head rises and falls, as I cry into his chest. His heartbeat is fast, but his breaths are steady, so I use them as an anchor and try to slow my breathing, to control my sorrow.

"The girl…" he whispers with a look of horror on his face.

I nod, feeling sick. "She was so young," I whisper. The memory of the dream surges through me again and again like waves crashing down on a sandy beach.

It takes us a moment to collect ourselves, and afterwards we mechanically get ready for school. Ivy walks with us, and Chris greets us, hugs Ivy, and goes back to his friends. Shortly afterwards, Will, Ivy's boyfriend, comes over to see us, and she goes off to spend the remaining minutes before school with him, leaving us to sit on a bench in front of the school while we wait for the doors to open.

We're talking quietly as a large guy comes over and grins at Jacob, followed by four others.

"Hmm… You smell that, boys? Fresh meat," he smirks. I almost laugh at the remark. The way he says it makes him sound like a boy trying to play man.

He's tall, maybe taller than Jacob, his black hair short with a buzz cut, and his arms thick with muscle. He's notorious for flirting with the no-violence Aether code. Amazingly, he hasn't been arrested for fighting yet, and he isn't old enough for the death penalty. He must know people in high places. I search my mind for his name. *Ah, yes, Todd.* Todd is that guy who picks on all the people who actually have plans for their lives. It's rare for him to take on someone Jacob's size. Maybe he decided he'd have the upper hand with Jacob in crutches. I almost laugh at that but remember Jacob's cover.

I stand up in his defense, glaring at Todd.

"Aw. Look, the girl is coming to save him. Get out of the way, sweetheart," he laughs. Anger flares up inside me. No one calls me sweetheart. Not even my family, not even Aaron. They all know the dangers that come behind that name.

"Don't you dare call me sweetheart," I grit my teeth, my voice full of force and my eyes lit with anger.

"Or what?" he mocks, his gang laughing.

"Or you'll find out the hard way," I growl, straightening my back to be as tall as possible. I'm trying to do what people call 'manning up,' but since I'm not a male, I'm struggling to act like one.

"Haha, move, bitch. Get out of my way," he orders. My hands are slightly raised, to cut the distance they'll travel in half, making for more speed and faster hits with harder impacts. Speed over strength. He will not pass me. He will not reach Jacob. Healed or not, he's still hampered by his heavy cast.

"No."

"Come on, honey. Don't make me force you."

Anger erupts in my mind. No one calls me honey either. It's all I can do to not hit him. All I can do is tell myself to save it for when it'll be helpful. He's pushed too many of my buttons. I'm going to blow at some point, and it's not going to be pretty.

"I'm not moving," I glare.

He sighs and reaches out to grab me.

I slap his arm away, bring my fists up, and get in my defensive fighting position. My leg wound howls in protest at the position, but my adrenaline is starting to flow and numbs the pain.

"Madrona! Keep your cool," Jacob tries to deescalate the situation, as he moves to stand up next to me.

"Don't even *think* about *trying* to touch me or him ever again," I rage.

"Don't tell me what to do, little girl! This is *my* school. This is *my* town. I can do whatever I want," Todd informs me. "Boys," he says, looking at the guys behind him. "Why don't we teach our friends a lesson on who they don't mess with?" They smirk, and my eyes go wide. I didn't want an actual fight. Just wanted to prove a point. This is going to suck.

At least I'm following Aether rules. No violence unless absolutely necessary. As long as they attack first, I have the right to defend myself.

One of Todd's grunts runs at me, trying to grab me, while the other heads for Jacob. Jacob braces to face him, but I find the strength to spin away with a shove, sending my challenger with his momentum into his friend. They collapse in a heap of tangled limbs.

The guy I knocked down recovers to run at me again. I hold my ground until the last second, spinning away, so he runs past me straight into a wall. Damn, they are really stupid. The next guy comes up, trying to run into me also. There's a bench to my right, so I go to the left, and he misses. I feel arms wrap around my torso, trapping my own arms at my sides, and realize the first guy is back. I struggle and struggle, but I can't get out.

"Madrona!" Jacob yells, but he's trapped by thugs three and four. He whacks them with his crutches before passing a crutch to his other hand to throw a punch. He is careful to always have one crutch on the ground to make it look like he needs it. It's an impressive display of agility and coordination.

Todd saunters over to me now that his boys have me contained and backhands my face. The impact is horrifying. My eyes water and the whole side of my face stings viciously. I try to kick him, but my captor is too strong, and Todd just moves out of reach.

"You little bitch. Tried to show us who's boss? Tried to threaten me?" he fumes. "Oh, why don't we have a bit more fun?"

Oh no.

He punches my leg, right at my thigh. My injured thigh. I scream in pain as it surges through me. There's yelling, but I can't hear it. All there is, all there ever was, and ever will be, is the pain. I can feel blood streaming from my wound, smell the coppery scent of it tarnishing the air. "Oh, did that hurt? You have a little scratch? Why is that?" he asks and reaches down to yank up my pant leg. I struggle and kick, because if anyone sees this…

"What the hell?" he shudders at all the blood.

"Jacob…" I gasp. Where is he? I struggle more, but the guy holding me tightens his crushing embrace and squeezes the air out of my lungs. My eyesight starts to go. I can't breathe, not well enough. Not enough to get the required amount of air.

I go into full panic mode when I feel a physical shift in my perception. My view narrows to potential hit zones, my brain mapping out a counter-attack plan in microseconds. The flood gates fully open, adrenaline surges through my veins, and I forget the pain. My body executes the plan almost on autopilot. I knock my head back into my captor's face, and he instinctively reaches for his broken nose. Without him restraining me, I'm free. Taking a deep breath, I spin and land a power punch to his solar plexus. He goes down hard, still holding his nose, gasping and wheezing. His friend quickly follows him down after I kick his knee from the side, dislocating it. As he lowers his head to grab his knee, I deliver a tap-tap right to his temple. Then he's off to slumberland.

Todd makes another grab for me, but I've had enough of this shit and kick him hard in the groin. He doubles over, and I punch his exposed face with an uppercut. He's on the ground in seconds when Jacob comes over to me, having finished with his two guys. Surprise is written across his face, but a wave of anger clears it, surging through his eyes as he sees my blood, dark and red against my light-blue jeans.

"Are you okay?"

I nod, as my surge of adrenaline ends, and the hyperfocus leaves my vision. I am met with horror at what I've just done. Half the school is standing around us, staring, utterly quiet in their shock. I collapse on the ground, blood flowing through my exposed cut. Jacob quickly moves my pant leg back down it to cover the stream of blood.

"We need to get you home," he tells me. I don't have enough energy to nod. I'm exhausted from the adrenaline spike, and the blood loss is taking its toll on me fairly quickly. With one arm, he scoops me up and fireman-carries me home using one crutch to support him. Everyone's watching us, looking at my blood all over the concrete and trailing us as we move away as quickly as possible. My vision starts to disintegrate due to pain, blood loss, and the fact that I'm flat out tired.

All I can manage is, "Shit, I… I think I'm about to pass…" *out*. Darkness greets me with warm and open arms before I can even finish my sentence.

I wake to pain and a table. A hard cold table. Without straining my leg, I tilt my head up and see I'm in the living room, lying on the most uncomfortable table in existence. Jacob's next to me holding an ice pack.

"Not yet," he shakes his head and pushes my head back down to the table, and I notice there's at least a pillow. Jacob holds the ice pack to the left side of my face. I groan as it touches the tender skin, but the cold feels good after the first couple seconds.

"Are you alright?" I ask. He nods. Of course, he's fine. He's a warrior, and he heals like ten times faster than a normal human being.

"You lost a lot of blood before I could stitch it back up. You might be using one of my crutches for a day or two." He's quiet for a moment, then goes into full pissed off mode. "That was so stupid! You shouldn't have stood up for me!" he lectures. "I can handle myself!"

"But how long until people are suspicious? What do they think when you have a bruise form and heal in less than an hour? They will start to notice. Students pay attention to new people, and soon they might figure it out," I argue. "Plus, I couldn't forgive myself if I let you get hurt when I could have prevented it."

"Still, it was stupid and reckless and got you hurt. You ever think about how I'd feel if *you* got killed?" He pauses to let that sink in before continuing. "When they started beating you, I wanted to kill them. I wanted to hurt them all, and I could have. All that kept me grounded was you, and what you'd think of me if I did. Don't do that to me *ever* again," he goes from all but yelling to whispering in seconds.

I nod. He's right. He could kill them all and destroy his cover. Sometimes I forget he's Erebus and not one of us.

He sighs. "Sorry, you just really scared me back there," his voice is soft and filled with regret at his outburst.

"I'm sorry," I answer. "You're right."

The table's cold against my back. Wait. I look down at myself, finally noticing. "What the hell?" My shirt has been removed, but luckily, I'm still wearing the sports bra I had on earlier. The bruises surrounding my ribcage are new though. I still have pants on, but they're rolled up so he can reach my cut. In other words, I'm showing a lot of skin.

"Sorry," he flushes. "After you passed out, you were groaning every time I bumped your ribcage, so I needed to check it out." I nod.

"Well, I guess I did cut off *your* shirt," I reply, and he chuckles in response. The ice pack feels good on my face, but when he moves it to my bruised ribs, I flinch at the cold before a wave of relief hits me.

"That guy squeezed the hell out of your lungs, giving you these bruises. I'm proud of you, though. You held your ground against two guys who were larger than you, and you were injured. Also, I didn't teach you how to break a hold. How the hell did you get away?" he asks.

"I... I don't know. I kind of... lost it. It felt like someone shoved me out of the way and took over the controls, but at the same time, I was in control, just hyper-aware and focused, and..." I'm not sure. I still don't know what it was.

He looks at me with his eyebrows curved in, showing a look of confusion.

He stands and paces, murmuring to himself. I catch pieces of words, bits of sentences. He uses the word "impossible" multiple times.

I reach out and grab his hand to stop his pacing. "What is it?"

He stops pacing and looks at me, shaking his head. He sits in front of me. "I have a guess, but it's not… it can't… it shouldn't be…" he seems at a loss for words. He shakes his head for a moment in consideration. "You're different."

"No shit, I'm different. I'm an *Aether* who throws *punches*."

"No, I mean, you're *different*. Ignore the sides for a second. You're different from everyone else who knows how to fight: guards, Erebus. You're *different*."

I feel myself go stiff. "What do you mean?"

"I wondered before, when you fought M93, but dismissed it as impossible. But today, I saw it and have no doubt." He sighs. "That feeling, it is a sign of something. Where you feel disconnected from the scene, as if you're watching it in third person. Where you just… *know*. You know what to do and where to hit and how hard and fast. Like someone took over, but is letting you tell them what to do, just not *how* to do it. Like someone grabs hold of you and is telling you to *move*, telling you to *fight*."

I shake my head, confused, but understanding all at the same time. It felt like everything he described.

"On my side of the wall, we have a word for this, for fighting without effort. For being able to see ten steps ahead in a fight. For your body to react instinctively, almost without thinking, and it makes you a much better and faster fighter," he explains.

"Madrona Carter," he says, looking deep into my eyes. "It is my belief that you are one of these people. You're... you are what we call a Nightshadow."

"A Nightshadow?"

"Yes."

"So... I'm someone who feels... *that*, and this makes me a better fighter?"

Jacob moves his head back and forth. "...Kind of. I mean, yes, that's the gist of it. Most people have to think before they hit, before they block or dodge. A Nightshadow doesn't have to consciously think about it. The Nightshadow part of you takes over and moves your body for you. It's caused by adrenaline and something genetic in your blood that we haven't quite identified yet."

I nod slowly, wrapping my head around it. "Are you a Nightshadow?"

He chuckles. "Yes. So is M93, but we're rare. One of a hundred thousand people will be a Nightshadow, faster, quicker, and better than other fighters. It takes time to learn how to use the ability correctly, but once harnessed, a Nightshadow could take out five to ten *highly* experienced fighters at once. They won't come out unscathed, but they'll survive and win," he explains. "M93 and I are still learning how to harness the ability. He's known for ten years, while I've only known for six months. I had only just started learning my abilities before coming over the wall. M93 has learned much more and can harness it well enough, but it's typically a slow process."

"Is it even possible for me to be a Nightshadow?" I frown. "I mean, if it's genetic?"

"No, it shouldn't be. Most, like M93 and I, spend years fighting before an internal switch pops at some random time, often in a fight or in a time of high stress. Our scientists believe it's a genetic trait that only shows every two to three generations, passed down through the family but largely inactive. We have no way of tracing who the switch will flip for, no way of telling why it happens, we just know it's there.

"As far as I know, the only way you could be a Nightshadow is if someone in your family was one before you. The only way that is possible is if one of your parents, grandparents, or so on, were Erebus," he unravels.

I can't wrap my head around it. *I'm related to an Erebus.* It can't be true. But no, it *has* to be true. There's no other explanation.

"There's been no evidence of any Aether having it. I suppose it's possible one of your great-grandparents snuck over the wall and made a home here without anyone knowing. That would explain how you carry some Erebus blood, making you both Aether and Erebus in the same moment," he muses.

I'm Aether. But I'm also Erebus. I'm Aether *and* Erebus, by blood. We have a moment of silence after that while I process my new reality. Jacob continues caring for my injuries while I lay on the cold hard table.

"Are I32's group all Nightshadows?"

"No," he answers. "None of them are Nightshadows." He moves the ice pack to my lower forehead, brushing a lock of hair out of the way. His hand is warm as his fingers brush my face and lightly hold the ice pack.

"What time is it?" I ask. "How long was I out?"

"Three hours. It's just past eleven," Jacob replies. I try to sit up, but his hand meets my shoulder and pushes me back down. "Not yet. Don't want to reopen those stitches, do we?"

"Thank you," I tell him.

"For what?"

"For everything. For taking care of me, for being here, for stopping me from going insane, and for helping my family…" I trail off.

He looks at me with a soft smile before leaning over to kiss me. "Anytime," he whispers when he breaks away, our breath still intermingling.

He continues caring for me for the next hour, when I remember what we were supposed to do today. "We're supposed to get Q08 those supplies," I sigh.

"Oh, right," he frowns.

"Can I move yet?"

He sighs, then gives in, "I guess so. But you're using one of my crutches. I only need one to keep up the act anyway."

"Fine," I say, and he helps me off the table, handing me my shirt and one of his crutches. After adjusting the height, I travel up the stairs and change out of my blood-soaked pants. Along with the new stitches, he put a fresh bandage on it for another layer of protection.

After a few struggling attempts, I finally get clean pants on, easing them up and over my wound. Rejoining Jacob downstairs, we head out the door, driving to the nearest grocery store to get the cheesy-poofs Q08 so desperately desires.

When we return, I print a map of everything within a three-mile radius of the POT. The facility is built into the wall, so both sides have equal access, and each side is responsible for protecting its own half, meaning we're obviously entering through the Aether side.

"Okay. Cheesy-poofs, check. Map, check. Guard rotations, well, I'll have to ask my uncle," I tell Jacob.

"Do we need to go see him?" Jacob asks.

"No, he's quite a ways away. I'll just call him." I pull out my phone and start typing in his number.

"Wait, won't he be suspicious?" he points out.

"Not if I approach it correctly. He's been trying to convince me to work as a POT guard when I graduate. If I ask him for more details on the place, so I can look into it, he'll be happy to provide," I smile, and Jacob nods his approval.

The phone call goes well. My uncle asks how I've been, I tell him about recent things with my family. He knows about Aaron, so I avoid the subject, and so does he. Then I tell him I'm wanting to know more about the job as a POT guard. He tells me everything. The lunch hours, possible shifts I could have, all of it. He explains they never change the hours because the schedule couldn't be more efficient. Plus, a hundred years of peace can make people a bit lackadaisical. I thank him for his time, and we say our goodbyes.

"Well, there we go," I chuckle, "Easy." I'd been writing down the times and schedule while he spoke, so now we have a list.

"Done, done and done," Jacob checks them off. "Okay, now back to being lazy until tonight." It's just past two, so we have an hour before my parents pick Lily up on their way home from work, and six hours until it'll be time to meet up with the other Erebus.

"Aww," I say as he practically pushes me upstairs and into bed. I wince when I pull my leg up, as a new spike of pain hits my nerves. He sits next to me, playing with my hair while I wait for exhaustion to take me away until we must see the other Erebus.

THIRTEEN

Jacob wakes me when my parents call us down for dinner. It's nearly seven, and the sun is working its way to the horizon. It'll be time to leave after we eat.

The four of us, my parents, Jacob, and I, are sitting at the table waiting for Lily. There are bags under my parents' eyes, as if they're not getting enough sleep.

"Is everything alright at the hospital?" Jacob asks, and I remember when we eavesdropped on them a couple days ago. Clever wording, I think. Not showing that we know anything but acknowledging the obvious.

"No," Mom carefully answers, glancing at Dad, who nods. "A few people haven't been showing up to work recently. That's all. We've been filling in for their shifts."

Jacob nods, glancing sidelong at me. I meet his gaze. It's still happening, and more people are finding out. More people are going missing.

At sunset Jacob and I drive to the library and meet the Erebus.

"Did you get the supplies?" Q08 questions once we enter the conference room.

Jacob hands him the three bags of cheesy-poofs, and I pass him the guard rotations and map. He smiles and opens one of the bags. He digs in before passing it around.

"Were they just to be eaten, or did you really need them?" I ask.

"We actually do need a bag, but yes, the others are so we can eat them."

"They are just so delicious! They are rare on our side of the wall," Y17 chimes in with a mouth full of cheesy-poofs. We all take a seat at the table.

Q08 lays out the blueprints he'd been holding and begins. "This is the Place of Truce. As you know, we have less than three weeks to break in and find out why they're throwing people over the wall." He grins. "Let's get started."

Each day of the next two weeks is all structured similarly. First, Jacob and I attend school, where Todd - who's supporting a matching nasty bruise on his face - has learned to leave Jacob and I alone. Chris hangs out with me at some point during the day like we used to, Ivy and I have our girl talk at lunch, sometimes including Jacob, then at sunset, we meet the Erebus at the library to plan our break in. The plan is, amazingly enough, coming together over such a short period of time.

First, I32 and Y17 will dress up as guards. They'll steal uniforms from two guards the night before we go in. This cover will allow them to get close enough to the outside guards to take them down. When it's their guard station's turn to rotate inside, I32 and Y17 make their way to the master security room. I32 will provide a distraction while Y17 will quietly grab a keycard from an upper-level guard and use it to access the security room. Surprisingly, the big guy has the most nimble fingers.

Once inside, they will take out any remaining guards. Then Y17 will insert a thumb drive into the nearest computer, allowing Q08 access to hack the whole security system and trigger alarms in specific parts of the building to lead the remaining guards away. He's been working to create fake camera clips to make it look like we'll be exiting on the Erebus side, while we'll actually be exiting back to the Aether.

Once Q08 controls the security system, I32 and Y17 will head to the roof, taking out any remaining guards, and drop a rope over the side from a nearby storage closet. M93, Jacob, and I will use the rope to climb the exterior wall and enter the external air vent shafts, opened by Q08. We will each take a separate air shaft and film the representatives' meeting from different vantage points. Once the representatives leave, we'll ease back out the way we came. N87 will be waiting with the get-away car, as Q08 sets off alarms and replaces camera feeds with false clips of us making our way through the building. The guards will follow the false trail to the Erebus side, while we make our way out on the Aether side, avoiding various guard rotations. N87 will drive us away, using evasive maneuvers to ensure no one follows us, then we'll head back to the library to review our footage.

Each night, Q08 works on the thumb drive programming while the rest of us memorize all routes and exits within the POT building off the blueprints. We also try to get our hands on weapons and other supplies needed, like a new license plate for the car N87 will steal tomorrow, since I told him to keep his filthy hands off my baby.

Only one more dream has come to Jacob and I in the past two weeks, which is a relief. It showed more explosions and us in the bunker, arguing with two guards and helping the medical staff.

My parents now know Jacob and I are a couple but seem to be relatively glad about it. I got an abbreviated talk from my mom like the one I got when Aaron and I started dating. Basically, be smart. Got it, Mom. Thanks.

Jacob no longer needs his crutches. His original cast was swapped out for a new walking cast, one that allows the wearer to move around more freely. He's scheduled to get it off the day before we go to the POT. The doctors claim he has healed incredibly fast, and his bone has already recovered, but they want to be sure. Some were questioning his healing, but they decided it was just strong genetics and moved on.

My knife wound is almost fully healed. Jacob removed the stitches for me after the first week. There will forever be a scar there, but I'm almost glad it's there, because it'll remind me of this experience, of my time with Jacob, should it ever end.

One night, Y17 cut himself on a thorn bush, and the shallow cut healed in five minutes. It was almost mesmerizing, watching the skin on his hand patch itself together slowly, scabbing over and disappearing. They still won't tell me why they can heal so quickly, but I'm at peace with it. Everyone has their secrets.

Every day I wear the spearhead necklace, my courage having finally returned after Aaron's death. I've finally accepted my grief. I'm not whole, and I never will be again, but I can get close. Luckily, Jacob's here to fill in the patches I cannot.

The final week we spend training. Deep in the woods, away from watchful eyes, Jacob teaches me to fight with my new abilities. Sometimes he will demonstrate with M93, and I can see the true meaning of Nightshadow. It's incredible. When trained, they can move at almost inhuman speeds, leaping around and bouncing to dodge blows. Once, M93 jumped over Jacob, who was only partially bent over, using his shoulder as a step when he started falling. This pushed Jacob to the ground and allowed M93 to climb higher and gain more space between them, using the time Jacob needed to stand as an advantage. Sometimes higher, more advantageous, ground can be made.

Not once have I won against Jacob or M93, but I did win against N87 once. He's our weakest fighter, hence the fact he's on get-away driver duty.

Usually I spar with Jacob, while M93 counsels us both. Sometimes it's a planned attack and defend, while other times Jacob will lunge at me without warning, trying to catch me off guard.

"Remember, the enemy won't wait for you to be ready before they attack. You have to always be ready."

I listen and learn. And I learn how to control and wield my Nightshadow.

Jacob suddenly runs at me and throws a punch. I catch it and pull his arm back, so I can hit his exposed side. He pulls free and dodges my hit, throwing one of his own at my back. I spin and duck, throwing out a leg to trip him, but he jumps and kicks me in the chest. I tumble backwards somersaulting, but I catch myself and jump up to dodge his next hit.

Finally, I land a punch in his left side. He backs away slightly before coming for me again. I try to throw him off by running at him, spinning to the side at the last second, swinging onto his back and pulling him to the ground. He shakes me off and lands a punch in my side. I deflect his next hit, giving his kidneys two quick jabs, causing him to shrink back. I follow them up by going low and throwing out my right leg, knocking his legs out from beneath him. On the ground, he spins and kicks my own from beneath me. I land on top of him with an "oof". He looks at me and we both burst out laughing.

Standing off to the side, even M93 is smiling. I've learned this is a rare sight to behold. "Maintain the space, Madrona," he directs, quickly back to business. I roll off Jacob and help him up. "Jacob, you need to keep your balance. Spread your legs slightly farther apart. A stronger stance will strengthen your punches as well.

"Madrona, keep the distance. The less space you have, the less you can do. You will likely be facing bigger and stronger opponents. You'll need to rely on speed and stealth. Make your hits count. Aim for those vulnerable spots. And stay off the ground! A hit from a larger, stronger opponent may do significant damage, so evasive maneuvers and blocking are key for you. Nightshadow will further emphasize your speed. Use it.

"Both of you, try a feint low to gain shots at the head. This will stun your enemy and give you more time to land a more crucial blow," M93 instructs. We both nod. "Madrona, you'll fight I32 next. Fighting another female or smaller male will require a different fighting technique than someone with L26's build."

I32 walks into our training clearing with a swagger and stops directly in front of me.

While we've gotten on better terms over the last couple of weeks, I gotta say I'm still looking forward to getting a chance to punch her.

I32 charges first, throwing a punch at my face. I duck and land one in her stomach. She kicks up her leg, but I'm already spinning out of the way, landing my own foot on her back. She pivots to punch my side, but I deflect her arm before grabbing it, pulling it high up her back in a punishing hold. She pulls us toward a nearby tree and spins to push me into it, but rather than fighting, I carry her momentum in a full circle, and she hits the tree instead. She elbows me in the side and kicks off the tree, pushing us both to the ground.

We leap up and circle each other warily. While it is tempting to practice some of my moves meant to incapacitate my enemy, I hold back. We need I32 to fight at the POT, so I can't hurt her *too* bad. I fake a jab with my right to get her distracted, but pull back and give my left momentum, landing it in her face. I follow it up with a quick right to her solar plexus.

With the wind knocked out of her, it's easy for me to get her on the ground. I hold my arm to her throat, pinning her. Game over.

Jacob starts applauding, since this is the second time I've beat an Erebus, and the first time I've beaten I32. "Great job, Madrona," he cheers.

"I noticed you're both ending up on the ground a lot. Both of you need to work on balance and strategic falling if you're tripped," M93 comments. "Let's review some fall techniques that allow for quicker recoveries."

After M93 is satisfied with our progress, we take a break. I walk over to where Q08's working diligently on his laptop. Grabbing my water bottle, I nearly drain the whole thing. I study Q08 while I chug; he looks tired and stressed. He flinches when he sees me watching him. I'm sure he feels a lot of pressure right now because the success of our plan and our very lives are dependent on his hacking skills, and I feel a little bad for him.

"One week until we break in," Q08 announces, finally looking up from his computer screen. "For the amount of time we had, I don't think we're doing too bad." N87 and Y17 stop sparing and come over to join us as we all gather around Q08. "I want you all to agree on something. If one of us is left behind, we can't go back to get them. If something goes wrong, some of us might not make it. While this plan has the best odds of success, we can't anticipate every variable. We must be ready to leave each other behind if we can't save them."

No one moves or says anything in response. I believe we all have someone in this group we'd die to protect. N87 and I32 have something between them, whether they know it or not, and M93 was Jacob's stand-in father when his true father wasn't there after his wife's death. I would die to protect Jacob, and I'm confident he'd do the same for me. Q08 and Y17 are like father and son figures. It must be troubling Y17 that someone he grew up with, who swore an oath to protect him with his life, and he the same, is saying this. But everyone is quiet.

"No," I blurt out.

"Excuse me?" Q08 asks.

"I'm not doing that."

"Me either," Jacob follows. "You get caught," he tells me, "I'm coming after you." He's smiling at me, a sad smile. I smile back and can tell he knows I'd do the same for him. The thought that he'd risk getting tortured or killed to save me warms my heart, but there's no way in hell I'd let him sacrifice himself.

"If either of you two get stuck, I guess I'm coming back too," M93 smiles and shrugs. "I'm not leaving Jacob, and if you're caught, he's definitely going back for you. Plus, I'd have to be a monster to leave you to that fate." He looks at me and I tilt my head in his direction to acknowledge the mutual feeling.

"I hate to agree with these fools, but I'm not doing that either," I32 steps forward. I'm not fully surprised she decided to say it in this way. "If N87 gets stuck in there, I'm sure as hell going back for him."

"And vice versa," he replies, and their eyes meet. I think they'd be kissing if there wasn't an audience.

"And if you were stuck, I swore I'd do the same. So did you," Y17 points out to Q08. Sounds like I was right. And Y17 is calling him out on it.

"Yes. I did," Q08 sighs. His statement worries me, though. He always seemed to me like a loyal person who would die for his friends, but here he's saying the complete opposite. I look at my watch and notice the time.

"We should clear out," I tell them. "It'll be full dark soon. No one needs to get lost in the woods after dark."

"Alright," Q08 agrees. "We'll continue training tomorrow. May the moon be with you."

"With you as well," we all say individually and head off. As soon as they're dismissed, I32 and N87 instantly move off together. I grin and follow Jacob through the trees back to my car.

Once we get home, everyone's already in bed. Jacob scoops me off my feet and carries me up the stairs, both of us laughing quietly.

"You know I'm perfectly capable of climbing the stairs by myself now, right?"

"I know," he chuckles. "But it's fun. Good night," he whispers, letting me down at my door with a quick kiss.

"Night," I respond and slowly close the door.

I keep the lights off and walk over to my window.

'Your mental state is doing much better, which makes me happy, except for the fact you're getting ready to do the most stupid thing ever,' Aaron's voice breaks the silence.

"I am doing better. I'll always miss you though," I whisper quietly.

'I know, and I you.'

"Thank you," I say softly to the empty shadows. "For being here."

But he's already gone, leaving me alone in the dark.

The next few days we continue training. It's only when we're three days out from operation POT that something happens. Jacob, Lily, and I are spending a quiet morning at the house while Mom and Dad are at work. We have Lily's favorite game spread out on the coffee table.

Abruptly the front door opens, and Mom and Dad run inside, panting, slamming the door behind them.

"Jeez, Dad. You alright?" Lily asks.

"Everyone needs to go pack their bags. If they're watching us, it means they know where we live and will come here soon. Grab only the things you need, including a sleeping bag and pillow. We can come back later, hopefully, but for now we need to move," Dad orders, moving towards the stairs.

Mom is already pulling backpacks and suitcases out of storage. The three of us just sit there stunned, not moving, just watching our parents run around gathering stuff.

"Dad, what's going on?" Lily asks, her voice shaking slightly.

"Later, honey. We don't have time. Please just go pack some clothes and any necessities you need to last a few days." He glances back at us. "Move! Now!"

Jacob and I share a quick look before each grabbing a suitcase and running up the stairs, me urging Lily along.

"What if they found out about you and are tracking my parents down because they're unknowingly hosting an Erebus? Maybe they caught you mentioning it on cameras somewhere else or someone tipped them off?" I whisper to him.

"That's definitely a possibility, I agree. But we'll have to deal with that later. There's no time for 'what-ifs'. Right now, our biggest priority is to get out of here," he says.

I grab things I need: clothes, toothbrush and toothpaste, along with a hairbrush - followed by tampons, of course - and stuff them in my bag.

I'm about to leave when I see the photo on my desk. We might never be coming back. I already have the necklace around my neck, but I reach out and stuff the picture of Aaron and me in my bag. I search for anything else I might need and grab the box hidden under my bed to stuff it back in my bag also.

Dropping my bag in the hall, I enter Lily's room and help her finish packing her things. We head back downstairs as Jacob joins us, bag slung over this shoulder.

"Put your bags in the car; it's already running. Then come back and load up food and sleeping bags," Mom instructs us.

We head outside. Not only is the car running, but my parents had backed in, so it was pointed heading out the driveway. We return to the house quickly and gather the pile of sleeping bags, blankets, and pillows Mom had stacked up. She has the pantry just about empty, food bags filled to go, and Dad comes racing out of their bedroom, suitcases in hand.

Everyone is in the car, bags and necessities crammed inside. Dad throws it in drive, and we lurch out of the driveway. As we are turning the corner down the block, I look back to see Law Enforcement cars pull up to our house, sirens blaring. Turning back around, Jacob and I share a look over Lily's head, as she sits in the smaller middle seat between us, raising our eyebrows. *That was close.* I release my breath, but my heart rate doesn't slow, adrenaline still fresh and relentless in my blood.

The car is quiet, other than Mom telling us to fully shut off our phones, as Dad doesn't waste time getting on the road heading out of town. I notice he pushes the speed as much as he can without drawing unwanted attention.

"Can you talk to us now? What happened at work?" I ask hesitantly.

"Law Enforcement. They came for us after we got out of surgery this morning. They had us locked in a room, waiting for someone to come and question us. We've been very careful, never talking at the hospital, but they must have found out that we've been questioning our colleagues' disappearances. Do you remember Dr. Ali? Super great guy, good neurosurgeon?" Dad hardly pauses to wait for an answer before continuing. "No, well, it doesn't matter. He disappeared last week. Just poof. Gone. But worse, his whole family, all five kids, his wife, also gone. Your mother and I couldn't wait for that to happen to you. We snuck out a back door and ran home to grab you."

I mull over his words. What are the chances Law Enforcement found out my parents were questioning their actions? What are the chances of them discovering my parents were, granted unknowingly, fostering an Erebus? Jacob and I had been careful as well, at least up until the altercation with Todd. Could word of our fight have gotten back to Law Enforcement? Did that spur their interest in my parents? Or did another Erebus get caught and forced to give us all up?

Turning to Jacob, I ask, "Can you check in with-"

"Already on it," he replies as he pulls out his phone and fires off a quick message.

Looking back out the window, I recognize where we are, only a couple miles out of town but in a densely forested area. Weighing our choices in my mind, I stare back at the forest. *My* forest.

"Everyone is accounted for," Jacob quietly informs me.

Decision made. "Dad, there's an old logging road coming up in the next couple of miles. Pull off there."

"What are you talking about? No! I want to put more miles between us and those Law Enforcement goons until we can figure out what is going on."

"Dad, trust me."

"Our lives are at stake here, Madrona."

"*Thousands* of lives are at stake, Dad," I reply emphatically.

He frowns. "What are you talking about?"

"Just turn off at the logging road. It's a long story. I'll explain when we get there."

"Get where exactly?"

"There's an abandoned hunting shack in those woods. I found it months ago. No one will think to look for us there, especially not so close to home. They'll figure we will want to get away as far as possible," I send Dad a knowing look. "Plus, I *know* these woods. There's water, food, and shelter."

My parents look at each other, indecision all over my dad's face. Mom shrugs, "She has a point," she tells my dad.

Dad's shoulders slightly drop, and he sighs. "Fine. I suppose the sooner we get off the main roads, the better."

Once we are on the logging road, I have Dad follow it for a couple miles before turning off onto an even smaller road. Road being a euphemism for this small, cleared path, barely large enough for our car. After a few minutes, I have him turn into a narrow clearing.

"Here. Park here. We can hide the car from the road with branches. It's only a short hike from here to the cabin."

The woods are quiet after Dad kills the motor, and I step out of the car. The wind rustles the branches, the occasional bird chirps, and I already feel more confident about my decision. About my plans for getting us out of this mess.

"Stay with the car," I tell my family, as Jacob and I prepare to head out. "You can stack up branches between the car and the road until we get back."

"Where are you going?" Dad calls out, as I slam my door shut on his questions.

We rush into the woods to the coordinates Jacob sent the other Erebus as a meeting spot. M93 is already there, and I can hear I32's group working through the dense undergrowth even before we see them.

"They found us," I explain to him. "Law Enforcement. Either they caught us on camera, or someone tipped them off. But we're all in trouble."

M93's face turns grave, and he pulls a knife out from his waistband, handing it to Jacob. Then he passes me another one. "You think it was one of us? Who would have done that?"

Before Jacob and I can answer him, I32 and N87 emerge from the trees and approach us. "What the hell is going on? What's with the cloak and dagger routine?" she asks, eyeing our new knives. "Why are we deviating from the plan?"

"Where are the others?"

"Back at the car. Q08 was finishing up something on his computer, and Y17 decided to wait for him. He's probably afraid Q08 will get lost in the woods without him. He's not known for his sense of direction," she snorts.

"They found us," Jacob cuts in. "Most likely someone tipped them off about our location. They're at our house now," he practically snaps at her. I32's eyes go wide, and she is momentarily speechless. I've never seen this happen, so I'm trying to memorize her face so I can laugh at it later when we aren't all in danger.

"Who?" she asks, almost defensively.

"Someone who's willing to leave everyone else behind and run," Jacob growls through gritted teeth. We all lock eyes. There's only one person who'd do that.

"Q08," she finally growls. "Are you sure?"

"Not a hundred percent. It's still a guess at this point, but he has been especially on edge lately. We'll need to take precautions if he is guilty. But right now, we need to get a safe location set up for my family," I tell her. "There's an abandoned cabin not far from here. We'll lay low there until we can make a new plan."

"N87, go back and make sure the car is hidden from view" she directs, and he runs off. "Lucky for us, I wasn't kidding when I said Q08 is terrible with directions. He won't be able to rat out our location without his computer, so I'll just take it from him until we get to the bottom of this mess," she tells us.

For once, I'm happy to have her on our team.

After giving her directions to the cabin, she lopes off to rejoin her group, deal with Q08, and grab their supplies.

Jacob and I quickly walk back to rejoin my family. They've done a good job in our absence of spreading out branches to disguise the car's location.

My dad turns toward us when he hears us approach. He does a double take when he sees me.

"Do you have a *knife*?"

"I'll explain later."

"It's a knife!" he shouts, upset in his eyes. "And not a kitchen knife, either! Are you trying to get a death sentence?"

"One knife against Law Enforcement's guns!" I retort passionately. "I think it's a death sentence either way, but I'd rather go down fighting!" I pause and take a big breath to regain my composure. My dad's shock has momentarily muted him. "Please. Please trust me. I will explain everything to you once we are safe in the cabin."

My mom reacts first, pulling her shoulders back, dropping into mom mode. Directions issued to everyone. "Lily, you grab all the sleeping bags. Michael and Jacob, help with the heavier food bags. Madrona, you and I can grab the backpacks and suitcases. Let's move out!"

The short hike to the cabin is silent. We move around a particularly thick cluster of trees, and there it is, just as I remembered. It is small and quaint, with log siding and a shingled roof that is starting to cave in. It's a single room inside with a fireplace and cooking stand but not a lot else. It's going to be cozy with all of us there together.

I32's group emerges from the tree line to our right and moves to join us at the cabin door.

"Who are these people?" Dad demands.

"What's going on?" Y17 questions, setting down the bags he was carrying, followed by everyone else.

"We were betrayed," I blurt out. "Law Enforcement came after us."

Everyone goes quiet, and their faces all go pale. Suddenly everyone is shouting the same thing all at once. "Who?" Everyone except Q08. Everyone notices at the same time. I simply glance in his direction; his head is down in dejection, his body still. The answer is obvious now.

He's bombarded with questions and accusations when I yell over the top. "Quiet!" Surprised, everyone stops talking and turns to me.

"Q08, why?" I interrogate through the silence.

He stares at me in anger, regret, and shame all in the same moment, then finally spits out his words. "They caught me. A week ago. They told me they had a connection over the wall who would slit my family's throats as they slept if I didn't cooperate. They told me if I tipped them off who was helping me and where you were, they'd spare me and my family. I had to give them something! They were happy to spare me and mine for information about Aether traitors, so I followed you one night and told them where to find you," he looks away.

My face starts to heat up, anger boiling in my blood. "You sent them after my family!" I shout. "You saved yours by almost killing mine!" My vision is red. My rage blinds me until he whispers the truest words ever spoken.

"A man will do anything for his family. *Anything*," he murmurs, a tear rolling down his face. "And I didn't send them after your family. I didn't even know you had a sister," he glances over at Lily. "I sent them after you and Jacob. I asked them to spare your parents, but they said those harboring an Erebus didn't deserve mercy."

"Madrona, what in the hell is he talking about? Who are these people" Dad jumps in. "What Erebus?"

I turn to my family who is still standing behind me. "I need to tell you all something. About the day I met Jacob." They're silent, confused. "I was in the woods, grieving privately, when I saw him fall… over the wall." I hear a quiet gasp from my mom as I continue, "I was going to run away and report him, but… he just… I couldn't. I couldn't watch someone else die. Not after Aaron. So, I helped him. I made a makeshift cast, stitched up his wound, which was from a knife. The next day I gave him a haircut and Aether clothes before bringing him to you. I disguised him as one of us, so he could heal and go home. Only it wasn't that simple. His own people attacked and threw him over the wall. Why did they do it? Why are so many other Erebus being thrown over? Why did they kill his family?" I pause and see a look of grief in Jacob's eyes. Only for a moment, then it's gone, hidden beneath an emotionless mask.

"Aaron had mentioned some odd happenings going on at the hospital to me before he died, but I had forgotten about them until you started whispering about disappearing colleagues. We figured other Erebus must have also survived the fall. Our search led us to meet I32 and her group," I explain, gesturing to the group.

I catch my family up on our plans for breaking into the POT and what we hope to learn there. Afterwards they step back slowly.

"You're Erebus?" My parents ask Jacob. He nods slowly, cautiously. "Madrona, you knew, and you *helped* him?"

I nod. "He's not a killer. He didn't want to be here in the first place. He's just like those you helped in the hospital, another person who was forced to come here against their will," I defend.

"J-J-Jacob?" Lily stampers. I can see the hurt on his face.

"I'm still the same person I was, Lily. I was simply born on the other side of the wall. So were all of them," he motions to the Erebus behind him. My father steps forward.

"You're right. You are still the same person you were yesterday, the same person who's been part of our family for weeks. You are the same person who saved Madrona from her grief when we couldn't reach her and the same person who helped save our family today," Dad smiles, surprising me with the quickness of his acceptance. My mother follows his lead.

"You're still the same Jacob, Erebus or Aether. You taught our daughter how to laugh again. We could never hate you for that alone," she starts to tear up.

"Jacob!" Lily simply yells and runs to give him a large hug. He smiles.

"Thank you," he whispers. "For everything."

"Sorry to break up the family love fest, but what are we going to do about Q08?" I32 impatiently interjects, bringing us back to the current issue.

"For what it's worth, I did not give up our POT plans or any others. I gave what I had to in order to spare my family. I also spent the drive here reformatting N87's phone and masking our trip from the city traffic cameras. They can't find us here… wherever here is," Q08 said. Turning to my family, he adds, "If you give me your phones, if you trust me with them, I can mask your location as well while still allowing you use of the device."

I stare at Q08 and then look at Jacob. He gives me a small shrug as if to say, *"Your call."*

My anger has dissolved, but I let Q08 sweat it out a bit longer before slowly speaking, "We'd all do anything for our families." Everyone's staring at me, surprised at my response. "I forgive you. As for trusting you again, I'll leave that up to your fellow Erebus. If they can still trust you to carry through with our plans, then so can I."

My gaze searches the group. One by one, each member gives an affirmative nod.

"Then we're following through with the plan." Everyone gives a small cheer, then starts to gather up their dropped bags, turning to enter the cabin.

"We'll help," Dad steps forward.

"No!" I protest.

"What?" he frowns.

"No, you can't help. You are going to take Lily and Mom and stay far away from the POT when we enter," I say.

"But what about you?" Mom frets.

"I'll be fine," I grin. "I've got the best fighters the Aether have ever known behind me."

"You're one of them," Jacob reminds me. I return his smile, proud of the recognition.

"We'll find out why all this is happening, then we'll go home when it's safe," I assure them. My parents don't try to convince me otherwise. They know I'll go no matter what they do, and it'll be safer without them. Jacob's hand meets mine.

"Together?" he asks.

"Together."

FOURTEEN

Everything continues as planned. Well, except the fact that we are living in a cramped, slightly dilapidated hunting cabin, in the middle of the woods, sleeping on top of each other, and hoping spiders decide not to make webs on our faces while we sleep. Luckily, I32's group was cautious and brought all our supplies with them when we were discovered, so the blueprints and map and all the stuff we need - including the cheesy-poofs, of course - are here with us now.

My mother removes Jacob's cast, and he can now walk and fight more easily. Q08 reprograms all our phones, and everyone sleeps a little better.

Each day I train with Jacob under M93's watchful eye. He gives tips and corrections on both our fighting techniques. I learn how to fight with a knife. Now I can beat N87, I32, and Q08. Y17 is huge, and I highly doubt I'll ever beat him, though Jacob's optimistic. He's been impressed with my learning speed and says I am grasping the nuances of Nightshadow even faster than he did. While I don't fully believe him, the praise leaves me with a warm feeling inside.

It's the night before we break into the POT, and I can't sleep. I quietly climb out of my sleeping bag and walk out to where my family's car is parked. I climb on top of the hood, lean back on the front windshield, and look up at the stars through the small break in tree branches. Stars always fascinate me. They're so far away, yet they still can be seen. The light shines no matter how far you go.

At home, I can't see very many of them due to all the city lights. But out here, in the middle of nowhere, I can see *all* of them. Billions and trillions of stars, light years and light centuries away. And in the middle of all this wonder, the moon, shining bright despite the darkness that surrounds it. Because it's never alone, always followed by these infinite stars to keep it company.

I don't hear Jacob walk up to me. His cast is no longer there to weigh his steps down and alert me of his presence. I only know he's there when I see him climb to join me. I lean into him, and he puts his arm around me. His warmth and smell are comforting. I close my eyes and breathe it in.

"Can't sleep?" he whispers.

I shake my head. "It's hard to get any rest with everything hinging on tomorrow."

Jacob rubs my back in comfort. His touch is calming, always there to tell me I'm not alone in the world. I look back up at the stars above us and notice him doing the same.

"We have stories on my side of the wall," he says quietly. "Fairy tales, essentially, but they've always stuck with me. There's one tale of the night sky. Once there was a mighty dragon, who soared through darkness, always alone, completing tasks for the almighty Chaos. One day, he stayed out later than usual, into the dawn, and encountered another dragon, one who soared through daylight. They fell in love, and he made her the world, anything she wanted was hers. Their union angered Chaos, as his orders were no longer being fulfilled.

"Chaos went to the mighty dragon and said, 'You cannot be together, as you are causing problems for the world, setting the universe in disorder.'

"The mighty dragon cried for many days and nights before he finally came to a decision. If he could not be with her, he didn't want his life. He gave his love the last thing he could and cut out his heart to stop the heartache. His heart became the moon, and his splattered blood became the stars in the sky, illuminating the dark and allowing his love to see him every night she was alone.

"They say that Chaos was angry at first to lose one of his prized dragons. But seeing the lady dragon's grief brought him remorse. So, after much thought, he sent the lady dragon out into space, in the form of a comet, to be closer to her love. Now the two former dragons were both the same, both permanent fixtures in the night sky, together for eternity."

I consider his words. It's a wonderful story of love and hope, grief and suffering, and rebirth.

"It's beautiful," I say. "Sad, but wonderful." He nods, and we continue to look up at the sky. I wonder why he picked this story, as I'm sure the Erebus have many. I think for a moment before I realize what he's trying to say.

We are not allowed to be together, as he's Erebus and I'm Aether. Law Enforcement came to us today intent on keeping us apart, just like Chaos came to the dragon.

Jacob kisses me and I forget my thoughts on his story and what it could mean. It doesn't matter now. Right now, this moment could be the last we have together. It could be the last night we ever have, period. The last time we see the moon before the sun chases it away. The last time I see him before the Aether chase him away.

"I have fallen in love," Jacob whispers. "But I wish to know if my love feels the same way."

I smile at him. "She does," I answer and kiss him. His warmth, his strength, his protection, his comfort. I love him for all of those things. I remember all the moments I've been with him. They play like a video reel inside my head, highlighting some of my favorites. Watching Jacob play the guitar. Having him do my hair for my date with Chris. Playing games with Lily. He has fought for me and my family. Cared for us. And now, this moment beneath the stars, he has loved us. Loved me.

I kiss him, and he kisses me back until we finally sleep. I'm safe in his embrace, my nose buried deep in his chest, breathing him in. His warmth will not let me get cold. He's Jacob. No, he's *my* Jacob. And as far as I know, he always will be.

Jacob's arms are still around me when I wake. The sun's just breaking dawn, and the moon is still in the sky. The light sneaks over the horizon, slowly chasing away the stars, one by one.

Reality intrudes gradually. *Today's the day.*

"We probably need to get up," I tell him.

Jacob looks at me, eyebrows raised, as if saying, *Do we have to?* I nod and he gives a small grunt. "Well, good morning," he greets and kisses my forehead.

"Good morning," I reply as Lily pops out of the woods and clambers up the car to lie across both of us.

"Oof," I chuckle, releasing a burst of air as she falls on my lungs.

"You two are so cute," she laughs, and Jacob follows.

"Can you get up please? I think we'd like to breathe," I gasp. She laughs and finally moves, pulling me off the car. I grab Jacob's arm and drag him with me.

Our jovial banter continues until we reach the cabin. The rest of the group is serious as preparations get underway in earnest. The Erebus are packing up our supplies, preparing to move out.

"Mom and Dad, I think you and Lily should consider staying here," I suggest.

"Absolutely not," Mom responds. "You may need a doctor after…"

Dad agrees with Mom, and I nod acceptance. While I'd like my family to stay as far away as possible from the fallout, Mom's logic makes sense. We may very well need medical care, but hospitals will be out of the question.

"Let's get moving. Once we get to the city, we can set up a new base camp, get some food, and then begin." Q08's statement gets us all moving again, each to our respective cars.

Continuing to drive our family car is, unfortunately, a risk we have to take. Luckily, N87 grabbed a few extra license plates, so we switch ours out. When I look at Jacob in surprise, he just shrugs at me as if to say, *"They're Erebus. It's what they do."*

Q08 will mask us from the traffic cameras as best he can, but our destination city is one of the largest Aether cities in the world and the governmental seat for the Aether due to its proximity to the POT. Needless to say, security is tighter there than in my hometown.

Named Eos after the Greek goddess of the dawn, the city looms over the hills as we approach. Yeah, it seems our founders were obsessed with ancient Greek deities. The city is enormous with a population of nearly three million people. Huge skyscrapers lord over the city streets, each rooftop containing a garden of some sort. Housing neighborhoods circle the downtown area, with yards getting smaller and buildings taller the closer they approach the city center. Apartment buildings, business offices, furniture stores, and grocery stores all match in perfect harmony, either light blue or white reflective glass bordered with yellow, the Aether colors.

We find an older hotel to check into, where the security cameras are nonexistent, and the desk attendant is lazy. We pile into three rooms and enjoy our first shower in three days. Once clean, we eat together in I32's room, go over the plan one last time, and do a final equipment check.

I had been worried about getting I32 and Y17 their necessary guard uniforms since our plan deviation didn't account for that. But I32 proves her resourcefulness in acquiring them while everyone else is showering.

"How'd you find the right sizes so quickly?" I ask her.

She shrugs. "Instead of getting them from individual targets as we originally planned, I just found the uniform supplier. It was easy enough when I had my pick of sizes to choose from."

I have to say, I'm kind of impressed.

Then it's time to head out.

"Promise me, Madrona. Promise me you *and* Jacob will both make it out okay," Mom begs.

I nod. "I promise, Mom." But deep down I don't know for sure. If either of us gets caught, we'll both go down in flames.

She smiles, pulling my mind out of the darkness. "My girl. I love you so much, and I'm so proud of you!" She hugs me tightly, then lets my father have a turn.

"We'll be waiting for you here," Dad tells me. "Don't. Get. Caught. I love you."

Lily hugs me. "You're the best sister ever!"

I see my parents make their way over to Jacob. "You protect her with your life. You hear me?" My father says strictly. "But don't you dare die either. You die and put her through that pain again, I'll revive you, so I can kill you again myself." They both chuckle slightly at his last comment. Anything to distract from the truth of how dangerous this really is.

"I will," Jacob vows.

"I'm glad I had the pleasure of meeting you," Dad smiles, shaking Jacob's hand. "Thank you for all you've done and all you've risked."

"I'm sorry for the danger I've put your family in."

"It is *not* your fault, Jacob. It would have found its way to us sooner or later given the happenings at the hospital. Our representatives' secret plans, or whatever they have going on, are the cause of this mess, not you," my dad assures him.

My mother pushes my father away and embraces Jacob. "I always wanted a son. You're the closest I'll ever have to one, so you promise me to take care of not just Madrona, but yourself also," she chokes on her tears.

Jacob nods, humbled. "Thank you, Michael and Anne," he dips his head. They nod, and Lily gives him the tightest hug she can manage.

"Aw, I love you, Lily," he embraces her back. "You take care of your parents for me, okay?"

"I will. I love you too," she answers and releases him.

After one last hug, I wave goodbye to my family and follow the Erebus out to N87's stolen car. I tell myself that I'll see them soon, but I have a strange feeling I'm not going to see them for a while. I push it aside, and we all squeeze in, before making our way toward the POT.

Phase one begins.

N87 backs the car into a small clearing in the forest, about a quarter mile from the POT. It was the closest location we found that provided a hiding spot for the car but somewhat easy access for a quick getaway. I32 and Y17 get out and quickly change into the stolen guard uniforms. They strap on their knives, and I32 slides the thumb drive Q08 made into her pocket. After a final radio check, they head out.

M93, Jacob, and I are quick to follow. Weapons check. Earpieces and radios check. Recording equipment check. N87 is ready at the wheel, Q08 in the seat next to him, computer out and ready to go once the thumb drive gets loaded into the system. We give them a brief salute and quickly follow the path to the POT.

From the cover of the trees, I get my first view of the Place of Truce. Built directly into the wall, the POT is a curved slab of white stone, jutting out in a half circle from our half of the wall. Four stories tall, the Aether side has multiple glass windows, even glass doors, to capture as much light as possible. According to my uncle, they are bulletproof, the perfect example of aesthetic meeting function. The curvature of the outer wall is such that outside door guards cannot see each other from their positions. They've cleared the trees a hundred feet back from the doors, so the guards can see anyone coming close. More guards watch from the rooftop, but they rotate ten minutes before the door guards.

As the roof guards go through their shift rotation, we watch I32 and Y17 approach the pair of guards by the east door. I32 is fumbling a bit with her uniform buttons, intentionally showing the two male guards a bit of skin. Their eyes are locked on her while Y17 sneaks up from behind and takes down the first guard with a quick, open palm thrust into the neck. The second guard jerks in response, but he's not fast enough to avoid Y17's choke hold. Ninety seconds later, he joins his partner on the ground, unconscious.

Grabbing the guards by the ankles, I32 and Y17 drag them over to us. Hidden by the dense undergrowth, we stash the guards, newly tied up and mouths covered in tape. I32 and Y17 grab the guards' guns and radios, the final bag of cheesy-poofs, then continue back to the guard post.

Outer door guard rotation comes just as expected five minutes later. The two of them are relieved from their outside post and make their way inside the POT. I can partially see them through the glass doors. They appear to be arguing over the cheesy-poofs as another pair of guards approaches them. I32 shoves Y17 and a struggle ensues, as Y17 holds the bag of snacks above his head out of I32's reach. The other guards quickly intervene and snag the bag of cheesy-poofs. During the scuffle, N87's hand reaches down and steals the security keycard one of the guards was wearing. He's so quick that I would have missed the move if I wasn't watching for it. After a quick reprimand, I32 and Y17 are sent on their way, without their snack; the other guards now enjoying their victor spoils. The Erebus continue into the building and out of our line of sight.

The three of us continue to wait at the edge of the forest for word of success. After the longest two or three minutes, Q08 cheers over our earpieces, "The virus has been activated."

"Finally!" M93 grins.

"Hacking camera feeds now..." Q08 trails off. "And... I'm in! Alarms, security codes, door access! It's all mine, bitches!" He gives a final maniacal laugh, and I can picture his fingers flying across the keyboard.

"Are we a go, pal?" Y17's voice murmurs quietly.

"Green light," Q08 replies. "Proceed to the roof."

"Where's the rope?" I32's voice is partially static through the radio.

"There's a supply closet two stories above you, near the roof. Madrona's uncle mentioned rappelling gear is stored there in case roof guards need to drop quickly to help ground units. Exit the security room and turn left. Go straight down the hall for fifty feet."

I try to recall the blueprints in my mind, envisioning the path I32 and Y17 will take to the roof. They will be passing guards on a regular basis as they work their way upstairs.

Q08 continues. "Take the next left to the elevator," he directs. "You have three guards on the next floor, coming towards you," he whispers into the radio.

"What are you doing here?" We can hear one inquire over the open link. "It's not time to change our rotations."

"Random security check. New policy handed down by Representative Spade in light of the increased Erebus sightings," Y17 promptly replies. "What's your status?"

"All clear here, sir," the guard answers, dropping the suspicious tone and assuming a more deferential demeanor.

"Excellent. Continue on."

We follow along the airwaves as I32 and Y17 move on, and Q08 programs a hold on the elevator, so no one else can access it. They move to the storage closet and find the rope and rappelling gear, as expected. This is the tricky part of the plan, as the number of guards on the roof may have doubled as Spade previously reported.

"I can't see you anymore," Q08 warns. "There should be ten to fifteen guards up there. Throw the rope down as soon as possible, so we can climb up to help you."

No response.

Jacob, M93, and I brace to sprint towards the building. A long, tense minute passes before we see a long black rope come flying down over the edge. Its arrival is enough to catch the ground guards' attention. We race over to the two of them, M93 neatly knocking them out before they can even blink.

Jacob pulls on the rope, making sure it's secure, then starts climbing. M93 follows, and I climb up after him.

Holding on for dear life, I climb as fast as I can, trying to keep up with the two guys who have no trouble at all. I fall behind as Jacob disappears over the roof, and a guard falls over the edge, nearly knocking M93 and I off the rope. *Shit*, I think looking at the body on the ground below. Our intention was stealth, to incapacitate and avoid killing whenever possible. These guards are no different than my uncle, just doing their jobs, wanting to go home to their families at the end of the day.

There's no time to go back down and hide the body either, so I push it from my mind as I reach the roof. Chaos reigns. So much for stealth. There's four of us and more than fifteen of them. I work to control the pumping adrenaline and give in to the calm darkness approaching my mind. Nightshadow. I grin. Now I understand where the word comes from.

I watch as my body moves for me, punching, jumping, leaping and striking, knocking out guard after guard with incredible speed. I focus on the knockout shots, trying to get the guards unconscious as quickly as possible before they can call for more help. Q08 is managing their lines and preventing any calls from going through from the roof. Luckily the close combat has prevented any guns from being discharged, as that would be harder to mask from the remaining guards on the ground below.

Two guards run at me. I feint to the left, causing one to hit the other, then I punch the exposed one in the side and kick the guard into the other. *Whack!* His head hits the pavement, and he's out. The second guard gets back up, pushing the first off him and comes at me with a knife.

I remember my brief training with knives. I let him strike first, since he has the advantage. He lets out a yell as he charges and slashes. I jump. And by that, I mean I jump *over* him. All the way over him, higher than six feet. Stunning him with my sudden disappearance, I land a punch to his kidney followed by a quick kick to his temple. The guard falls, joining his predecessor.

With three Nightshadows joining the fight, the battle doesn't last long. The roof is ours. I32 now carries a gash across her arm, but it's not deep and will heal soon. Y17 has a few nice bruises while Jacob, M93, and I are unharmed, the gift of the Nightshadow having saved us from taking a single hit.

Bloody and unconscious bodies cover the roof. I cross my fingers that no one is dead. But there's no time to check each one. We must continue with the plan. I can mourn them later, if necessary.

"Open the vents," I order Q08 through the radio.

"On it," he answers. The large vents to our right open, revealing a small airway through the whole building. "I can't keep them open, so once you're in, they'll shut behind you."

"Got it," Jacob responds.

"Y17, I32, you have our backs?" M93 checks. They both nod, picking up another gun from the fallen guards. They'll remain on the roof, guarding our escape route. "Well, ladies first," M93 gestures for me to go first.

"Why am I getting the feeling that you're going to be staring at my ass?" I turn to face Jacob. M93 laughs softly behind him.

"Would it make you feel better if I told you, it's a nice ass?" he deadpans. M93's cracking up now, struggling to stay quiet. My face turning bright red, I scowl at both of them as I climb into the small air vent, sliding down the slope to the inside of the building.

At the bottom, I check my video camera is running, and Jacob and M93 do the same.

"Receiving feeds," confirms Q08 with a whisper in my ear.

When everyone is ready, I try to crawl quickly, since it's embarrassing to have a guy staring at your ass. Suddenly we reach a split fork.

"Which direction?" I ask Q08.

"Right, followed by a left," he says. "Let me know when you're there." We turn right in the small air vent and then left, and we're over an opening.

"Shh," I wave quietly back to them. Looking through the grate, I can see guards on their lunch break in the mess hall directly below us. I make it over fine and so does Jacob, but when M93 crosses it, there's a hard sound like rock against metal. He hurries over the gap as all the sounds in the room below stop for a moment. We barely breathe until the activity resumes below.

We reach another turn in the vents. "Next?" I ask the radio quietly.

"Right, straight, and another left," he instructs. I continue to the right, quietly passing over another grate to a room beneath us.

We pass over a vertical vent, heading down beneath us. I stretch out and dive across as quietly as possible. Jacob and

M93 follow, not anywhere near as quiet as I was. We take a left and the vent opens up a bit, heading to the right and the left. I stay in the center as Jacob and M93 fan out of the vents in either direction.

"Where are you now?" Q08 asks through the radio.

"We're in position," I barely breathe through the radio. Through my vent, I can see a green indoor garden. Living walls grace the sides, as more lush greenery blankets the ground. Exotic flowers provide bright pops of color in the garden. A large skylight overhead provides the plants with the necessary sunlight to thrive indoors. A small, thin stream circles the entire thing, two bridges on each side. The one on the right, the Aether. And on the left, the Erebus. In the middle there is a patio with a table in the center containing a teapot and two cups.

The view is stunning. It's surreal to even be here. So few Aether or Erebus ever see this sight. We are *inside* the POT. And alive. At least for now.

Before I can check back in with the guys, two doors at the base of the bridges on each side open. Five guards enter, followed by the two representatives, trailed by five more guards. The two representatives take their seats at the table while the twenty guards circle them. Ten on the Erebus side, ten on the Aether side.

"A70, a pleasure to see you again," the Aether representative greets.

"You as well, Miss Spade," the Erebus representative answers. "How are you fairing on this fine day?" I look down and double check my camera is recording and is positioned to view through the grate slots.

"Well. And how are you?" she answers politely.

"I'm glad to say the same," A70 smiles.

I look at the man. He sports a thin, dark mustache and messy haircut. This is the man who killed Jacob's family and ordered him thrown over the fence. I can feel the hatred burning in my eyes and can only imagine what Jacob's feeling.

"Enough with the social niceties," Janice Spade cuts to the chase. "I'm afraid we must get down to business."

"Yes, we must," A70 sighs, pouring the tea and dropping in a sugar cube, Spade following in a similar fashion.

"Continue sending over the Erebus. It's sparking fear in the people that I can use to my advantage."

He nods. "Yes. I will do that... Also, the disease is spreading."

Spade stops all her movement, freezing on the spot, and sets down the tea, devoting all her attention to him.

I try to look at Jacob but can't see him from my position. *Disease? What disease?*

"We're getting rid of the people who are immune," he explains. "There are a few who can naturally survive it, and we're eliminating the carriers to prevent the continuation of those genes, so that no one else will resist it. Those who do survive..." Janice stares at him.

"What?" she demands. "What happens to those who survive the disease?"

A70 looks her dead in the eye. "Their cell regeneration rate increases astronomically, every single one gaining the ability to heal many times the normal speed. They get a shallow cut, and it heals in minutes. They fall fifty feet and can recover quickly if they survive the initial impact. They are rare, only five or six survivors per hundred thousand. However, all the Nightshadows are surviving the Moros. For every Nightshadow we find, five non-Nightshadows survive the virus and also gain this ability."

Janice goes pale. "Nightshadows with increased healing rates… you should kill them on the spot rather than send them here for me to deal with!" She lights up in anger, but behind the anger there's something else. *Is that… fear?*

"We can't tell the difference between an immune and an inexperienced Nightshadow," he says through gritted teeth. "Either we send over both Nightshadows and immunes, or no one at all. Besides, it seems you've had no problem so far. For a peace-loving people, you are remarkably efficient at killing." He's smiling. I shudder at the evil in his grin. "Anyway, outside of the few immune cases, the disease always kills its victim. Luckily, it's hard to transmit, and therefore isn't spreading too quickly. It's killed six million people in two decades so far, many of whom are expert fighters."

Janice is biting her lip. "Back on the subject of the Nightshadows, the plan isn't going to work if you have that many of them running around with special healing powers. Either throw them over here for us to deal with or kill them yourself, though preferably the latter. One Nightshadow can take out ten experienced men. But two working together can take out more than fifty. I can't imagine what would happen if they all worked together. Add supernatural healing to the mix," she scowls, "and you can forget about it. Keep the disease spreading, and get rid of those Nightshadows, or you're never coming home."

"Anything else?" A70 asks, sighing.

Janice glares at him. "Just keep your cover and influence. As I said, get rid of the Nightshadows and all others who can heal, except for Subject B3. I want daily updates on the status of your people and how many you manage to terminate," she says. "In the meantime, have your scientists continue their research on building massive shockwaves, and be sure that they are large enough to topple buildings. I had hoped to move operations, but I don't have the ability to work on it here without arousing suspicion."

"Ma'am, may I ask what you'll be doing while I'm working on all this?" He winces at her glower, but it softens quickly.

"I'll be building an army and collecting the necessary funds," she explains as if to a young child.

"Yes, ma'am," he nods. "What do I tell people when they ask what happened today?"

"Tell them that you're working with us, and our medical experts, to find a cure. Building the foundation so they won't question our presence later," she smirks. "I don't want any Aether citizens to know about the disease, so make sure you don't throw over anyone with an active infection." A70 chuckles at her tone. "Good luck. May you find happiness if you deserve it."

"And if you don't, may you work to earn it," he dips his head. They stand up and prepare to head their separate directions, as A70 adds, "Oh, and what of the guards?" The confused watchmen look at him.

"Kill them," she shrugs, tossing the words over her shoulder as she exits. She's about to walk through the door when someone enters, whispering in her ear. She turns and looks right at the vent grates. While I can't imagine that she can actually see any of us, two words pass through my mind, bright as day. *Oh shit!*

"Intruders! Find them, now! *No one* leaves this building alive unless I permit it!" she yells, sprinting out the door.

FIFTEEN

Jacob, M93, and I are in full panic mode.

"Q08, they know we're here! Get us out of here!" I demand, turning away from A70, who's systematically killing all twenty of the guards. In the split second I watch him fight, I notice something's off. He isn't a Nightshadow, but he's moving faster. Not in the way we do, smooth and graceful, but with hard and sharp edges, almost artificial, landing blows with an unnatural force.

"Okay, go to the right." Q08's voice pulls me away from this confusing image, and I obey, following Jacob, with M93 falling in behind me.

"Next?" Jacob calls from the front into the radio.

"Another right, followed by two straights and a left. There'll be an access grate into the restrooms. I'll set off the alarms on the other side and put the false video clips into the camera streams," he answers. "Y17 and I32, get ready."

"On it," I32's voice calls back.

I follow Jacob to the right and then straight through two forks, across another vertical vent and to the left. He stops to remove the grate, sliding it out of the way before sticking his head down into the room below.

"Clear," he tells us, then jumps down, catching me when I follow. M93 does an awesome stunt and pulls the grate back into place as he joins us.

"Okay, we're here," I whisper into the radio. "Tell us when we're clear."

"Three, two, one, now!" Q08 counts. We open the door and run down the hall.

"Take the next left, and you'll find two guards," he directs. Jacob and M93 knock them out in less than a second. "Straight, and… stop!" He halts us at the next hallway. I hear footsteps heading away from us, towards an alarm going off on the southern side of the building. We're to the north.

"Okay, now turn right." We obey.

"There's four guards straight and to the left," the radio blares. We head in that direction. I guide my body to land a punch in a guard's face and the other in his stomach, followed by a kick to send him to the side, out of my way. Unconscious. M93 and Jacob have cleared the others.

"Okay…" Q08 waits. "Oh shit! Alright, you're going to have to fight your way out. Go up the stairs, and you'll find two more on the next level." We follow his directions, entering the stairway after running to the right. One guard hears us and starts coming up the stairs to challenge us. Jacob braces himself between the wall and railing with his arms, lifts his feet, kicking the upcoming guard in the head, and he's unconscious.

Three punches and the next guard at the top of the stairs is down. I'm tired from running, but my life depends on it, so I run even faster.

"Straight and to the right, then you'll find the roof exit blocked by twenty armed guards. It's going to be ugly," Q08 warns.

Jacob, M93, and I grab guns from the knocked-out guards. As we're running, Jacob gives me a quick lesson. "Trigger, safety, reload," he explains. Pointing to each part and showing how it works. By the time we reach the end of the hall, I've got the very basics down. Point it at the bad guy, pull the trigger. End of story. But we'd all like to avoid using them if at all possible.

"Ready?" M93 asks us.

"Yes," Jacob confirms.

"Definitely not," I reply. M93 chuckles, then his face turns dark.

"On three. One, two, three!" We burst around the corner, all but leaping at the stunned guards. Q08's false trail with a southern ground escape was clearly convincing, as they were not expecting us. Ten fall in our initial attack and the rest run back around the corner for safety, but by then we're already there, knocking their weapons out of their hands. Once they're all disarmed, we begin the fist fight in earnest.

My body leads my mind, rather than the other way around. One punch followed by a hit to the solar plexus, while the guard is out of breath, another punch to the face and he's down. A kick to the groin followed by a punch to the temple, down.

A guard comes up behind me and punches me in the back. I absorb the impact and use it to spin and land one in his face. He stumbles back, stunned, and I land a kick along the side of his head, then he's out. Another guard comes behind me and squeezes me tightly. The air is pushed out of my lungs, and I can't breathe. I kick and struggle, headbutting and doing everything I can, but I'm pinned. Pain surges through me, my lungs burning, begging for air, and I let out a small cry, using all the oxygen I have left. The guy restraining me suddenly goes limp, releasing me, as Jacob knocks him on the head with the butt of his knife.

I gasp for oxygen, kneeling for a split second, then run and follow M93 and Jacob up a set of stairs and through a door, where I'm met with a wave of fresh air. We sprint to the rope still where we left it, and descend quickly to the ground, the rope burning our palms. Heading to the cover of the trees, Jacob and M93 are the first to make it. I'm following when a burst of pain in my leg causes me to stumble and crash to the ground.

A warm red liquid is bubbling from my thigh. I roll to the left, and the next shot bounces off the ground. I hear the shooter reloading and see Jacob running for me. The pain is like a fire raging in my leg. It's all I can do to roll back to the right to dodge the next bullet. I hear a grunt of frustration then feel warm arms around me. I stumble to help carry some of my weight, as Jacob half carries me into the safety of the woods.

M93 comes to help Jacob, and the two of them get us to the car in record time. N87 immediately puts his foot to the floor and drives us away as fast as possible. I hear yelling, but I can't see, and the noise is all blurred out, muffled. There is only pain. The horrible pain. And so much blood. And... Jacob. Jacob's here. He's holding me. If he's here, I'll be safe. I'll be fine. I give in to the darkness and it swallows me, leaving the pain behind.

When the darkness descends, she already knows what is happening. 'Ugh. Great,' she wants to yell into the empty gray space, but knows she won't be able to say anything anyway, so why try? Plus, anything is better than the pain.

A figure appears. One not of a specific physical shape, but more of many shapes. Not only ever-changing configuration, but constantly changing between dark and light. Chaos. The shape finally separates, the right being light, the left being dark. The figure in the center is gray, as if to show that it is neither light nor dark but both at the same time.

Two symbols appear at the source of light and dark. A sun and a moon. Aether and Erebus. Day and night. Opposites. Suddenly, the sun gains more power, and the figure in the center starts moving back to chaos. The sun goes back to its original form, and the figure moves back to center.

'Balance. You're trying to say we must keep the balance, as chaos is already erupting,' she thought.

Suddenly, the figure in the center grabs the sun and moon and pushes them into one form. Light and dark, day and night... the eclipse. The figure wraps its arms around the eclipse, and the symbols shatter. Joined, and then destroyed.

"You must keep the balance," *a voice instructs. There's a strange hint of recognition in her mind at the female voice.* "Keep the balance, else the world will fall into chaos. Once you gain unity, they must be destroyed."

"What? Who must be destroyed?" *she asks, suddenly surprised she can speak.*

"Destroy the Erebus and Aether?" *Jacob's voice follows.*

She turns toward his voice and realizes that for once she's in control of her dream-self. Jacob stands a few feet away from her.

"Yes," the voice confirms. "They will keep trying to merge. Become the eclipse, unite the sides, then destroy the wall, and give the people freedom."

"How?" Jacob's voice asks. "And how do we stop the virus?"

"I have already shown you how to stop the disease," the voice claims. "But you must figure out on your own how to merge the people."

"What are you?" she asks. The figure moves closer to her, materializing, gaining more definition. Her eyes widen as she sees the figure's face, the flowing hair and the scars.

The figure smiles at her.

"I am you."

I shut my eyes the moment I realize I'm awake. Every time I pass out, the moment I open my eyes again I'm hit with a massive headache, so I'm trying *not* to open my eyes until I'm ready to deal with it. I sniff at the air of the room. Cinnamon. Jacob. I sigh in relief.

There's something in my arm. I move my hand down to my arm and follow a small tube up to wherever it originates from. *Probably an IV. Why am I injected with an IV?* I almost open my eyes out of curiosity but remember the reason I'm keeping them shut. I sigh and realize I'm leaning against a pillow. Was it there before?

I open my eyes despite my common sense screaming at me to shut them, and a massive surge hits me. Memories flood back into my mind. I was shot! *Oh shit, I got shot!* I register a surge of pain radiating from my leg. I gasp and let out a small cry, my eyes shutting again before I can even see anything.

I hear yelling. "She's awake!"

"Put her back under!" someone orders. My mind is drowning in pain, too lost to comprehend who is speaking. "She's not healed yet! Put her back under now!" the voice says again.

"I'm here, Madrona, I'm here," this voice cuts through the pain enough for me to recognize it.

"J-Jacob," I whisper, clenching my teeth. The massive wave of pain.

"I'm here. It's alright, we got out."

"W-We did?" I manage.

"We did," he answers. I feel his lips meet my forehead. "They're going to make you sleep, okay? Get some rest."

"Wait, did you see it? The vision? Did you see *me*?" I ask. I can't see him with my eyes closed, but I want to.

"Yes, I did. We can talk when you wake," he strokes my forehead, then his hand leaves.

"Don't leave me, please," I beg, feeling someone fiddling with my IV and soon feel a sensation moving in my veins.

"I won't," he promises, his voice slowly fading as the darkness returns.

Black. Darkness, black and quiet. Peaceful. Then, light. Too bright. I squeeze my eyes shut, my hands moving to block the light. What happened to the darkness? It was a comforting solace. Empty, calm. Now, I hear more yelling and this bright light is shattering my peace, splintering my eyes.

I feel someone reach out and hold my hand. The person squeezes lightly, and I squeeze back. I keep my eyes shut as I run my fingers along the person's hand. Jacob, I realize when I hit the scar running from his thumb to his ring finger, from when he first started learning to fight.

"You stayed," I smile.

"I did," he smiles back. I let out a pained grunt. Someone drops pills in my hand, and I swallow without opening my eyes. *They better be pain meds.*

"What happened?" I force out of my mouth, still using one hand to shield the light.

"Hey, can someone turn that off?" he shouts. The light blinks off, and a wave of relief is instant. I can finally open my eyes and see Jacob. I wrap my arms around him, then regret it as a shock of pain hits me from my right thigh. But… It's not as bad as before. Less painful than the knife wound, even.

"You were shot," he says.

"No shit, Sherlock."

He lets out a chuckle, then continues. "M93 and I carried you back to the car, and we reached our safe house. You were bleeding out, the bullet nicked your femoral artery, and fast. We didn't know what to do, then your mom had a brilliant idea, and we transfused you with some of my blood," he says.

"What?"

"Your mom remembered that we're the same blood type from when I was in the hospital, and you needed to heal, so we injected you with some of my blood after pulling out the bullet. It seems to be working, since you look much better than you did before," he smiles. I look at the IV going into my arm and see a red liquid inside it.

"Thank you." He nods. "How long since the POT?"

"Three days, and you're already half healed," he explains. I was out for *three days!*

"How's my family?" I ask.

"They're fine," he assures me. I release a sigh of relief. "They were just here. We've been taking turns sitting with you."

"We have a lot to talk about," I remind him. He nods.

"Whenever you're ready, ask away," he agrees and sits on the edge of the bed I'm lying on.

"I'm ready now," I say immediately, making Jacob chuckle. "First of all, the disease. What did A70 mean by that?"

"Last year, a disease broke out. A deadly disease. Our healers called it Moros. I don't know what it is with people naming stuff after ancient Greek gods, but Moros was the god of doom and son of Erebus. It's funny because rumor has it that the Moros was designed in a lab by our own scientists, then released upon the population." Jacob doesn't laugh. "It's a disease that kills anyone who contacts it. Unless you're randomly immune or a Nightshadow, who all seem to have a natural immunity, both of which are extremely rare. A70 was right when he said that only one or two out of twenty thousand survive the Moros.

"We're guessing the immune were just lucky enough to have a specific kind of mutation or gene that saved them from the virus. Nightshadows though, our guess is the genetics giving us strength and speed are also strong against the virus. All of us, naturally immune or Nightshadow, still have a week or two of living hell, but afterwards… you know what happens. The Moros targets our regenerating cells. If you survive the virus, your body gains the ability to heal quicker and more efficiently, hence the reason that we all survived the fall."

"Damn," is my only response. "This is the secret you weren't allowed to tell," I finally put the pieces together. "They didn't want me to know about the disease because it makes Erebus look weak?"

"Yes."

"It sounded like A70 was reporting to Janice… for an invasion?"

"We're not sure. This was the first we'd heard of an invasion. It sounds like the Aether are going to take over the Erebus after eliminating the bulk of the army and as many Nightshadows as possible," he says. "They want to weaken our people because we have the higher population. Hopefully, they have a cure stashed away somewhere in case it gets out of control."

I shake my head. "Everyone they threw over was immune, Nightshadow, or related to one of the two," I say. "So, all of you already had the virus?"

He nods in confirmation. "It sucked."

"It matches up with Spade being extra diligent about keeping Aether and Erebus separated. There's no way she'd want that virus spreading through the Aether population," I say. "What now?"

"I'm extracting enough of my blood for you to fully heal. Once I've donated enough… I'm leaving," he says it quickly, and it's so sudden that I'm hit with a wave of shock. I must not have heard him correctly. As I'm trying to process his statement, I see his mask rise, hiding his emotions. Is he ashamed of them? Is he *happy* to be leaving, or does he not want me to see him upset? Does he even care at all?

"Wait, what?"

"I have done nothing but harm you and your family," he forces out, and the mask comes falling down. His eyes dampen and he blinks furiously. "It'll… It'll be better, safer for you if I'm not here to drag them towards you."

"No, you can't go," I beg, feeling tears beginning to stream down my face. "You can't leave me."

"It'll be safer for you if I do," he straightens, pulling himself together. "Your fellow Aether will be more likely to help you if you don't have an Erebus hanging around. And you can always tell your government that I forced you to help me. It should be easy enough for most people to believe an Erebus would make violent threats against you." He looks away, not making eye contact with me.

"No, no…" I shake my head. More tears following the previous, and I can tell he's crying too, even as he looks away. He sits and wraps his arms around me. Both of us suffering, both broken.

"It's going to hurt a lot, for both of us, but I'll do anything to keep you safe," he almost chokes on his words, and I realize that's why he's leaving. He's going to put himself through this heartache for my sake. *No... no, no. It's just a nightmare, a bad dream. None of this is real.*

'It's real,' Aaron's voice whispers from the corner of my mind.

It's your fault! You made me fall in love with him! You're the reason I'm going through this now! I'm filled with anger at my hallucination.

'I didn't make you do anything. I just told you what you already knew and felt.'

I shut him out of my mind. Not now.

Jacob kisses me, wiping away my tears. I should punch him for leaving me, scream at him for hurting both of us like this, but I can't. He has the look in his eye that shows when he's telling the truth. He has been fully honest so far. Plus, I don't want to spend my last moments with him raging, shouting, and screaming at him. Even if I wanted to, I couldn't do it.

"You... you can't leave."

"I have to."

As much as I wish I didn't, I understand his reasoning.

"Is this why you told me the dragon story when we sat on top of my parents' car?" I choke on my tears as I say the last few words. He nods. I gulp down the pain. This hurts worse than the punches and beatings, worse than the knife wound, and worse than the bullet that tore through my thigh. I can feel what's left of my heart being ripped to shreds, and I can see on his face that his does the same. I guess this is the consequence of love. The heartbreak that follows when one leaves or dies. "You'll come back, right?"

"I don't know," he holds me closer. "It would be better for you if I didn't."

"Stop. Stop saying it's for me," I want to hear a lie. The lie will be easier than the truth.

"But it is," he looks at me and dries my tear-soaked face with his sleeves. "I'm cutting out my heart, so you may see the night sky more times than you might with me nearby."

I understand now. The pain the female dragon lived with every day. Knowing your love is near but being unable to reach him. Perhaps I'm also destined to always be separated from those I love.

"How long until you leave?" I murmur my question.

"I'm going tomorrow," he sighs, wiping his own tears. "The longer I wait, the harder it is to leave." He kisses me again, and I wrap my arms around him, doing the best I can to hold him in place.

"If you're going, I want to give you something." I remove my arms from him and pull off the spearhead necklace. It was originally made for boys, so it won't look strange on him. I place it around his neck. "I can't give you much, so I will give you my courage and my heart."

"I can't take this," Jacob shakes his head. "I know how much it means to you."

"You should know by now that you mean far more to me than a piece of metal on a string. Take it." He dips his head in acceptance. I would be angry with him for leaving, but I'd do the same for him. "I love you," he whispers.

"I love you back," I smile. I savor his scent and touch since he won't be here much longer. We don't stop crying, not that day, not that night when I move over to give him space, and he lies with me, keeping me warm in the cold room.

During the night, I sleep well, having cried all day. My eyes were tired, and so was I. We sleep through the night, and when I wake, he is gone. And just like that, it is over. The only thing he left was a note: *I love you, and I always will. Remember that. I'm sorry.*

I stop crying quickly, having spent all my tears, and end up sitting in silence for that day and the one that follows. I guess I'll always have a piece of him in me, literally, since he gave me his blood. That night and the next I spend lying awake and cold.

Lily and my parents come in to check on me a few times, but I can't talk to them about Jacob yet, and they know I simply need time. I remember why I decided not to love anymore. I had made a decision and yet almost instantly went against it. But… is it worth it? Are love and memories worth the pain? No, I tell myself. But as every memory of Jacob flows through me, as his smell lingers on my pillow, as my time with Aaron flashes by, I know it is. It is worth it. I wouldn't change anything that led me to L26, that led me to Jacob Thomas.

The next day, there is no pain in my leg. By the sixth day of my recovery, there is no trace of the wound, except for a small scar. I'm glad for the scars though, from the knife and from the bullet. They'll always remind me of Jacob, so I'll never forget what we did, so I'll never forget him.

I32 and her group have been checking on me occasionally, but they know better than to mess with a heartbroken Nightshadow, so they don't speak to me.

Once, M93 comes in and says Jacob will return. He tells me that Jacob has never been able to leave family behind, and that my family has been his since he first moved in. We took him in, forever tying him to us, so he'll have to return. No matter how long it takes, he will come back. I decide to believe M93. To believe in hope. I will wait. Even if I wait until my death, I will wait for him. Even if I wait for all eternity, I will wait. Because if I lose faith in love, Jacob wouldn't be happy. He won't be happy about me waiting either, but he can't have *everything* his way.

I survived heartbreak before. And I can do it again now. Resolved, I slowly climb out of bed and take my first step in six days. I walk around the building that my parents had rented for this week. I head down the stairs and grab a knife. Slowly, I drag it lightly across my palm. I want to know if his blood, his gift, will stay with me. I hope it does. Not for its ability, but because it'll mean there's a piece of him in me that will always be with me.

I wait and watch the cut. I stare at it for a minute, and I'm about to give up when the ends of my cut slightly move. I look back down and stare at it for five more minutes as it stitches together and slowly mends. I smile and wipe the blood off my unscathed palm once I'm sure it's done healing. No cut.

Jacob is here with me, and he always will be. He will be safe and brave, as I've given him my courage, and I will be strong, as he's given me his strength, his will to stand up, even when the world pushes me down. We will survive, together or apart, and neither of us will forget the other. I remember the day Jacob asked if I believed in fate.

Looking up at the night sky, the moon and stars, the symbol of Jacob's heart and his sacrifice, I nod.

"I do," I whisper to the chilly night breeze, as it takes my words and scatters them among the stars. "I believe."

SIXTEEN

All I can think about is Jacob. I know he's probably feeling something similar, somewhere out there. I trust him. I trust him enough to know that he wouldn't leave me unless it was necessary. But still, the heartache hurts in my chest, and the pressure of unshed tears aches behind my eyes. But I remain strong and do not fall back into the dark pit of despair I found myself in after losing Aaron.

"Hey, Madrona?" Dad knocks on the door before poking his head inside the room. "We're going to the market to get some more food. Should be back in half an hour or so."

I nod, glad everyone finally stopped trying to comfort me. I just need space to absorb the loss. Pain and grief never truly leave you. They simply carve out a space to live inside you always. One must learn to live with them as constant companions.

Dad backs out the door, and I move over to my window. I take a deep breath. In and out. Slow and steady. *I am Nightshadow. I am Aether. I am Erebus. I am…*

I look out over the city. Eos is an almost mystical place with all its buildings light blue to white, often with yellow borders and trim. The whole city design is fantastic, a true engineering marvel. I see the forested area hiding the POT and remember the day I was there.

"What do I do?" I whisper my question to the open sky. "What the hell do I do now?" Birds continue chirping from the tree beneath my window on the second story. "It hurts. So damn much. All I see when I close my eyes is his face.

"I want to distract myself with the task at hand, but I don't know what to do about that either. He would have known what to do next." I sigh at the open sky, feeling lost. I can see the sun making its way across the sky. The moon goes to meet it halfway, slowly arching across the blue dome.

I watch for the next half-hour until they meet, forming a solar eclipse, covering the land in darkness and light at the same exact time. Balance. Not day, but not night, for one short moment. I think of Jacob in this instant. He's the moon, and I'm the sun. Erebus and Aether. He meets me in the center of the sky, aligning for a brief moment, and then… he's gone. No, I think, as I continue looking up at the eclipse. It's not him and me. It's just me. My Erebus part aligns with my Aether part. I look up at the sky. I am…

I am the eclipse.

·〜· ✦ ☾ · ☼ · ☽ ✦ · 〜·

I stare at the sky for another hour, long after the eclipse has ended, when M93 runs into the room.

"Where's your family?" he demands.

"They went to the store."

"They were supposed to be back over an hour ago." He shakes his head, and a surge of fear races through me.

I try calling their phones, but no answer. I have Q08 check their phones' locations, but they've been turned off. All of them. I run down the stairs as M93 chases me, trying to get me to stop. Bursting out of the building and onto the street, I suddenly realize I don't know what to do now.

There's only one possible answer for what happened to them.

I fall to my knees and sob. I've failed them. My mother, father and even Lily, are now missing, likely claimed by Janice Spade and her secretly commanded Law Enforcement. I never should have let them leave the hotel. I should have made sure it was safe for them. They were only in danger because of me and my actions. This is all my fault.

M93 puts his hand on my shoulder.

"Hey, we'll get them back. They'll be fine," he tells me. "We're going to save them, okay?" I shake my head.

"It's my fault they're gone. It's my fault Jacob's gone; it's my fault Aaron died," I whisper to myself, even though something inside me knows the last statement is false. I push it aside. It's all my fault. The world would be better without me in it.

"No," M93 answers with a forceful and stern voice. I look up at him. "It's not your fault. But you know what? If you *don't* go save them, if you *don't* take the chance that they're alive and need your help, then their deaths *will* be your fault." He almost snarls at the end of his sentence.

I gulp down my sobs and will my tears to stop. I nod. He's right.

Slowly, he helps me stand. "We're getting them back," he tells me. "And we're going to have a heck of a time kickin' ass and taking names while we're doing it."

The edges of my mouth tilt up in a half grin, my face already back to its regular color. "Yes, we are."

I'm about to head inside to see what I can do to find them when a static rumbles over the city. The broadcast speakers have been turned on.

"Fellow Aethers, greetings," It's a female's voice, and I instantly recognize it as Janice Spade's. "We are looking for a teenage girl named Madrona Carter. If you have seen her, please report her location to the authorities. She is a criminal for helping Erebus break into the Place of Truce and is currently on the run. She is guilty of hiding these Erebus criminals amongst our people, teaching them to look and act like us.

"Madrona Carter is sentenced to death for treason against the Aether people. Miss Carter, if you'd like to make it much easier on us, you could turn yourself in, for the sake of your family and friends. If you turn yourself in, we will stop hunting them as well. Anyone who brings us Miss Carter will be rewarded enormously.

"Thank you for your time. May you find happiness if you deserve it, and if you do not, may you work to earn it," the speaker shuts off. Suddenly, all screens light up with a parade of faces, and I realize Spade has taken over every screen in the entire Aether population. All the billboards, computers, phones, electronic watches, surfaces, TV's, are hers to command. All over the Aether world, people are seeing my face. First, my face, then Jacob, M93, I32, and Y17's faces. Only spared are N87 and Q08 who were never seen by POT security cameras. All the photos are captioned, 'Wanted, reward'. All but mine. My picture is labeled 'Top Priority'.

There's only one response to this.

"Fuck!"

We run inside and everyone exchanges silent glances.

"I'm turning myself in." I speak first before anyone can stop me.

"No, you aren't!" 132 snaps.

"Yes, she is!" Q08 supports.

"Of course, she is. It's her or her family. There's really no decision to be made," N87 throws in his opinion.

"She isn't going," M93 growls at him.

"I'll turn her in myself if you won't let her," N87 snarls. I can see they are about to fight when I cut in.

"I'm going, and none of you can stop me!" I shout. They all stare at me. "This is *my* decision. Not any of yours!"

"I promised him," M93 mutters, slowly gaining volume. He's looking at the ground. "I promised Jacob I'd keep you safe while he couldn't."

"I'm *going*. I'm doing this for all of you, for my family. If I don't, they'll *all* be dead! Plus, my capture will be enough distraction for the rest of you to escape, to get far away from here. When," I refused to consider *if*, "I rescue my family, please help them get away from here if you can."

"Of course, we'll help them. But what about you? They plan to kill you!"

"It's not like I don't deserve it!" I snap. I probably killed a few guards in the POT. I have betrayed my home and culture and have helped Erebus infiltrate the community. I have hurt and killed other people. A shudder goes through me at that, but I don't have time to mourn. Silence follows. "I'm going *right now*. Don't try to stop me." I start walking out the door, and no one follows. I sigh in relief. They're letting me go. I feel a small twinge in my heart but push it aside.

I walk out the door and onto the street. With my hood pulled up and my head down, I walk briskly away from the bright yellow hotel. I weave through the city foot traffic as I make my way to the largest public square in town. There's a deli down the street with a line already gathering for lunch. Window signs flash words like "fresh" and "made to order". Next door is a bakery putting delicious, yeasty smells into the air. My stomach rumbles even though I'm not actually hungry.

The public square is one of the busiest in the city. Multiple screens are mounted high above the street, many of which are still displaying my face. Others flash commercials for the latest and greatest gizmos and gadgets. There's a hum in the air, from car engines and horns honking, pedestrians talking on their phones, music coming from speakers and random performers on the corner. People yell or whistle to catch a taxicab driver's attention. Mothers scold their children and push strollers down the sidewalk. Into this commotion I stand, still and silent, letting the world pulse around me, as I remove my hood and wait.

Everyone can see me now. It doesn't take long for the recognition to set in. That's the thing about being a redhead, we tend to stand out. Everyone knows I'm being hunted. They know who I am. But most still hesitate to approach me. I may look like a normal teenage girl, but my shoulders are back, my back is straight, my eyes are alert, and I am watching the crowd, relaxed but ready. Everyone hangs back, forming a rough circle around me, just watching and waiting to see what happens next.

Finally, four large men push through the wall of bodies and walk up to me. Young and healthy, these guys strut with confidence. The leader's chest is wide, his arms thick with muscle. His three sidekicks are only slightly more diminished. In jeans and matching shirts, they look as if they are coming off a construction job. They come to a stop a couple feet in front of me. The crowd surges forward to close us in a tighter circle.

"They'll pay good money for you," the leader smirks with a southern accent. I smile my most wicked smile at him, as he continues. "Aren't you just a pretty little thing! Why don't you come along all nice now with me and my boys?" He nods at one of the men behind him, who reaches out to grab me. I spin quickly, grabbing the outstretched arm, yanking backwards, dislocating his shoulder. He cries out in pain, as I force him to his knees, still applying pressure to his arm.

"You'll have to make me," I seethe, anger flooding into me.

I am Aether. I am Erebus. I am a Nightshadow. I am the shadow of the sun.

I am the eclipse.

The other two men charge at me, while the leader stays back to watch. I feel the Nightshadow fully slip into my veins, my muscles, my mind, and take over my body as I shift into my fighting stance. I kick one away and punch another in the face, while dodging his reaching grab. The first guy recovers from my kick and tries to tackle me, but I duck and roll, then kick his legs out from beneath him. He goes down hard on his back and the second tries to jump on me while I'm still on the ground, but I spring up and land a punch in his stomach, followed by a rapid two-punch to his solar plexus. He falls to the ground, struggling to breathe. The first guy staggers back up off the pavement. I knee him in the groin, and he howls in pain as he doubles over. A follow up kick to his temple sends him right back down, unconscious this time.

Moving slightly away from the downed three bodies, I look over at the leader who's still standing out of reach. I beckon him with my hand with a slight smirk on my lips. He hisses back and tries to charge me. He's surprisingly fast for someone so large. Startled, I can't quite move out of the way fast enough, and he knocks me to the ground. He lands one punch, then another, pinning me down with his weight. I feel each punch and take it to heart. I deserve this pain. I deserve it for putting my family in danger.

When blood finally flows from my nose and my lip splits, I decide that's enough punishment and pull up my hand to catch his next throw. I can feel my lip slowly healing, and his eyes go wide. I smile at him, then land one to his face so hard it throws him off of me, and I stand. Four bodies on the ground. All brought down by a slip of a girl.

The people on the street are staring at me. Fixing my hair and brushing off my shirt, I smile back at them and continue on my way. The Nightshadow portion of me is still controlling my body as the next group attacks. Now that I've warmed up, I take out the eight of them all at once. They aren't as good as the four from before, but there are more of them. I take a few blows I could normally dodge, mostly from trying to fight on multiple fronts, but I easily recover a split second later.

When the last attacker falls to his knees and hits the ground, I swear I can feel the pulsing of Jacob's blood flowing strong through me, his cells blending with mine, healing my minor injuries and regenerating quicker than ever.

The two have become one.

Law Enforcement officers finally arrive and surround me, as I stare them down. They stare back. They know why I'm here, that I won't put up a fight against them because I *can't*. Twelve in total, three come to me and zip tie my hands together behind my back. I could easily break out of them, but I won't.

"Hand restraints? Are those necessary? Why not kill me here and now?" I ask, a swollen lip healing as I speak, clearing my voice as I talk.

"No questions."

I growl at one of the guards and watch him flinch slightly as he searches me for knives or any other weapons. Like I need a weapon to escape and knock them all out. I roll my eyes at them, making sure the troop leader can see it. I want to be the biggest pain in the ass I can. Four guards surround me now, two holding my arms, plus one in front and one behind.

I feel a small sting in my arm and only see the needle as they pull it away. Quickly and quietly, I slip into a dead sleep, collapsing in the guard's arms.

My vision goes in and out as my body fights the serum, but they just keep injecting more wherever I come to. The first time I start to come back a guard is carrying me to a large law enforcement truck. I look at his face. He's young, just like all of them are. Maybe only five years older than me, still in his twenties. I give him a look of empathy and am hit with surprise as he returns it right before I'm stuck with another needle, and darkness takes over again.

The second time I start to wake up, we're in the truck. My hands are still tied behind me and appear to be secured to a ring on the floor, forcing me to lay on my back. The floor is cold beneath me, being the first thing I feel. I let out a grunt as I register my arms are asleep from being trapped under my body, pins and needles pricking me mercilessly, but only for a moment as Jacob's blood fights it off.

"They have my family. You don't have to knock me out as a precaution. If I don't obey, they'll die," I say to the guard who's about to stick me with another needle.

"I know," he whispers into my ear as the truck rolls over a bump. "We don't have a choice either."

What? I slide back into sleep before I can formulate an explanation.

The next time I wake, I'm ready.

"Damn, how many of those things did you bring?" I laugh. "You must have filled the whole truck with them." One guard chuckles, then instantly stops as stares, sharp as daggers, are aimed his way.

"This is the last one," another guard answers.

"Lucky me!" I reply, only somewhat sarcastically.

"Why did you help them?" the guard, who keeps sticking me with needles, asks.

"I…" I don't want to speak, but I guess it won't hurt to tell them. "I fell in love. My boyfriend had died recently, and when I found the Erebus, in the woods behind my house, he was wounded and I just… couldn't let him die. I couldn't put someone else through the grief that I was currently drowning in.

"The Erebus aren't what we've been taught. They only fight because if they don't, they die. Over the wall, they live in poverty, stealing food for survival. They aren't mindless, killing brutes. They're people, just like us.

"Jacob, my name for the Erebus, has since saved me many times over, first from the grief consuming me alive, then later giving me his blood to survive a bullet wound that bitch Janice gave me. He plays guitar better than any professional I've seen, enjoys cooking, is the funniest guy I've ever met, and he would *always* play games with my little sister when none of us would. I couldn't help but love him.

"I knew what I was putting at stake, the risk, when I helped him. I imagine that a few of you are married. What would you do if you discovered your husband or wife was Erebus? Would you now hate them, simply because they were raised on the other side of the wall? If they were the same exact person, simply from another place, would you still love them?

"To answer your question, love. I fell in love," I shake my head, tears streaming down my face as I remember how he left. They're silent for a moment, staring at me with empathy, probably trying to imagine loving someone you aren't allowed to keep. Then, mercifully as the memories flood back into my mind, the guard sticks me with his last needle, and my mind goes blank.

The next time I wake, the young guard is carrying me again. The truck is nowhere in sight, only a brightly lit, white hallway in front and behind us. I have no idea where I am or how far we are from the city square. The guard glances down at me with sad eyes, probably trying to wrap it around his head that I'm only sixteen and the whole Aether population was sent after me. Only sixteen but sentenced to die.

The needle-happy guard must have found more serum because he instantly sticks me as soon as he notices my eyes are open. I feel like the injections are wearing off faster and faster, but without a clock, I can't be certain. I go limp in seconds.

I'm slowly rising out of my unconscious mind when another poke enters my arm, and I slip away again. They must have figured out how fast my body can overcome the serum by now, and the rate of decreased time spent unconscious, because this time I'm out much longer before I wake.

· ∼ ◦ ✦ ☾ · ☼ · ☽ ✦ ◦ ∼ ·

I'm greeted with a nice headache. They must have hit me with quite a few more needles, or something much stronger, because I get the sense that I've been out for a while. I feel the cold, hard ground beneath my body, but something soft covers me. Slowly opening my eyes, I find one of the guard's coats lying over me. I smile slightly at the kindness. He could get fired for his considerate gesture, but I greatly appreciate it.

Blinking sleepily, I try to reorient myself as I glance around. I'm in a holding cell, metal bars on three sides with a solid wall behind me making up the final side. Everything is bright and sterile. White walls, white ceiling, white laminate tile flooring all illuminated by cheap fluorescent lighting. It's shockingly hard on the eyes for being so bland. There are no windows, so I can't judge where we are in relation to the rest of the city. There's a single door into my cell and a single door into the room.

Twelve guards stand between me and the door exiting the room, and I see the guard missing his jacket. It's the same one who carried me so carefully and almost apologetically. I try to stand but collapse instantly. Whatever they hit me with must be real damn strong if I'm still recovering from it. My knees are weak, so I drag myself over to the bars and hold the coat out for him. He smiles gently at me as he takes his jacket back. Two or three of the guards glare at him, but he seems to take no notice.

"Thank you," I whisper to him, then slowly force my body to crawl back over to the wall, leaning against it for support. My head is killing me, my body having no strength due to whatever the injection was. I lie back down, realizing how much energy it took to fight off all the serum, as I'm dragged into a peaceful, natural sleep.

SEVENTEEN

"You sleep like the dead," someone snorts. I grunt at them. My thoughts are fuzzy as I crawl out of the depths of sleep, but it recedes as I stretch, seeking to remove the discomfort from lying on a hard floor all night. Any aches and pains quickly dissipate, and I find I have most of my strength back. I hear the clang of metal on metal, then peek open one eye to see food. Stomach clenching in hunger, I roll off the floor and regret it instantly, swaying unsteadily, as I become light-headed.

The person laughs, "It seems that you act like the dead also."

"Oh, shut up," I grumble back without any heat, dragging myself over to the food and shoving it down. Only when I've eaten do I look up to see who has spoken. It's the guard who carried me here. "How long was I out?"

"Twenty-six hours," he informs. I drag myself into a sitting position against the wall and put my hands to my temples, trying to clear my head. I sit in silence, hardly moving, as I feel Jacob's blood rushing through me, kicking out the rest of whatever the hell it is that managed to keep me down and out this long.

With the quick meal and special blood working its magic, I feel back to normal in no time. I stand and walk around. I'm not sore from fighting. I'm unscathed, again.

"Were you watching me sleep?"

The guard shrugs as if to say, "What else am I supposed to do?" Sighing, I start pacing. I don't want to sit. I want to move, but my ten-by-ten-foot cell doesn't allow for much movement. "So, what now? You've got me, now what?"

A new guard speaks. "Representative Spade has arranged for a little… interview… for you with her head inquisitor. After she's gotten whatever she wants from you, you'll be executed in the city square as an example. It will be televised to all Aether people, so they won't make the same mistakes you did."

I yawn, trying to irritate the guard. He wears a sour expression at the best of times, but now he almost looks gleeful at the thought of my questioning and execution. Chest puffed up, scar across his cheek, and a sadistic gleam in his eye, he seems to be the type to get off on others' pain.

Channeling my inner bitch, I dryly retort, "Well, that sounds like jolly fun. When do we start?"

I'm pacing by the bars when the guard reaches through and nearly strangles me.

"Do you have a death wish?" He asks when he pulls my face into the bars, his own face an inch away, putrid breath blowing into my face. Ahh, I see. He's also into that whole 'me-man, you-woman' male-dominance bullshit.

"Actually yes, I do. By coming here, I signed myself up for my own death to protect my family and friends. So yes, I believe I do have a death wish," I blandly reply, then almost burst out laughing when I see his face. He practically growls at me before pushing me back and slams my head into the metal bars. I collapse, and the darkness returns.

"Damn, either you're wanting to be the biggest smartass on the planet, you're a dumbass, or you really do have a death wish," the first guard chuckles, shaking his head.

"How about all of the above?" I push myself off the cold floor. There's blood all over it, but when I reach up to feel my forehead, there's no mark. I use my sleeves to wipe the residual blood off my face as I finish sitting up.

"Why, though?" he asks. "Why not even *try* to live?"

I try to figure out how to put it for a moment, then finally reach a conclusion. "But at what cost? As long as I'm alive, my family might as well be dead. They don't deserve that; they're only here because of me. I've faced enough loss to know I couldn't survive losing them too, so I'm going to die the way I die, and I can't do shit to stop it."

He's silent.

"What's your name?" I inquire.

He waits another moment before speaking, probably carefully planning his words, since we have an audience with the other room guards. "You ask a lot of questions." I shrug. I know I do. I hear it a lot. "Luke."

"It's a nice name," I compliment and smile at him. "Why talk to me? Won't you lose your job?"

"We get bored," he chuckles, glancing at the other guards. "And besides, no one wants this job, so they have to hold onto the people they get."

Oh. So, I'm the entertainment. Great.

"Madrona, but you already know that."

He smiles, nodding.

I don't speak for the next couple of hours. I stare at the ceiling, a song stuck in my head. Not specifically one I like either. Luke is correct about boredom quickly becoming an issue when stuck in a small room for hours on end. I'm hungry, but I refuse to ask for more food.

A memory of Jacob hits me. I close my eyes and turn away from the guards. I curl up against the back wall and place my head on my knees. The pain returns, but not the physical pain I can overcome, ignore, or heal.

"Aww. Now the poor girlie is finally grieving for herself," that son of a bitch guard croons upon his return. I'm up next to the bars where he's standing before he can react. I grab his coat and yank him against the metal, splitting open his forehead, returning his earlier treatment.

"You will not taunt me," I growl, the Nightshadow creeping out. "Maybe I'll decide I've had enough of this place and bust open this door to teach you a lesson. I could get out easily if I wanted. You're lucky you have something to hold against me. Because if you didn't…" I slam his head against the bars again, and fresh blood spurts from the gash in his face. "I think you get the message," I grin, baring my teeth. Three guards come over and pull him away, one pushing me away through the bars after landing a single punch I didn't bother blocking. I smile at the physical pain. Something I can defeat. I feel a bruise swell, then disperse, leaving me without a mark. The bloodied guard is hauled away as I return to my place in the corner.

Head down, I let myself cry. Not for me, but for Jacob. He'll probably be pissed as hell when he hears I turned myself in. I cry for my family, I cry for Jacob's family, I cry for Ivy and Chris back home, and finally, I cry for Aaron. For once, I wish I was hallucinating, if only just so I can see his face, but he's gone.

Finally, the cell door opens, and my small space is flooded with guards who grab my arms and yank me out of my cell. I punch one and knock him out for good measure, receiving a few blows in return. I feel a needle pinch my neck, and I go limp as the guards catch me to drag me off to who knows where.

When I wake, I'm lying face down on a table, in yet another sterile looking white room. I try to turn my head to look ahead, but a thick leather strap runs across the back of my head, smashing my face against the hard surface, securing my head, and severely limiting my range of view. I quickly test my arms and legs, but they are strapped down tightly too. I guess I'm not going anywhere.

"Hello and welcome! I'm so happy you've decided to join me!" someone announces with an enthusiastic tone. I groan. If the person torturing me is going to be this chipper, it's going to be far worse than I imagined.

"Hi," I respond blandly.

"Are we ready for day one?" the person asks, but then carries on without waiting for a reply. "I hear you're a unique person and seem to heal twice as fast as it would usually take." I chuckle internally at that. Jacob's blood heals much faster than double. "I'm so excited to see it in action. Front row seat, right here!" he crows as a face finally pops into my vision field.

My interrogator is a slim man in his mid-thirties. His skin is pale, almost translucent as if he's never seen the sun. He has sharp cheekbones and blonde hair, almost as devoid of color as his skin, with bangs that hang low over his face. He wears a large smile that doesn't comfort me in the slightest accompanied by a look of malicious madness in his dark brown eyes, which scare me most. He wears a white smock, and altogether at first glance could be mistaken for a ghost. I wonder briefly if he likes the symbolism he projects, his victim's final view of this world is otherworldly.

"Alright," he clasps his hands, moving back out of my sight. "Let's get started. I'm going to be asking you some questions. You're going to want to answer them truthfully. I'm afraid I'll have to do some not nice things if you choose to lie to me," he sounds giddy at the prospect. "But I never like to just jump right in. Where's the fun in that? So I've prepared a little warm up. A welcome party, if you like, just for you."

I hear some clattering on another table, then hear something sizzling. That can't be good.

He pulls up my shirt to reveal my bare back and giggles, "I'd give you something to bite on, but that'd destroy the purpose of this, wouldn't it?" I sigh, frowning when my wish for him to shut up is denied. "You're pretty chill for a teen."

"Not like I can do anything about it," I snort.

"Good point," he chuckles and suddenly pain erupts from my back. After a split second of shock, a scream fills the air. *I'm* screaming, my brain dumbly informs me. He put burning coals on my skin. The smell of burning flesh is sharp and acrid in my nose. My screams continue as the coals burn through my skin layer, touching upon fat and muscle. Searing pain blinds me and erases all other thoughts. There is nothing but the pain, the suffering. It continues on for what feels like days, but I know it's only a few minutes.

"Now, how was that?" he checks in after removing the hot coals. "Are we properly *warmed* up?" I wince at the pun, still gasping for air. The pain is slowly receding as my body's defenses take over, cells regenerating, creating new skin and muscle, reforming nerves. He lets me lay there for a moment poking and prodding the healing injuries, muttering things like "miraculous" and "amazing". The tapping of a keyboard echoes in my ears, and I assume he's taking extensive notes.

I slip into sleep but wake up still in hell. Still strapped face down, but the table has been tilted to stand vertically, and I'm not wearing a shirt.

"Now, Miss Carter. Shall we begin?" he smiles.

"I haven't got all day," I reply sarcastically, and he bursts out laughing.

"Actually, we do! Have all day that is. Let's see if you are ready for a little game I call Truth or Pain. Here's how to play: I'm going to ask you a question. If you answer with the truth, we'll move on to the next one," he sounds disappointed, "but lie to me, and I'll make it hurt so good." Ah, much more cheerful with the thought of getting to dish out punishment.

While talking, my overly upbeat tormentor has been attaching small probes all over my body. Best guess, I think they are measuring my body's response to his questions, some kind of high-tech lie detector.

"Let the game begin! First question, how did you get into the POT?"

"Your mom let me in."

"Sorry, wrong answer. Hmmm...first prize...Let's try the whip first. I've always favored the cracking sound it emits."

I can feel myself turning paler than a ghost. Tied to the table, the first lash strikes, leaving a welt on my back. A second lash quickly follows, splitting open my skin where it overlaps with the first, and a scream flies out before I can bite it down.

"How did you get into the POT?"

"By walking."

"Walking how?"

"On my feet, of course."

Lash.

"How did you get into the POT?"

"I said, 'Knock, knock.'"

"Who answered the door?"

"Your mom."

Lash.

"What did you hear in the POT?"

"Your mom gettin' busy."

Lash. Lash. Lash. Lash.

I lose count of the lashes as the questioning continues to go in a circle. I think he throws in a few extra strokes when he notices his truth-o-meter didn't flag falsehoods when I mentioned his mother. My back is a patchwork quilt or minced meat depending on how you look at it. The coppery scent of my blood is strong enough to taste in the air, making my head spin in torment. With every lash, my body is thrown into the table by momentum. I feel bruises developing on my front as the whip ravages my back. Maybe I will be really lucky and all of Jacob's blood cells will leak out of my body, so I can just die...

Just as I feel as if I'm about to go under again, he stops. I can hear him breathing hard from his spot behind me. He walks closer, grabs my hair, and pulls my head back, so I can see him. His face glistens with sweat, nostrils flaring, as he breathes in my face. Apparently whipping someone is hard work. With a slight huff, he slams my head back down and walks off.

Time has no meaning as I continue to remain tied to the table. The lights remain blindingly bright, making sleep difficult. Not to mention I have a fire blazing on my back, stiff muscles from being tied up, a sore throat from continuous screaming, and a full bladder. As my body starts to heal, my brain is finally able to process something other than pain.

After some time, I sense the presence of someone behind me. I almost cry in relief when I realize it is the guard, Luke, and not my interrogator. Luke holds out a water bottle, and at my quick nod, holds it up so that I may drink from it. The cool water is comforting, sliding down my throat.

"Thank you." My voice is hoarse, quiet.

Luke has trouble meeting my eyes, and I can tell he's uncomfortable seeing me in such a state. Seeing the conflict in him, I decide to push my luck. "Do you know if my family is alright?"

"They're doing ok. All attention is focused on you right now, so I think they've been largely left alone," he informs me.

I feel a surge of relief; they are still alive. "Where are they? Are they nearby?"

"They are being kept in a holding cell in the basement here. I don't think they'll be released until after your execution… if at all." The last part is barely a whisper.

I almost forgot to mutter a quick thank you, as Luke exits the room, my mind too busy contemplating his words.

·〜· ✧ ☾ · ☼ · ☽ ✧ · 〜·

The reprieve from pain, however, is short lived. "Extraordinary," the interrogator murmurs in awe, running his hand along the nearly invisible scars on my back. I shiver under his cold touch. "Most people would die from so many lashes, and you're healed in a few hours' time!" I growl at him like an animal. He simply laughs.

"Don't. Touch. Me."

"You are so feisty! I love it! Since that didn't do much to encourage you to talk, why don't we try something else?"

He pulls out a needle and injects me with a green liquid. I let out a scream as the most painful thing I've ever experienced follows. My vision turns black, but my tormentor has managed to find the perfect amount that suspends me in consciousness, and I lay there for hours or days, screaming, as the chemical rages through my body. It burns, deeper than fire, sprouting in my core and feels like I'm being incinerated from the inside out. Whatever he put in my system is *strong*. My whole body is screaming at once, and I can't think of anything *except* pain. Every second feels like days as the pain shoots through me. My cries are barely audible by the end. Once the serum finally wanes, I nearly pass out in relief.

"Hmm..." he muses. "I always have to give the antidote, otherwise it continues for days, weeks, even. Whatever is in your system is extremely strong. How are you able to heal so quickly?"

I can barely talk through my clenched teeth. "I don't know."

He injects me with more green liquid. Instant pain.

"Try again. How are you able to heal so quickly?"

"I. Don't. Know."

"Wrong again." Another shot. Blinding pain.

"How are you able to heal so quickly?" He has to repeat himself even louder to penetrate the screaming inside my skull.

Gasping, withering in pain, I cave slightly. "The blood," I mumble.

He perks up. "Blood? What about your blood?"

"Blood... transfusion... healing," I am almost incoherent in my suffering.

"Interesting... very interesting. And how did you discover Erebus were coming over the wall?"

I hesitate to answer until I see his arm lifting the green syringe.

"The Erebus... almost fell on me."

"Why were you next to the wall?"

"I was walking in the woods, grieving for a recent loss."

"Who died?"

"My boyfriend."

"Why there?"

"It's private. And peaceful. Or it is until bodies almost fall on top of you." My voice is gaining strength as the time from the last injection grows. I can tell my latest answers bore him; his eyes start to glaze over, and his shoulders hunch as if he no longer has the energy to hold them back.

Sure enough, my interrogator soon returns to his subject of interest. Blood. He moves out of sight, and I hear clanging and rattling behind me. Returning, he has a metal tray in his hands with more syringes and small glass collection tubes. "I think I'll just grab a sample or ten and see what I can see."

Another needle pricks my arm, this time taking my blood in neat little tubes. After he's done draining me, he picks up the first syringe again. "A little something to keep you entertained while I just look your blood over. Don't want you to be bored waiting for my return, now do we," and in goes the green serum.

My entire body seizes with the newest chemical onslaught, and I lay there in agony, wishing I could die, and it could just be over.

A millennium later, he returns. "I'm told our time has come to an end. It's the executioner's turn to play with you," he sighs in disappointment. "I'm going to miss our happy little visits. They were so very interesting. But," he perks up here, "at least I have your blood to keep me company for a while. In return, I got you a little parting gift." He holds up a syringe with a red liquid. "I'm particularly proud of this agent. Developed it myself with extensive studies on human subjects, of course. I call it *Inferno*. Enjoy!"

I wake with a start, freezing in my cell. After a sigh of relief to be out of the torture chamber, I quickly scan my body for trauma. I see no marks, but I swear my skin started shriveling during those long hours. I could see it split open in places at the command of that serum, almost like being skinned alive. Green is liquid fire. Red is near dead. I shudder and don't care that I'm pale. I'd probably be dead a dozen times over if I didn't have Jacob's blood in me.

I curse my torturer under my breath. I'm going to kill that man; I swear on it. Of course my pending execution puts a slight kink in those plans. I lie back down, to rest and regain my strength. As I drift back off to sleep, I forget my plan of dying as quickly as possible and set a new one in motion.

I'm woken by a guard banging on my bars.

"Get up, pretty face," the son of a bitch guard, my nemesis, taunts, hitting the metal with his wooden knife hilt, causing the sound to ricochet off the walls.

"Oh, you think my face is pretty? Thank you!" I lightly puff out my lips and bat my eyelashes to add to the effect.

"How's *your* face, by the way? I think that splash of color and the split lip really brings out the asshole look you favor."

Behind Private Dickhead, another guard throws a hand over his mouth to keep from laughing out loud.

"So the interrogator didn't break you, eh? Maybe we ought to throw you back down there for a few more days," he grits his teeth, eyes full of anger.

"Oh, that'd be delightful! We've become such good friends," I force my mouth into the widest smile I can achieve. "But then, I'd hate to be late for my own execution…" His face turns red in anger and several guards lose their battle to stay quiet and burst out laughing. I can't help but join them as Dickhead storms off.

Luke sighs. "Well, you *do* need to move. They're going to pretty you up for your death. I guess it doesn't look good for people to know the Aether are so good at torture," he frowns, but I smile. *Perfect.*

He sends me a brief glance that says a thousand words. He suspects what I'm going to do. I send him one back, knowing he'll get the message. *Don't be there when I get started.* Luke looks away and opens the door. All twelve of the guards surround me, leading me down the hall and into a room with three girls waiting. I sigh. This might suck.

The guards leave, though I can hear two standing outside the door while the three girls get me into a dress. Grey and white, since black is forbidden, but it's close enough, and I almost smile at how perfect it is. I'm the eclipse.

They do my hair, pulling it out of the way for me. I thank them and stand. They try to get me to sit back down, telling me they aren't done, but *I* am. I am done with this place.

I thank them for their work and walk out the door like I own the place. The guards are too surprised to react, then I'm already gone, sprinting down the hall and to the left, ignoring the girls calling out behind me to come back. I run through the building and knock out a squadron of guards, all nine of them.

I'm pissed and allow the rage and Nightshadow to fully take over, removing any and all obstacles between me and the surveillance room. After making quick work of the security guards, all the cameras and the building layout are at my fingertips. I memorize the camera locations just as twenty guards round the corner. I may be able to take most of them, but I doubt I can take all of them at once. I glance back into the room and see my family in a holding cell on the first floor, in the southern wing of the facility.

Looking back at the guards running toward me, I curse. "Looks like we're just going to have to make do." With the Nightshadow in charge I launch toward the guards, kicking two backwards and landing a backflip.

"*Holy*-" I begin, but I'm interrupted by someone throwing a punch. I dodge to the side and land three return punches in less than two seconds, using each impact to channel the rebounding energy into the next blow.

I land two more punches in another guard's face, and he falls on top of the next guard standing too close behind him. Two run at me, and I land my next blows on each of their noses, the pain and blood momentarily stunning them. With their eyes watering, they can't see my follow up power punch to their solar plexus. This might be my favorite attack. Out of breath, it's easy to slam the two guards' heads together. I jump off them as they fall, using their shoulders as a step to boost me higher, just as M93 once did with Jacob. I jump over several guards and use the remaining guards' heads as steps, moving over them before they know what happened.

I continue, landing on my feet and running toward the southern part of the building. I reach a flight of stairs and jump before thinking, grabbing the handrail, and using my arms to swing me into the door below, kicking the oncoming guards and sending them back through the door. Landing on their unconscious bodies, I run down the open hall, landing two punches to the face of the guard coming around the corner. I take a left, then a right and see a row of cells, each covered by two guards. They stare at me in surprise.

"Hey, boys! How are you all doing this fine day?"

"She's out! Get her!" someone yells.

The Nightshadow grins, and I'm consumed in a flurry of punches and landing hits. I watch my body dodge hits that shouldn't have been dodged, and deal blows that are so fast they shouldn't have been possible. The hallway becomes a blur of bodies falling as I make my way through. They were going to kill my family. You don't attempt that and make it out unharmed.

I haven't seen Luke, so I'm assuming he followed my unspoken advice.

I look down the hall, the Nightshadow subsiding, having done its job. Twenty-five guards in total, all taken down by one person. I shake my head, remembering what Jacob told me once. An experienced Nightshadow might beat ten experienced fighters. Even if they weren't experienced, there were still twenty-five of them. I push the thought aside and run down the hallway until I reach my family's cell. Opening the door, I see the surprise written all over their faces.

"Madrona," Mom's eyes are wide. "You shouldn't have come!"

"I've been here for a few days," I tell them. Their expressions turn to looks of horror, but I push them out the door.

"What happened to you?" Dad asks.

"Later. Right now, we have to get you out," I remind them, leading us down the hall and towards the exit that's supposed to be a few hallways down. I lead Lily and my parents down the hallway, to the left and back to the right when more than forty guards show up.

"Go," I tell them. "To the left there should be an exit. Run to the safehouse. The Erebus will help you get away from there. If Q08's smart he'll be keeping tabs on all the Law Enforcement facilities, and I think I set off a few alarms." I look at the guards running at us.

"But what about you?" Lily turns to me.

"Just go!" I yell. They won't make it out unless they leave now, when all the guards are in this part of the building rather than on the streets going after them. I'm their priority anyway.

Finally they leave, and I watch them race down the hallway. This will be the last time I see them. At least I know they're going to be safe. I turn my attention to the guards who are almost to me.

"Alright, alright. Sorry, I had some stuff to take care of," I chuckle. I see the son of a bitch guard and wave at him as he sprints toward me. I release the Nightshadow portion of myself. I won't make it, but I sure as hell want to go down fighting. I flood myself with memories of Jacob, my family, and Aaron, all the times I smiled and laughed, all the happy moments I can remember. I don't fight out of anger. I don't fight out of hate. I fight out of love.

I meet the attack head on, and it all becomes a blur.

I wake up back in my cell, my hands and feet cuffed. I have bruises all over my body and realize they must have happened in the last few minutes, otherwise they wouldn't be there. I bet they beat me after I passed out, after some genius shot me with a dart gun. My head hurts, and my dress is torn. Honestly, I think it looks better this way. More dramatic and badass. Makes me look tough with all the bloodstains on the gray and white dress. The red adds to the mixture, really making it pop.

I notice the whole hallway is filled to capacity with guards, all of them staring at me, most covered in bruises.

"Ouch, you guys don't look so good," I wince for them. Almost all of them either snarl or growl at me. "Aw, you guys are so nice." They open the door and drag me out in the hall. I take notice of every detail, every picture, everything I see in one of the last moments of my life.

The stone hallways are decorated with details in light blue, white and yellow. Some are painted with art of the sun, others of unity underneath the daylight. I note all the guards' faces, young and old, as they escort me down the hall, my head held high. Most are male, but there are a few women among the ranks. Exiting the door at the end of the hallway, I breathe in the fresh air, sucking in the cool mist, the fog that covers the sun. I listen to the city pigeons coo. They make me remember listening to the birds in the forest with Aaron.

"I'm coming," I whisper to him.

I savor every stone my feet glide over, the smoothness of the breeze on my face, the sun hidden from view. I feel them push me up onto the stage, I feel all the eyes on me as I'm dropped on the floorboards of a platform, hurriedly thrown together with nails. The whole city must be in front of me, as there's people as far as I can see.

I remember none of these people know what's happening on the other side of the wall. They don't know how many people are dying, how many are being killed simply because a family member was immune to the virus. They don't know the Erebus suffer from starvation and poverty.

I watch their faces as the person behind me begins his speech. They either can't watch or can't *not* watch. All of their eyes are either filled with hate or empathy. At first, I think it is their hate for me and their empathy for all the guards I've hurt, but soon I realize what it really is.

I'm sixteen, and I'm about to be killed for saving someone's life, for saving my family. They're showing me their empathy, their empathy for *me*. A warm feeling enters my body, my heart. *They care.* The Aether understand and don't agree with Law Enforcement. But what can they do? Nothing, and they know it. We were always told we were free, but we aren't. I look up at the sky as the man behind me loads his gun. The fog disperses enough for me to see what's above. Not the sun, but the moon. The moon, out during the day. Almost as if it is here for me. As if Jacob is here for me. Jacob's heart in the sky, not the dragon's. I think of Jacob, as the man behind me holds his gun to my head. I close my eyes and accept my fate.

Just before he pulls the trigger, there's a whistling sound, then a whack in the wood wall behind me. Everyone gasps, and I open my eyes, realizing the gun has moved away from my head. Above me, a cable stretches from the top of a building on the nearby block, a grappling hook holding it to the wood backboard behind me. A zipping sound follows, and I see a small shape come into view. Everyone's silent, trying to see what it is.

The light from the moon reflects off it, and I see something I never thought I'd see again. My courage and strength, the spearhead necklace. The one I gave Jacob before he left. I look up at the building and see a figure in *black* attached to the line, speeding towards me.

The return of the mighty dragon. The return of my heart.

I smile.

I am not dying today.

REVIEWS

Thank you so much for giving me a chance to entertain you. If you enjoyed *Nightshadow*, please consider writing a short review on Amazon. Reviews are vital to every writer but especially important to self-published writers like myself. It allows others to find my books.

ACKNOWLEDGMENTS

First, I would like one thing to be known before I start: I have never written an acknowledgments page before. The only reason I am doing so now is because of my incredible parents, family, friends, and everyone else who was either directly or indirectly involved in making this dream come true.

Now, for the people who helped make this brainchild a reality.

My editor (A.K.A. my mom) Kristin Rogers has spent more hours on this book than anyone else, even me. From fixing grammar and spelling mistakes to helping me re-organize the whole timeline, she has been there for every step of the process, even as I was writing the first draft.

The 'person-who-did-a-little-of-everything' award goes to... (drumroll) my dad, Curt Rogers. I remember he was always there to keep us moving forward when my mom and I started losing determination. He taught me the basics of hand-to-hand combat, so I could include it in the story. Along with being one of my beta readers, he also set up the business portion required to publish this book. I'm so grateful for everything he has done.

My fabulous beta readers include Curt Rogers (my dad), Sue Monaghan (my grandma), and Jamie Rogers (my aunt). These people helped revise and edit by looking for grammatical and spelling issues, logic problems, and inconsistencies that my mom and I wouldn't have found. Thank you for taking time out of your lives to do this for me.

My family has been supportive from the beginning. Ian and Alyssa have always been there to give a supportive thumbs-up, along with my extended family.

Shout outs to my incredible non-family support team: Siena Frost, Rizzy Black, Maggie Miller, Tierney Wells, and many others who 'bothered' me almost daily for updates on *Nightshadow*. Special thanks to my friends and teachers, along with everyone in my BLOC class, for all the support and encouragement.

With all of these people, *Nightshadow* became what it is today, a book born from my family. It wasn't easy to juggle writing this book with being a thirteen-year-old girl in middle school, but with their support, help, and encouragement, I did it. We did it.

Along with all these people, thank you to the warm summers on the water, reading *Twilight*, *Divergent*, and *Throne of Glass*. My love for fantasy/dystopian novels helped inspire my own story.

Finally, there is one more person I'd like to thank: you, my reader. You reading this book means the world to me. I believe that when someone writes a story, they include a piece of themselves within the pages. Thank you for sticking with me, for sticking with the characters as they pull themselves out of the incredibly different holes they fell into.

Orson Scott Card, the author of *Ender's Game*, wrote the following in his introduction: "The story is one that you and I will construct together in your memory. If the story means anything to you at all, then when you remember it afterward, think of it, not as something I created, but rather as something that we made together." I could never state how I feel about you reading this book any better than that, and so I hope you enjoyed it enough that it will stay with you well after you read it.

Thank you for reading the first part of Madrona's story. I hope you'll join me again in the next portion of her journey, as we are only just getting started.

ABOUT THE AUTHOR

Living in the Pacific Northwest, Mia has always loved the forests and water around her. She started writing stories early on, beginning *Nightshadow* at the age of 12. Mia currently lives with her family and dog in western Washington. *Nightshadow* is her first novel.

Stay up to date on my latest books at my website;
https://www.miarogersbooks.com/

Nightshadow Duology
Nightshadow
Untitled Book 2: Coming Soon

Made in the USA
Las Vegas, NV
31 July 2023